RETROSPECTIVE

A GRAEME JAMES NOVEL

The Awakened Press

www.theawakenedpress.com

RETROSPECTIVE
A GRAEME JAMES NOVEL

Huw Evans

Copyright © 2022 by Huw Evans

For information about special discounts for bulk purchases, please contact The Awakened Press at books@theawakenedpress.com.

The Awakened Press can bring authors to your live event. For more information or to book an event contact books@theawakenedpress.com or visit our website at www.theawakenedpress.com.

Cover design by David Moratto
Interior design by Kurt A. Dierking II

Printed in the United States of America
First The Awakened Press trade paperback edition

ISBN: 979-8-9860377-2-1

RETROSPECTIVE

A GRAEME JAMES NOVEL

The Awakened Press

Table of Contents

PROLOGUE

It was a Tuesday morning. Outside was cold and gray. A light drizzle had started and was now tapping monotonously against the windowpane.

Sitting at his cubicle desk, staring out at the dreary cityscape, Graeme James was reflecting on his life—again. At thirty-five years old, he was starting to wonder if there was much of a point to anything. Here he was, stuck in yet another dead-end job (his sixth since graduating from college) and working for his worst boss yet.

Reports were due but there was little enthusiasm for getting them done, especially since said boss, Doug Richards, was out, taking one of his famous long business lunches that seemed to achieve little results.

Winfield Technical Management Services was failing. Once a rising star in London's IT consulting field, over the last two years, both business and the firm's reputation had been on a slow, steady decline. Not that Graeme really cared; perhaps losing his job might be a good thing, *especially if it meant not having to deal with that arsehole Richards anymore*, he thought. That said, he was barely making ends meet. His divorce with Karen was crippling him financially and he was struggling to pay the rent on his very average flat in Shepherd's Bush. If he did lose his job, Graeme wondered how he'd simply be able to get by.

After grabbing an overpriced "gourmet" sandwich and a can of Coke from the young Australian who always seemed sickeningly cheerful, Graeme decided it was time to get those reports done. He was just finishing the last one when he glanced up and saw his portly, bearded boss, back from his lunch, heading straight towards him.

"James, have you done those reports yet?" Richards snapped.

"Just finishing up the last one now," Graeme replied.

"I want them on my desk in ten minutes, understood?"

Graeme shot his boss a quick glance.

"Well, what are you waiting for? Get on with it," Richards snarled, before turning around and marching towards his corner office.

Not long after Richards had gone, Graeme heard a sympathetic voice from behind him. "I don't know how you put up with it, day after day. He must really have a hate for you."

He turned around to see a slender young woman with long, straight brown hair, and an oval face with big brown eyes. It was Clara Davidson, the one person he could truly rely on the fifteenth floor of Centrepoint.

"You're right, Clara," he sighed. "Barely a day goes by when he doesn't have a go at me, just because in his first week I asked him a question he didn't like. Between you and me, I don't know how much more of this shit I can take."

"Look," she said, "fancy grabbing a drink after work? I know I could use one."

"Sounds like a plan. Let's meet downstairs around 5:30 p.m. In the meantime, I'd better give the bastard those reports he's been hounding me about."

Twenty-five minutes later, armed with the completed documents in hand, Graeme knocked on Richards' office door. As he entered the room, its only defining characteristics the almost floor-to-ceiling windows, he could see his boss lying back in the big leather chair, arms behind his head, feet on the desk. *In a typically arrogant pose*, Graeme added in his mind.

"You're late!" Richards blurted.

"I wanted to make sure the reports were completed properly. I hope you find them to your satisfaction."

"Was that a trace of sarcasm I detected, James?"

"Not at all, sir."

"You know what, I've just about had it with you; you've got a bad attitude and it drags morale in the office down. You're staying late tonight. I've got a presentation that needs doing for Friday," he yelled, barely changing posture. "Come back in half an hour and I'll give you some material to get started on." Richards raised his arm as though he was shooing Graeme away like some stray cat off the lawn.

"Anything else? Sir?" Graeme was finding it hard to contain his growing anger. He was about to turn and leave when Richards said something he wouldn't soon forget.

"I'd watch your step if I were you, James."

It was the last straw. Graeme turned around, his fists clenching, the culmination of a lifetime's worth of rage and frustration finally bubbling to the surface. He knew this was it; there'd be no going back.

"Or else what? What are you going to do about it, Richards?"

The man was stunned. He sat bolt upright and was about to say something but was cut off by his angry employee.

"You know what, I don't care anymore," Graeme declared, surprised at his own assertiveness. "You can take this job and shove it up your arse. For three years I've put up with your shit and I can't take it anymore."

Richards was speechless, perhaps for the first time in his life.

"And another thing," added Graeme as he slammed the reports on the big oak desk. "You're a bully. Somebody, someday, will be a lot less forgiving than I will."

He stormed out of the office and headed back to his cubicle, stopping by the storage room to grab a few boxes. He'd already started packing items from his cubicle desk drawers and walls when Clara came by.

"What happened in there?" she wondered. Her kind, oval face and sympathetic, chocolate eyes revealed a genuine curiosity. "I guess it wasn't good."

"I did it. I finally did it." Graeme shook his head in disbelief. "I told Richards to stuff this job up his arse."

Clara's eyes widened and she placed her right hand over her mouth briefly. "Wow! I can't believe you actually *did* that."

"Neither can I, really," Graeme continued, "but I felt I had nothing to lose. I basically hate my life and I'm tired of this crap; I have no idea what I'm going to do, but anything's better than this shit." He turned away and continued packing.

"You still want to meet for that drink?"

"You're damn right I do. Look," he said, rotating his body to face her again. "Why don't we just meet at the bar? I need to cool off and I don't want to put you in a bad mood, as well. I was thinking of a place called Porto's just off Leicester Square. Do you know it?"

"No, but I'm sure I'll find it. I'll see you in a bit." She smiled, lightly squeezing him on the arm before heading back to her desk.

Graeme continued packing his last few personal items from the cubicle. As he headed out of the office carrying the two cardboard boxes, he glanced at his colleagues as he walked by.

Many stopped what they were doing and looked at him with disbelief. A couple of them smiled and gave a thumbs up, while one of them, Andreas Calvin, whispered under his breath, "You've done the right thing mate. You'll be okay."

"Thanks man, appreciate it," came the reply.

Andreas winked and shot Graeme two thumbs up.

Reaching the front door, Graeme glanced back at the sea of cubicles. *I can't believe I devoted three years of my life to this.*

Stepping through the door and out into the lift corridor, he was now in uncharted territory.

Down at street level on Tottenham Court Road, he flagged down a black cab. "Leicester Square, please."

"You've got to be joking, mate," laughed the cabbie, "on your bike."

As the TX4 sped off, it started to drizzle again. Graeme was wearing his wool overcoat and had forgotten his umbrella; both he and his boxes were going to be soaked by the time he reached Porto's.

What the hell, nothing can get worse at this point in time, can it? Did I do the right thing telling Richards to shove it? It sure felt good at the time, but I have no clue what I'm going to do now. For Christ's sake—I don't even think I'm going to be able to pay rent at the end of this month! Some merry sodding Christmas this is going to be!

It took him about thirty minutes to reach his destination, by which time he was damp, cold and thoroughly miserable. The boxes in which he'd gathered his few personal possessions from the office were barely holding together.

Walking through the entrance to Porto's just off the square, he headed downstairs and turned right into the bar.

Porto's was a small basement affair with no more than half a dozen bar stools and a cluster of tables, though for Graeme, in the last six months, it had essentially become home.

The beer always tasted fresh (unlike so many other establishments in the West End) and Paolo, the Portuguese bartender, always lent a sympathetic ear. And the ambiance; it always felt great every time he went there. His troubles would simply melt away and for a few hours, he felt like someone else—somebody who was confident, happy, and full of life.

However, this being a Tuesday afternoon, things were quiet. A middle-aged couple sat at one of the tables talking in low, hushed undertones; at the end of the bar a young girl, probably not more than twenty-one, was busy texting away on her phone.

"How are you, my friend?" Paolo came forward as Graeme set down the boxes by the edge of the bar. "We don't usually see you at this time of day."

Graeme stripped off his coat before taking his place on one of the stools. "That's because I quit my job today." He had a manic look about his face. "I just couldn't take it anymore. I'm at the end of my rope, Paolo. I've got an ex-wife who hates me, no money, few prospects—and as far as I can see, very little to look forward to. Most of my friends and family live far out of town and these days I simply can't afford to travel."

"I'm sorry, my friend," said Paolo sympathetically. "Perhaps things will work out for the better, eh? Look, you've been a good customer, so today your drinks are on the house."

Having poured Graeme a fresh pint, Paolo went into the small storage room and emerged a few seconds later with what looked like a bottle of port. "This might help you forget about your troubles," he mentioned. Grabbing two small glasses, he poured the liquid and both men toasted each other before downing them.

Loosening his tie, Graeme reached into his jacket pocket and grabbed his Blackberry. *Might as well check my messages; bugger all else to do.* Scanning through the latest raft of spam emails and now irrelevant Winfield company notices, he found one from Karen. He decided to open it.

"*I'm pregnant,*" it read, "*and I believe it's yours. That said, I don't want us to contact each other anymore except through my solicitor. This baby deserves a better life and I want Martin to be the father, he'll be able to provide everything the child needs.*"

Graeme slumped his body forward, resting his arms on the bar. As he exhaled, he could feel tears starting to swell. *What else could possibly go wrong today? Nothing like kicking a man when he's really down! What the hell? I mean, really? It's my sodding child, too, and she does that. Could there be anybody more heartless in this world? Maybe I should just jump off Tower Bridge or something; I'd probably be better off at this rate.*

He glanced at the Blackberry for a quick second. Then, in a fit of rage, he threw it across the room, watching it hit the hard stone floor. He hated mobile phones, anyway. *The curse of the modern age*, he grimaced.

"Hey, what is going on?" Paolo spoke compassionately, surprised and perhaps a little angered at Graeme's uncharacteristic outburst. "Look, my friend, you don't need it, any of this. I know you're a good man, but you have to learn to control the anger, otherwise it will kill you. Trust me, I speak from experience. Remember, I'm Portuguese; we are known to be a bit, how do you say, *fiery* at times!"

"I know." Graeme took a full exhale for the first time all day. "I'm normally the most mild-mannered person in the world, but I've just taken so much on the chin in recent months. My bastard of a boss at work, my ugly divorce with Karen, and *now she says she's pregnant* with my baby and doesn't want me to get to know my child! Honestly, Paolo, is there any justice in this world? Any, at all?"

"More than you think, my friend." The bartender winked, as if he, perhaps, knew something Graeme didn't, before setting down a fresh pint and another glass of port on the bar. He promptly disappeared into the storage room.

After taking a few sips from his pint, Graeme swore he could hear a phone ringing. He looked towards the entrance of the bar. *It can't still be working, can it? Especially after that?* Curious, he got up and headed towards the direction of his Blackberry. He'd forgotten it had a hard case and although scuffed and cracked, it was indeed ringing.

Picking it up, he saw it was Clara's mobile number.

"Hello?"

"Graeme; it's me, Clara."

"I'm glad you called."

"You sound a bit better."

"Must be the beer. Are you coming?"

"That's why I'm calling," she said, a hint of anxiety in her voice. "Look, my sister called me not long after you left the office. It's my mum, she's been taken into hospital. It looks like I won't be able to join you tonight, I'm really sorry about that."

"I hope she's all right. Your mum, I mean," replied Graeme. "Look, if I can help in any way please call me. As you know, I haven't exactly got much else going on at the moment. And Clara—thanks for everything. You're one of the few people in this world I can really trust at the moment."

"You're alright, Graeme James. I know better things are ahead of you, for certain. You just need to believe in yourself." Clara's response and tone felt solid and reassuring. "Listen, I have to go now. Take care and have a few drinks for me, okay?"

Graeme was about to say something, but she was gone. He turned the phone off and headed back to the bar, jamming it in his coat pocket before taking up his stool.

A couple of hours later, two more pints and three (maybe four) glasses of port, he was definitely feeling a little more relaxed. Paolo was telling him he'd come to Britain in 1983 and how he felt it had changed and generally not for the better, especially since New Labour came to power. "Even with this government now, we are still picking up the pieces," he reflected sadly. "The taxes on property and alcohol…and now these new regulations and austerity measures. They are killing the business—I mean, this recession, I don't see when it will end. When I first came here it was a land of opportunity, now I am not so sure. I really miss those days."

Taking another sip of his pint, Graeme thought about that for a minute. He'd only been a little boy in 1983, but he'd long held fond memories of the era and even today, in the present, remained fascinated by it. To him it seemed to be an age that somehow just made more sense and as his adult life unfolded, thinking back to those times provided a kind of sanctuary from what he viewed was an increasingly bleak, cynical world—one with few prospects, at least for him.

Sitting at home in his flat, listening to Japan or Roxy Music, or perhaps watching an episode of *Bergerac* or *The Professionals* on his cheap DVD player along with a bottle of his favorite beer, or a glass of red and nights at Porto's, was the only relief from what he saw was pretty much a wretched, mundane reality. He loved the dialogue, the action, the car chases—the political incorrectness and sometimes wafer-thin plots of those old shows, no matter how far-fetched and ridiculous they might have seemed at times.

Thinking about old TV often brought him to his other main interest: cars. He had a real fondness for what were now classics—machines from the 1960s through the 1980s—and considered himself somewhat of a petrol head. Sadly, he'd never managed to scrape together enough dough to buy something he really wanted, like a classic BMW or Mercedes. His last car, an old Citroën BX, had given up the ghost a few years ago and he'd elected not to replace it.

Thanks to taxes, fuel, and parking permits, owning a vehicle on his wages had become just too expensive and now, with seemingly no wages at all, at least in the short term, he wondered how he'd be able to make ends meet. He was reflecting again.

I sure wish I could escape all this crap. My life has turned out pretty shit and every day it seems something happens—either directly or indirectly—that serves to piss me off even more. I definitely feel like I was born in the wrong age. I could have done so much more with my life. I wanted to be a pilot, a copper or racing driver, but I'm just a sodding failure; I'm a timid, nervous wreck. I barely scraped through school, I can't get a decent job, I'm fucking useless when it comes to relationships and now I'm out of work. Perfect.

He kept drinking.

Looking up, Graeme saw Paolo smile at him before pouring another glass of port.

Screw it! I'm getting drunk tonight. What have I got to lose? Exactly! Plus the beer's on the house. Why the hell not?

The bar was starting to fill up as people got off from work. A couple of acquaintances acknowledged Graeme as they walked in before sitting down at one of the tables.

Graeme stood up and went over to talk with them. He'd known Alan and Dave for about six months, since he first started coming to Porto's. The three of them would get together here, usually on a Friday night and talk about life, women and other matters. Dave worked at a bank near Covent Garden while Alan was an estate agent in West Kensington.

"Alright Graeme old son?" asked Alan, with heavy brows creased inwards. "You're looking a bit haggard tonight."

"Walked out on my job today, just had it with everything."

"*Jesus*, I'm sorry to hear that." He could see that Dave was genuinely concerned. "Look, have a pint or two on us, alright?"

"Cheers."

Graeme explained the details about his miserable day, and the three of them ventured on to other topics. Dave, who was single, liked to go on about women.

"—*There's this bird*, Angela, who's just started at our branch, she's gorgeous, can't be more than thirty-one and blonde. She's been giving me the eye I'm certain of it. I think I'll ask her out next week and, she's got a crackin' pair of tits."

Alan laughed. "You've got a better chance of winning the lottery than getting a date with her, mate. She's out of your league."

"What are you on about?"

"Well, she's a clever bird, isn't she? Articulate, funny, and every bloke in your branch is fawning over her, at least that's the impression I got when I stopped by to see if you wanted to do lunch last week, remember? I can't imagine what she'd see in the likes of you!"

"Shut it, you tosser."

Both men guffawed. Graeme, enjoying the light relief, found it hard not to break into a smile. *This is what I need!*

Although it was all harmless banter and Graeme knew Dave to be liberal with the truth, especially when it came to matters of the opposite sex, this girl he was talking about did, nonetheless, sound like Graeme's ideal type. Blonde, beautiful, intelligent and funny. Then again, with his lack of confidence, how could he possibly hope to meet a girl like that? He thought Karen had been the best thing since sliced bread. That was until he found out about her and Martin. Worst of all, she hadn't seemed very sorry or even that bothered after realizing Graeme knew about the two of them. It was almost as if she'd used him to get to Martin. Graeme started thinking back to the times the three of them had been together. *Come to think of it, she always seemed a bit chummy around him. Bollocks!*

Despite trying his best to stay involved in the conversation with Alan and Dave, once the two of them started bitching about the government, taxes and tube fares, Graeme found himself tuning out. After saying he'd catch up with them in a bit, he got up and headed back to his stool at the bar. By now the place was buzzing. A bunch of young twenty-somethings had arrived and Porto's was packed, to say the least.

Normally Paolo didn't play music, but tonight he'd had a change of heart. The tune was new wave synth pop, OMD's "Souvenir," something that really surprised Graeme since it was hardly a popular tune, yet one he loved, recalled from years back.

The slightly haunting, melodious tone was feeding on his senses, making the hair on the back of his neck stand up. After a few moments Graeme felt himself beginning to perk up, drawn into the music, like it was cleansing him of the worries he carried on his shoulders each day.

"I thought you might like this," the barman said. "It was one of the first songs I heard when I came to England. I think you need another drink, my friend."

Graeme looked up and nodded emphatically, breaking into a huge smile.

After a couple more pints and yet another glass of port, his mind began to blur. Music was still playing and a few of the lively twenty-somethings had started to dance in the corner of the tiny bar. One of the girls, perhaps feeling sorry for Graeme, grabbed his hand and led him across the floor, just as Spandau Ballet's "Lifeline" was starting. *Wow, another rave from the grave,* he reminisced. *Paolo must be on a nostalgia trip tonight!*

For Graeme, as the alcohol delved further into his system, he felt his senses merging; the music and people were starting to blend together. His head was spinning but he couldn't remember enjoying himself this much in a very long time. After a while, he went back to the bar.

"Graeme, my friend. I trust you are enjoying yourself, yes?" Paolo was grinning.

Graeme nodded slowly. He was smiling, but found it too difficult to actually open his mouth to speak.

"I propose one last drink," said the barman. "But you are pretty drunk, my friend. After this, it will be time to go home."

Paolo set the fresh glass down on the bar. This one was bigger than the others and the port seemed to taste different, perhaps sweeter. After a couple of swigs, he looked up. Paolo was still smiling at him. Graeme's surroundings continued to blur, as if he was being taken somewhere. He turned around and thought he saw Clara coming towards him, beaming. *But I thought she couldn't make it tonight?*

Shortly afterwards, he blacked out.

CHAPTER 1

When he came to, Graeme felt cold. He was lying in the small corridor that led to Porto's. It was dark and the door to the bar was locked, as was the entrance above the stairs.

His head was spinning like a top. It was at that moment when he realized he'd left his belongings and his coat inside, including his wallet.

Shit, I'll have to wait until 11:00 a.m. when Paolo comes by to open up, he remembered. *Might as well just stay here a while.* He looked at his watch, an old 1970s vintage Rolex his grandfather had given him as a birthday present. It showed the time as 4:25 a.m. He fell back asleep.

When he awoke again, Graeme could see sunlight streaming in through the door at the top of the stairs. He was absolutely freezing now; perhaps walking out into the rays would help. He stood up, struggling somewhat to keep his balance. Finally summoning the effort to move, he started making his way towards the door, stumbling up the stairs as he went. Despite the pounding in his skull, he observed that the further he climbed, the more the chill inside him dissipated. Fumbling for the bolt, he unlatched the door and stepped outside. As soon as he did, he noticed that something wasn't right.

A rush of fairly warm air hit him as he stumbled out onto the pavement. *But it's December? Sure was when I went into the bar.* Graeme looked around. The sun was shining, leaves on the trees were in full bloom and it was balmy. *What the bloody hell? It feels like it's almost twenty degrees—what's going on?* Despite the temperature, it appeared, according to his eyes, to be morning.

Leicester Square was slowly coming to life. A few early risers were already up, heading for the office, while city workers were still clearing away the rubbish left over from the night before. As he looked around him, Graeme could see that nobody was wearing winter clothes. In fact, what they were wearing seemed a little strange.

Glancing across the square at the theater, he took in the huge display above the doors. As always it was advertising a major motion picture, only in this case, it was the original third saga in the *Star Wars* trilogy. Graeme couldn't believe his eyes.

He turned around; a pair of city workers were placing refuse into what seemed to be an ancient yellow Dodge truck with roll up side shutters parked nearby. He couldn't see a single person talking on a mobile phone. *It can't be,* he thought. *It's got to be a dream.*

Stumbling through the square, Graeme headed north towards Lisle Street. Still bewildered by his surroundings, he almost slammed into a parked car, causing him to lose his balance and fall over.

He noted the vehicle; a brown 1977 BL (Austin) Maxi, registration number TGF 267 R.

A bloody Maxi? My junior schoolteacher used to have one of those. I haven't seen a car like that in years.

As he struggled to stand up, Graeme's head was still pounding, only now he was starting to feel dazed, too. *No doubt the effects of dehydration kicking in.* His thoughts were racing. *What the hell is going on? Am I hallucinating? Just what did Paolo give me last night?*

No matter where he swiveled his head, it appeared that his surroundings harked straight from the early 1980s—from the shop fronts and people's clothes to the double-decker buses and black taxis. *I know enough about the era from those old TV shows and memories, but it just can't be.*

Graeme carried on walking down the street, almost staggering. People were staring at him as he passed by, many with a look of confusion, others perhaps with sympathy. The dizziness was getting worse; he felt himself losing balance and falling forward, then suddenly, everything went dark once more.

When Graeme came to, he was lying on a bed. It was soft and comfortable and the sun's rays were gently beaming on his face. The sensation was soothing, but it still felt like he'd gone ten rounds in the ring. Slowly opening his eyes, he looked around. The room wasn't familiar. White seemed to predominate, from the quilt to the pillows and walls, intermingled with pine furniture and watercolors in glass frames. On the wall facing the window was a big analogue clock; it showed the time as being 3:17 p.m.

He heard footsteps outside the room and suddenly the door opened. A young woman, who looked to be in her early thirties and slim, walked in. She had piercing blue eyes, an elegant face, lightly tanned complexion and blonde, shoulder-length hair. She was wearing a white, tucked-in blouse and what looked to be vintage designer jeans. In her hand, she held a mug of tea.

"Look at the state of you!" she proclaimed, in crisp Queen's English, with a velvety, slightly matronly tone, peppered with subtle hints of a Dutch accent. It was something Graeme noticed since he'd spent six months in Holland after high school.

"What on *Earth* happened?" She walked over to the side of his bed and set the mug down on the nightstand before sitting on the edge of the duvet, facing him.

"*What?*" Graeme sputtered, sitting up and rubbing his eyes. "I don't understand. I've never seen you before and just what the hell are you talking about? Also, where the hell am I?"

"Your flat," she replied abruptly.

"What? This, most certainly, is NOT my flat. I've never seen this place before. My flat looks nothing like this, it's a dumpy place in Shepherd's Bush, plus last I recalled, I didn't have a job, so how on Earth could I afford the money for a place like this?"

"This *is* your flat," she went on, clearly irritated. "I know because not only have I been here several times, but this was the address that was on file for you when we found you this morning, and so you were brought here. There are some bills on the nightstand in the foyer with your name and address on them. Would you like me to fetch one for you just to make sure?"

"I don't understand." Graeme shook his head. "I don't recognize this place at all."

"I think you must be," she sighed.

"Must be what?"

"Suffering from amnesia. You went missing forty-eight hours ago and none of us could find you. Donaldson and the entire department almost had a fit."

"What? Who's Donaldson and just who are you?"

"Come again?" she replied, perhaps with a hint of irritation. "Who am I? Don't give me that, I really don't have time for it right now."

"Look, I really have no idea what you're talking about! I—I've never been here before and I have no idea who you are. Just what the bloody hell's going on?"

"*I don't know,*" she stated slowly, shaking her head, "perhaps we need to get you to hospital and get you looked at—the damage is probably worse than I originally thought. I can't be having a partner who doesn't remember who he is—especially at this juncture. We've got a major crime to solve and our boss wants us in the office, pronto."

"Major crime?"

"*Yes,*" she affirmed authoritatively. "You and I have been working on a case involving a spate of violent jewelry store robberies over the last few months, and so far we're coming up short. I need you to be focused, James."

"James—that's my name—*Graeme James?*"

"What else would it be?" she retorted, chuckling a bit.

He studied her for a second. She was beautiful, clearly educated and staring straight at him. *I must be dreaming. This is easily the most gorgeous woman I've ever laid my eyes on. She's here in "my" flat, and I'm giving her the nth degree. I have no clue what's going on. Perhaps I should just see where this hallucination or fantasy takes me.*

"So this really is my flat, then."

"Y-e-s," she said slowly, indicating that her patience was starting to ebb. "I'm glad we've been able to establish that. And, as you can clearly see, it's far from a dump, even by my standards."

"And I have a job, then?"

"Yes—but you've been skating on thin ice over the last few months, not in the least because of the Southwark incident."

"Southwark incident?"

"James, I'd rather we not talk about it at this moment in time. We've got work to do and you need to get cleaned up. For God's sake, *look* at you! You look like shit. Go and get ready and I'll wait in the kitchen. See you in ten."

With that, she turned and got off the bed, walking out of the bedroom without glancing back.

As her footsteps grew fainter, Graeme managed to summon enough energy to slowly raise himself off the mattress, making his way to the rather substantial looking wardrobe to the left of it. Opening the big heavy doors, he found a pair of suits—which looked like expensive ones—a couple of sports jackets, and four shirts hanging up. He pulled out one of the shirts, a striped Van Heusen, and tossed it on the bed. Below, in the drawers, he found a pair of dark blue jeans, underwear and socks. He quickly took off his old clothes—noticing that his shirt and trousers were different from what he remembered wearing—and got dressed before dashing into the bathroom.

Looking into the glass cabinet above the sink, he had a shock. The image staring back at him wasn't quite what he thought he knew.

He recognized his own reflection, but his skin was darker, his face leaner and hair lighter. He quickly turned away, looking for deodorant, a comb and a toothbrush. Graeme found them soon enough. Cleaned up as best as he could for the time being, he ventured out into the smart, tastefully furnished corridor. *This is nice, and it's mine? Where the hell did I get the money for a place like this?*

Moving past the kitchen towards the front door, he caught *her* glancing at him as she donned what looked like a Harris Tweed sports jacket.

"Are you ready?"

Graeme felt tongue-tied. Still trying to take it all in, he just looked at her like a child on their first day at a new school.

"*Look*," she huffed, clearly growing impatient. "We'd better get a move on."

Graeme found what looked like a pair of old-fashioned Reebok pumps by the front door, though they appeared to be barely broken in. Having put them on close to the entrance, he grabbed his wallet from a small shelf next to the coat stand. He was about to reach for what he thought were his car keys when her hand grabbed his.

"No you don't," she retorted. "You're still obviously in no fit state to drive. We'll take my car."

Having descended the stairs, through the lobby and onto the street, Graeme glanced over his shoulder at the structure they'd just come out of. He shook his head in disbelief; it was a handsome building.

"Very nice," he muttered to himself as they got into the blue Mercedes SL parked across the road from his flat. "This is yours, is it?"

"No, it's the bloody milkman's! James, what's wrong with you? Don't you remember? You borrowed it last Monday."

"*Borrowed* it? For what?"

"*That stakeout in Fulham*! I'm actually *amazed* you got it back in one piece. Next time, I'd appreciate it if you could actually *tell* me you plan on using my car for official police business *before* you take it."

"Sorry."

She looked at him with a slight smile.

Police work, pretty girl, 1980s-style surroundings, Mercedes-Benz R107. Was Graeme somehow indulging in his wildest fantasies? It certainly seemed that way—but if it was just a dream, it was the most realistic one he could ever recall. He could feel the air, the light breeze, the sun, the scent of leather inside the Mercedes and her perfume; it all looked and felt so real. *I'll just have to see where this fantasy takes me.* He shook his head once more. *It's already* far *better than* my *reality…*

It took them approximately forty-five minutes to reach their supposed destination. The roof on the car was down, allowing Graeme a chance to truly ingest his surroundings.

Wherever they were, it was clearly the height of summer. Glancing around at the cars, buses, lorries and people—even the buildings—it appeared as though he was indeed back in the early 1980s. In Graeme's eyes, everything seemed absolutely period, nothing out of place. Part of him was scared; uncertain, yet another part was strangely happy and content. In fact, he could feel satisfaction growing from within him, a sensation he could barely recall in recent times, except during his nights at Porto's.

They pulled into a cul-de-sac just off of Maddox Street in the City of Westminster. At the end was a gate. Showing her pass to the on-duty guard, they drove into the courtyard and parked.

The building in front of them appeared nondescript, blending in with most of the Georgian architecture found throughout this part of London. Graeme decided it was probably best not to ask questions, for although he had little clue what was going on or where he'd end up, he didn't fancy making himself look like a total fool…especially in front of *her*.

Whether a fantasy or not, she was already starting to grow on him and he was increasingly feeling more excited about what might happen next. He hadn't felt like this since he was a teenager. If this was indeed a dream, it was certainly one of the most vivid ones he could ever remember.

Inside, the building seemed like an old-fashioned government institution. And the smell… There was a scent only found in places like this—*official buildings*, he realized. It reminded Graeme of his days as a child in primary school and the hospital when he broke his arm at the age of seven. Various people scuttled along the corridors. He followed her up a flight of stairs and into a fairly large room. Scattered around it were several desks, three of which were occupied. Graeme noticed a couple of the workstations had early desktop personal computers. Dominating the room was a large table in the middle. It was devoid of clutter, contrasting with most of the desks, which were piled high with papers and files. There was also a glass door and partition at the far end of the room—what seemed to be part of an enclosed office.

A young, lanky, late twenty-something man with very dark brown hair saw them and got up from his desk. Graeme studied him. Sporting brown corduroy trousers and a white shirt, the man was wide-eyed, almost as if he was surprised to see him.

"My God, James—you look like you've been dragged through a hedge!" he bellowed.

His partner quickly cut in. "Believe me, Tim, he looks better now than when I first found him."

The two of them were just about ready to carry on their conversation when suddenly, a voice boomed from behind the glass at the far end of the room.

"Judging from your idle chatter, I would say you've found our missing-in-action hero!"

The door opened and a stocky man, sporting a military style crew cut and mustache, stomped out, puffing on a cigarette. Dressed in a three-piece suit sans jacket, he clearly looked to be in charge of the whole operation and, judging by his facial expression, was not amused.

"Just where the hell have you been James?" he scowled. "We've had people looking all over town for you!" He turned to Graeme's partner. "Okay, Braithwaite, *do tell* how you found him."

"Call it intuition, sir. I found him passed out on Cranbourn Street at about 9:30 a.m. this morning."

"What the bloody hell, James?" the older man boomed, taking another drag of his cigarette. "We're knee-deep in a major robbery investigation, and you decide to go on a bloody bender. You've already been skating on thin ice because of the Southwark incident back in April."

"Southwark incident?"

The man quickly glanced at Graeme's partner before staring him straight in the face with a look of disdain.

"Alright," Graeme turned, "I guess we won't talk about it now. She said the same thing back at my flat." His own assertiveness surprised him.

Graeme studied the man for a hot second. He stood around 5'10". Although he wore a Savile Row pinstripe, judging by his haircut and presence, this obviously wasn't somebody to be messed with. From the scent and wisps surrounding him, he also appeared to be a heavy smoker, a trait Graeme had all but forgotten.

"Alright." The man scratched his crew cut and took another drag. "Since you're both here, fill me in. What's been the latest on our jewelry thieves? Sergeant Braithwaite, have you managed to dig anything up from your roster of informants?"

So her last name's Braithwaite, and I'm presuming she's a police sergeant, Graeme deduced. He couldn't get over how stunningly beautiful and sophisticated she was. Then he remembered reading something about the Braithwaites, a prominent family from Suffolk, in the *Daily Mail* back in his teens, though he wasn't sure what, exactly.

"Well, sir," she said in that prim and proper Queen's English, "not much to report, I'm afraid. Things have been really quiet since last week. Not much action, though one of my sources—and he's been fairly reliable—says they might be planning something next week. Possibly big."

"Any *more* details?" the man pressed. "We must have something to go on Em, surely."

"I'm afraid not, sir. The most solid lead I have is from one of my best sources in Vauxhall."

So that was her first name, Grame put together in his slow, yet gradually awakening brain. *Em—short for Emma, or Emily, perhaps?*

"Alright," the man sighed, scratching his crew cut again and taking another drag of his cigarette. "Why don't the pair of you take one of the unmarked cars we have downstairs and follow up with this lead of yours? Em, there's got to be something we can get our teeth into. Let's reconvene here at 8:30 a.m. tomorrow and pray that we have more intel. Go on, get going!"

"Right sir," replied Em.

The man studied Graeme for a second, eyeing him up again, before turning around. He shook his head slightly in disbelief and headed back to his office at the far end of the room.

"You'll be all right, James."

Graeme turned to look at Tim, who was smiling.

Half-smiling back, Graeme nodded his head, trying his best to acknowledge the fact that he appreciated the comment from the young lad.

"I'm guessing that was Donaldson," Graeme said under his breath as they sauntered down the stairs to the parking garage in the basement of the building.

Em said nothing. She just glanced at him and rolled her eyes.

Opening the fire exit to the parking garage, she walked over to the on-duty officer standing by the entrance who handed her a form. Graeme noticed three cars parked nearby: a beige X registration Ford Cortina and two dark blue, Y registration Ford Escorts—all of which looked virtually brand new.

"Look," she started, passing the now signed form back to the officer and receiving the keys, "it's probably best if I drive."

Graeme wasn't about to protest.

Climbing into one of the Escorts, they quickly pulled out of the echoey garage. Beyond Maddox Street it was starting to get busy as people headed home, both on foot and by car from another day at work. As they drove towards Westminster Bridge, Graeme did his best to soak it all in. He just couldn't fully believe he was here. It all still seemed like a dream...yet the scent of summer and the traffic fumes...

it was all just so real.

Once across the river, Em steered the Escort south, down the Albert Embankment Road towards Kennington.

The "source" was waiting for them on the edge of Kennington Park. It was almost 7:00 p.m. now, and warm outside. The car windows were open and neither Em nor Graeme were wearing jackets. Pulling up across the road from Kennington Park, they both got out of the Escort and made their way on foot to the rendezvous point.

"So what do you know about this '*source*?'" asked Graeme curiously as they walked through the leafy, green and quiet park.

"He's been one of my most reliable informants over the last several months relating to almost any criminal activity in South London. If something's about to go down, he's the one most likely to know about it."

"Can you trust him?"

"He's never let me down before. And besides, I think he secretly wants to come in from the cold."

"Do you mean *join us*?"

"Perhaps. I certainly don't think he wants anything to do with the lowlifes we seem to spend a lot of our days trying to keep tabs on. Can't say I blame him, really." She lowered her head briefly before turning to look at her colleague. "He's chosen to cooperate with SRI in turn for immunity."

Graeme noticed a slight irritation in her response, perhaps to suggest if he was questioning her source and sleuthing abilities.

She turned to face forward again before continuing the conversation. "He's got a wife and a little girl and he's afraid for them. This gang we're dealing with are not known for mercy, even when it comes to their own members, as you well know. Remember that tip-off we had a couple of months ago?"

"About what?"

She turned and looked at him, annoyed. "The getaway at St. Paul's, remember? The one where they crashed the van and shot the driver on the spot?"

Graeme sensed a slight shudder inside him.

Em continued, with sharp eyes looking into him, "Our source apparently turned his back because he obviously values his family and life more than the potential spoils."

"What's SRI?" blurted Graeme.

She looked at him as if he was from Mars. "My God, you really don't remember anything, do you? *Us*. What the hell do you think it is? What's wrong with you?" She just about snarled. "We've been partners in Scotland Yard's Special Response and Investigations Unit for almost fifteen months and all of a sudden, *today*, of all days—you *don't* remember. What the hell actually happened last night?"

It was then that he noticed it once more. He was starting to feel different.

Trying to come up with a suitable excuse for his actions, he found one he thought would work.

"Tequila, it must have been those shots of tequila."

"You mean that you were *drunk* last night? That Donaldson was actually *right*? Is that what this is all about?"

He could see that she was angry, but he simply did not know what to do.

"Can we at least focus on the task at hand?"

He nodded.

"Perhaps we should split up," she added. "Why don't you stand close to that nearby tree while I talk with my informant? There's still a chance somebody could be watching us, and if it's only me on the bench, it'll draw less suspicion."

Graeme nodded curtly and made his way to a mature tree not far from a bench where he saw a man sitting, sporting jeans, a blue, vintage-style sports top and a flat cap. The tall, leafy canopy of the big plane seemed to offer a secluded, yet fairly good vantage point. Meanwhile, Em approached the bench and sat down at the far end.

As he scanned the area around them looking for signs of any suspicious people or activity, Graeme could definitely sense changes inside him. The headache was just about gone but there was something else. He was more alert and focused, like he'd never recalled before. He also felt noticeably fitter and mentally more confident. There was a time, he remembered, when he was afraid of just about everything—but not here, not now. Graeme kept an eye on Em and her informant. She was indeed beautiful, but he tried to brush any romantic thoughts aside.

We're just partners after all, aren't we? Plus she—this—*can't be real, can it?*

The man on the bench, Em's informant, who called himself Del, was tense and jittery.

She studied him. Del didn't appear to be that old, but his thin face, solemn expression and nervous eyes made him look beyond his years.

"I'm really taking a risk being here," he huffed, in a heavy South London accent. "I wasn't even gonna do it, but I want out." He lit a fresh cigarette, trying to calm his nerves. "I'm afraid for me missus and me daughter, vey'll kill us all if they ever find out I was ever talking to a copper."

"Look, Del," Em spoke firmly, "I understand that you're in fear for your life, but if you want us to protect you, we need that information. When's the next robbery going down? What are they planning?"

"Dennison's Jewelers, *Marylebone*—it's supposed to go down on Friday afternoon at three, eight-strong crew, two Transit vans."

"Are you sure about this? Do you have any more info?"

"Vat's all I know."

She could see Del was trying to hide his shakes.

"Broad daylight? That seems a bit *bold*, especially in that part of town. All the others were night raids, and from what we've seen so far, it just doesn't fit the profile of the other robberies. You better not be lying to us." She turned her head slightly and gestured to Graeme. "Otherwise we'll be the ones not taking any prisoners. Got it?"

Del took another drag of his cigarette and exhaled. "Vey want to make a statement," he continued. "About four years ago, some members of this gang were part of anover one. Vere was a blag in Blackwall vat went wrong, vere was a police stand-off and the gang leader was killed in the line of fire, but not before he took two coppers wiv him."

"So what's this latest blag all about, then?" pushed Em.

"I 'ere vat the owner of the Dennison's chain 'appens to be a close friend of the deputy commissioner of the Met. Ve two of 'em goes a way back. Ve *Marylebone* location is his largest shop."

"And that's all you know?"

"I swear," Del stopped himself.

"Look, take this." She handed him a fiver. "Walk to Kennington tube station and take the Northern Line to Embankment. One of our operatives will pick you up from there. From then on, you'll be safe. Wait at least ten minutes until *after* we leave the park and try to be relaxed—if you're antsy, you'll draw suspicion. Maybe get a sandwich or something. We'll be off now."

Em removed herself from the bench and started walking back through the park towards the car.

When he saw her abandon the man on the bench, Graeme followed, still scanning the park for any signs of people watching them. As he walked briskly, his thoughts were turning. From what he presumed, there weren't many female detectives in the Met in what appeared to be "1983." *Especially ones attached to what appear to be an elite squad. She must be something special. But is she real? Is* this *real?* There were so many questions, yet as this apparent "fantasy" was unfolding, Graeme seemed further than ever from getting his answers. That said, despite being curious, his feelings of contentment—satisfaction, even—were continuing to grow. Could it be that a part of him was actually starting to enjoy all this?

"So—how did it go?" said Graeme curiously as they rendezvoused by the Escort.

"Not a lot of information, I'm afraid. What we *do* know is that Dennison's Jewelers in *Marylebone* appears to be the next hit, and it's apparently happening on Friday, this week—3:00 p.m."

Graeme found himself speaking through a strong intuition. "*That* seems pretty bold for professional jewel thieves, especially in broad daylight, and in one of the busiest parts of town. Don't you think?"

"That's the first intelligent thing you've said all day, Inspector James."

He pondered the thought for a moment.

So I'm an inspector, and she's a sergeant? That must mean that not only am I a police officer *"here," in this world, but I also* outrank *her—one more clue to this mystery.* That said—the way she'd behaved towards him indicated that, for all her public-school mannerisms, she seemed a real no-nonsense kind of girl.

Perhaps that's why she seems to be the only female detective in "SRI"?

They hopped into the car and Em radioed Headquarters, asking their boss to arrange a pick-up for Del once he got north of the river. She started the engine and they headed towards Westminster.

CHAPTER 2

Once she'd left him on the bench in the park, Del sat there, thinking about what he'd just said. Had he done the right thing? He was only twenty-eight but now, with a young family, he knew that he wanted out of this criminal life and had a real chance to go straight. And he needed to do it now before he found himself sucked deeper and deeper into London's criminal underworld.

It all started at age fifteen when he dropped out of school. He'd pickpocketed here and there, stolen a few bicycles and clothes, but then he'd fallen in with some local riffraff in Clapham and started stealing cars. One thing led to another and before long, he was in over his head, working for a local professional theft ring. His last couple of jobs had brought him in contact with some pretty scary characters and when his daughter was born he knew that was it. He wanted his wife and little girl as far away from this life as possible. The only way to do that, he felt, was to work with the police. *They'd protect me, surely?*

Del did as instructed, waiting ten minutes before he began to make his way towards Kennington tube station. As he left the greenery behind and turned onto Kennington Park Road, heading to the tube station, he looked around. It was still warm out, with a steady stream of traffic in either direction and people going about their business, either walking or coming in and out of buildings on the street. Glancing at his Casio, he saw it was 7:43 p.m. and as far as he could tell, nobody was following him.

He passed by a silver, T registration Vauxhall Royale, parked on the southbound side of the street. He thought nothing more of it.

In the Vauxhall, two men had been sitting quietly, watching Del's every move. "It's almost time," said the older man in the driver's seat. He had a gruff voice, not helped by years of chain smoking, and the lines on his square face hinted a past of living hard. The one in the passenger seat, the thinner and younger of the two, nodded. Checking his 9mm Beretta, he carefully placed it in the holster under his jacket. Once Del was approximately fifty paces on, the man slowly opened the door of the car, got out, crossed the street and started to follow him.

Del was twitchy and nervous; he just wanted to put all of this behind him. He tried to reassure himself. *Once the cops have me in custody, I can rescue my daughter and wife.* He'd sent them to live with his cousin in Basildon just in case things got heavy, but in the back of his mind he knew that the gang could get to them, for its tentacles were spreading all the time. *They have people on the streets, bookies, informants...all kinds of lowlifes in their pocket now. I'm not even sure that the female police officer I've been feeding information to truly realizes how big this whole thing is.* The blags were just a part of it, a steppingstone to something more.

Arriving at the Victorian-era tube station, with its distinctive dome, he purchased a single ticket to Embankment. He proceeded down the stairs to the platform and had the notion that somebody was following him.

Oh shit, he thought, *now I've really gone and done it.* He turned around, but couldn't see anybody suspicious. A gaggle of people were behind him, making their way towards the platform. A young girl cackled as her boyfriend whispered in her ear. An older lady struggled with her shopping bags. *Stay calm.* He shook. *Nobody's following you, nobody even knew about the meeting in the park.*

On the platform, it felt like an eternity waiting for the train to arrive. Just before he boarded, Del took another look around. Nothing. But he still wasn't satisfied. The train was quiet. He grabbed a seat and kept his head down.

Graeme was starving; he couldn't remember the last time he ate. He looked at Em. She was peering straight ahead, eyes on the road as they crossed the bridge. "I could murder a pie or sandwich," he commented.

"There's a pub just off Trafalgar Square I know... Let's stop there for a quick bite." She lit up without taking her eyes off the road.

As they turned onto the one-way system that led from Pall Mall and around the square, past the National Gallery, she pointed the Escort down Duncannon Street and parked near St. Martin-in-the-Fields.

Entering the homely yet smoky establishment, Graeme noticed it was quite busy, accentuated by the din of multiple conversations and the clanging of glasses. The two of them grabbed a table not far from the long bar. It was then he discovered that he must have misplaced his wallet. This was probably why he hadn't realized that he was a "police officer" until their meeting with Donaldson.

"I had it when we left my flat," he told Em, feeling a tad unnerved. "It must have fallen out of my pocket in your car."

She looked at him, rolling her eyes again as she handed him a quartet of pound notes and two fifty pence pieces. Graeme examined them in his open palm with interest. The large fifty pence coins and the notes—he couldn't remember the last time he'd seen some like this.

"What's wrong? You're studying those notes like you've never seen them before." She tilted her head, trying to fathom his fascination with the change in front of him.

"Oh, nothing."

"Are you sure you're alright? You've been acting strange ever since I found you this afternoon and I'm not entirely buying the '*hangover*' scenario. C'mon James. Can you *please* just tell me what's going on? I'm your partner and I feel I have a right to know."

"No, honestly, I'll be fine. Feeling better every minute."

"J-a-m-e-s."

"No really, I'm okay. Please. Can you just trust me?"

"Alright... But I'm not entirely convinced. If not now, please tell me what's really been going on as soon as you can. I'm your partner. I need to know that you've got my back."

"Trust me, I most definitely have your back," replied Graeme with heavy assertion.

Despite Em's disapproving look, Graeme honestly did feel okay. In fact, for about the first time he could recall in his adult life, he knew he truly meant it, even though he was certain his partner still wasn't convinced.

"What can I get you to drink?" he pointed to the task at hand.

"Dandelion and burdock for me. *You*, on the other hand, look like you could use a pint on this occasion."

Graeme got up and made his way to the bar.

He'd been given a specific task: to follow the man in the flat cap and ultimately take care of him. He was being paid handsomely for this little job—£5,000, cash in hand. They didn't like anybody asking questions, and he'd seen the man talking to the pretty girl on the bench in the park.

She had to be a copper, he thought. *Too classy and well-dressed to be talking casually with the likes of him.*

He'd follow the man all night if he had to, until the task was done.

Walking down the stairs to the tube at Kennington Park, he saw the man's head turn. He was certain he didn't notice him; after all, he was dressed respectably. Trousers, shirt, and a blue blazer; nothing to give him away.

When the man boarded the train he slid in two coaches behind. At the next station, Waterloo, he'd change cars and move forward. There'd be more people about then, making it easier to blend in and get closer to his prize.

After finishing his chicken pie and the last dregs of his pint, it was time to go. Graeme had begun to notice that his partner didn't appear to smoke, which was quite a contrast from many of the characters he'd so far come in contact with "here."

Jumping into the Escort, they headed off towards Piccadilly Circus. Traffic was fairly light now. It would probably take them less than twenty minutes to get back to the office.

"So...what are your plans tonight?" Graeme inquired. "I presume we'll be clocking off after checking in with the boss."

"I'm not so sure about that," Em answered with more than a little emotion in her voice. "And besides, since *when* did you care about what I do after hours? You've never asked me about it *once* since we started working together."

Graeme held the thought for a minute. *Does she have a husband? A boyfriend?* She was already stirring feelings in him he didn't know he had, and he'd not even been with her a full day, as far as he could tell.

It was relatively crowded at Waterloo station. People piled on the train, ready to cross the river. Del was still acting a little shaky, his body betraying him. What if someone was following him? He'd be an easy target in this lot. He decided to move forward in the carriage, taking a seat against the bulkhead. Slowly, he looked up. There were people standing; it was getting busier. *Just one more stop to go now and I'm home free.*

The bustling platform at Waterloo had been the perfect opportunity to get a good view of the man in the cap. Now it was just a question of timing. If he played his cards right, he could get a clear shot once the train arrived at Embankment. It was another busy station with multiple tube lines; the crowds would provide the perfect cover.

As the train drew into Embankment station, Del got up and slowly walked towards the door. A feeling of uneasiness washed over him, only this time it was stronger. *I just have to get out of here; she'd said somebody would be waiting for me.*

The doors opened and he stepped onto the platform. Del got caught in the wave of people as they headed up the escalator towards the exit. Quickly turning around, the young lad saw a man in a blazer, discretely reaching for something in his jacket pocket. Del panicked. But it was too late.

"Sierra 3, Sierra 3, come in," it was Donaldson on the radio. "Shooting at Embankment, one casualty."

Em and Graeme looked at each other.

"Sierra 3 responding, we're on our way."

Dropping gear, Sergeant Braithwaite mashed the throttle of the Escort.

Wow, this girl can drive. Graeme looked at her and beamed. *I wonder what else she can do? Probably beat me to a pulp.*

It took them less than fifteen minutes to reach the station. Met Police cars and uniformed officers were already on the scene. Their worst suspicions were confirmed: it was Em's informant, Del. He'd died within sight of his freedom.

"What happened?" she asked, her voice shaking slightly, a hint of anger in it.

One of the uniformed officers stepped forward. "A single shot—in the back of the head. He was gone in an instant."

"Witnesses?"

"None, I'm afraid. This is one of the busiest stations on the entire network. Nobody really saw anything, just the sound of a gun and the body slumped on the platform over there."

"How long ago did it happen?"

"Less than twenty minutes, we reckon."

"Well I don't want you to reckon—I want you to find out exactly. Shit."

Graeme could see she was upset. Del appeared to be "just an informant," a working-class lad who had gotten in over his head, leaving behind a young family. *Why would they kill him like this? Maybe bigger forces are at work, something more than just an armed gang.*

"It smells of a contract killing to me," Graeme spoke. "But who else knew he was working with us?"

"Nobody, absolutely bloody nobody! I mean, we checked everything." He could hear the frustration in her voice. "And now we've got *nothing*. We only had his word that the next robbery was going to happen. I've been tapping Del for three months to get some information on this gang, and he ends up dead on a bloody platform! And I promised that we'd protect him."

"Look, I know this is shit, but there's got to be a leak somewhere. Somebody knew he was feeding us information, and we have to plug it if we're going to solve this thing," Graeme tried his best to ease the tension.

She glared. "Are you saying it had something to do with me, him being shot like this?"

"No—I'm not. Look, let's just go. There's very little we can do here now." His assertiveness was continuing to surprise him. "Give me the keys and I'll drive you back to the office."

She didn't say a word on the way back. He kept glancing at her, feeling he needed to find a way to reassure her that he was there for support, but she continued only to stare into the car's windscreen, arms folded.

Walking into their office, Em took a seat on the edge of her desk. Graeme leaned against what appeared to be his. Donaldson was there, suit jacket off, tie loosened, another cigarette in hand.

Just that second, the young officer named Tim Charles walked into the room, placing some files on the table in the center. They all gathered around.

The mood was solemn. Graeme glanced at Em; he could tell she was still sickened by the whole thing.

Donaldson began. "We should have a report from the coroner's office sometime tomorrow. Ballistics are already working on the bullet found at the scene. A single shot in the back of the head at close range. And both of you were certain nobody was watching at your little rendezvous?"

"Absolutely," said Em quickly. "That's why you asked us to take one of the unmarked cars. That's why we picked Kennington Park."

"Alright, Sergeant. Let's try and stay focused. What, exactly, did you find out?"

"He said the gang that's going to hit Dennison's will be eight strong... Two vans, one possibly for a diversion after the heist. He said the reason they're doing it in broad daylight is to make a statement. He said the store is the flagship in the Dennison's chain."

"Yes, it is." Donaldson rubbed his brow. "The chain is owned by Eric Thompson. He's the deputy Met commissioner's brother-in-law."

"Del also mentioned something about retaliation for a botched robbery in Blackwall," Em injected, "around four or five years ago?"

Donaldson pondered. "Ah, yes—the Midland job, I remember that one. That was messy." He scrunched his face inwards. "It was executed by the Grafton Gang, led by Mickey Barnes. Mickey was a South London hood. He'd run protection for a local gangster in Clapham, but developed a reputation for being particularly heavy handed, and soon graduated to armed robbery. In the spring of '78 he put together a crew of perhaps the worst pond life we'd seen in some time. A couple of members, Charlie Downs and Robert 'Pipe' Piper had done stretches for assault and battery in Wandsworth."

Donaldson went on. "I was part of the Special Patrol Group then. We'd had a tip-off that something was going down in Blackwall in the autumn of '79 and coordinated with local police. It was a bloody disaster. They jumped the gun and went in headfirst instead of waiting for support to arrive, strictly against our instructions.

"A standoff ensued; three hostages were shot, one fatally. Mickey and his mob blasted their way out, figuring it was only local police who called in, but the SPG had gone in as backup. Just as we were arriving on the scene, Mickey and the gang were exiting the bank, armed with shotguns. Gunfire ensued. Two police officers were shot and killed, but we got Mickey.

"It was carnage," Donaldson trailed off unexpectedly, his eyes moving upwards, and tone of voice indicating as if the incident had only happened last week. "Four members of the gang managed to get away by hijacking a passing car, including Downs and Piper. Just one was taken into custody, Harry Chatsworth. But it turned out he was just the getaway driver, hired for this particular job. We recovered most of the money, but the gang simply disappeared."

"So what happened then?" Graeme was curious to learn more.

The super carried on. "For a while things went quiet, then in the summer of '81 another bank robbery happened, this time in Bromley. It was a night job and they got away clean, the local plod came up with nothing and neither did our boys. It was as a result of this incident that our deputy commissioner asked me to form a special unit—SRI—to deal with thugs like this lot.

"Two more robberies followed last year, then we started hearing about jewelry heists north of the river, early this year. There were two in North London, one in Wood Green, the other in Islington. Then we heard about the St. Paul's job. We actually managed to get a tip-off on that one, but the gang appeared to be one step ahead. They'd already split by the time we got there. We found the getaway van not long after arriving on the scene—it was abandoned a few miles away with the driver shot dead at the wheel."

"Blimey," said Graeme.

"There's no question this lot are serious—ruthless bastards who clearly aren't afraid of killing their own. I want them caught, do you understand?"

Silence followed.

Donaldson evaluated his weary team, downright sullen. "I'm in discussions with the commissioner and deputy commissioner to provide this special department with all the resources it needs to catch them. We have to get these animals off the street. I just wish we had more to go on." He focused his gaze intently on Graeme and Em. "There are a couple of things, though."

Graeme seemed to awaken a little bit. Em was still working to shake things off.

"Your informant was right about those Transit vans that were stolen from that car dealer in Stratford a couple of months ago. One of them was used for the St. Paul's raid; the number plates had been changed, but the serial numbers matched."

Em perked up somewhat. "So you believe there's a good chance they'll strike on Friday in Marylebone?"

"There's a very good chance. And right now, we will make sure we're out there in full force come hell or high water. If the bloody axe has to fall because of it, then so be it." Donaldson was defiant, like a man with little or nothing to lose.

"And there's something else," he carried on, changing tone, with a deeper thought that had caught hold. "That driver who was shot dead following the St. Paul's job—the bullets that killed him were from a Walther P1, a standard West German Army pistol. Those aren't easy to get a hold of. This makes me think that these robberies are likely part of something that's actually quite sinister and possibly rather big. Something that maybe extends beyond the borders of our merry town and likely our own green and pleasant land."

Graeme turned towards Em. As their eyes met, he could sense she was scared and looking for reassurance. He tried to offer it as best as he could with a sympathetic smile and sensed she appreciated the gesture. But deep down, he was also scared, though not in the same way that fear had gripped him in his "real life." In fact, he somehow felt more frightened about this "dream" coming to an abrupt end and having to face his miserable existence in the twenty-first century. Threat or no threat, he was starting to like who he was here, in this world, even if it was a fantasy. And he was clearly starting to like her, too.

"Do you think any of Barnes' old mob are involved with these robberies?" Graeme asked.

"With not much to go on at this point, it's difficult to tell." Heavy creases in Donaldson's forehead wrinkled. "Piper and Downs are thugs, but they're no masterminds, and it's doubtful they'd be able to get their hands on military hardware like German Walthers. I also don't think they'd be bright enough to take out a contract on somebody like Del, or at least get away so clean. We simply need more to go on.

"Alright you lot," he rubbed his brow again, "let's call it a night. We'll reconvene at 8:30 hours tomorrow morning as originally planned.

"Tim, keep tabs on ballistics and the coroner's report from this latest killing tonight, that might give us a little bit more to go on. And Em, I'm sorry about what happened to your informant."

Donaldson headed back into his office, sighing and rubbing his cheek. It seemed he still had a lot on his mind. Meanwhile, Graeme and Em grabbed their things and made for the door.

"Goodnight, you two," Tim Charles sang out, who, as Graeme was beginning to notice, often seemed chipper, even at this hour.

"Goodnight, Tim." Em was weary. Graeme could tell she needed a rest.

"Look, I'll drive you home," he offered as they wound their way down to the car park.

She made no objection.

Graeme had never driven a Mercedes before and always wanted to, especially an SL like this with a 5.0-liter V-8 engine. *Wow, this thing's got some poke.* The car felt solid, smooth and effortless in motion, with a satisfying rumble from under the hood. He could hardly believe he was actually driving it.

"What's the best way to your place from here?" he mused.

"This time of night, take Piccadilly to Grosvenor Place and then the King's Road."

He glanced to see her nestled low in the passenger seat with her head against the window.

Chelsea girl, he figured out. *Now why didn't that surprise me?*

She was almost asleep as they cruised further down King's Road. He didn't know where she lived, so he prodded her. "Em. *Em*. Where to now?"

She quickly sat up, annoyed. "You've driven me home at least three times before."

"I know, but after this morning I'm still feeling a bit out of it."

"As you keep pointing out! Third street on the right, fifty yards up the road, it's number 16 Chelsea Square."

He found it soon enough. It was a three-story brick building with a driveway flanked by two large bay windows. He drove through, into a courtyard and brought the car to a standstill.

They sat in the vehicle for a moment, silent. He was longing for her to ask him in, even if it was for just a quick nightcap.

"Well, goodnight, Inspector," she said instead, sighing. "Seeing as you're driving my car, you might as well take it home. I'll call you in the morning and you can pick me up."

"What time?"

"The usual." She closed the passenger door, walking to the building entrance without glancing back.

I'll guess I'll find out in the morning what "the usual" is, he decided.

Never having driven a convertible before, he chose to keep the top down on the way back to South Kensington. It was still a balmy night by London standards and he was savoring every minute of it. He finally got back to "his flat" at about 11:30 p.m. and slid the car into the visitor's spot.

The porter was still on the door as he walked through. "Evening, Mr. James," he greeted with a cheerful smile. Graeme nodded before taking the stairs to the fourth floor.

Shutting the door behind him, he went into the living room, kicking off his shoes before sinking into the soft leather couch.

CHAPTER 3

*T*hud. Graeme jolted. He'd fallen asleep at his desk and the sound was Richards dumping a box of files.

Graeme looked up. Richards glared at him, and said nothing. He swiveled around and headed back to his office.

Graeme was in shock. Rubbing his eyes, he felt his heart sink. *It was too good to be true after all. Just a dream. A bloody dream!* The soul-sucking aura of the Winfield offices surrounded him.

Getting up from his seat and scanning the room, Graeme gazed over the sea of gray cubicles and walkways. People sat at their desks while phones rang and copiers whirred. He looked around for Clara. No sign.

He felt utterly confused. *How can I be back here? I swore I quit my job, so what the hell is going on?* He knew he couldn't face Richards, not yet, at least. Glancing at his Rolex, Graeme saw it was close to noon. He decided to pop out and grab a sandwich down at street level.

Pushing through the lobby door of Centrepoint, out onto Tottenham Court Road, the crisp chill and gray skies of winter greeted him. A quick glance down the street and the sign of Christmas decorations indicated that it was December.

Patting his pockets, Graeme quickly realized that he had forgotten both his wallet and Blackberry. Entering back into the building, he pressed the button and waited for the lift. Once it arrived and the stainless-steel doors opened, he got in and punched the knob for the fifteenth floor.

The doors were just about to close when a hand grabbed hold and opened them again. It was Clara.

"Graeme! Are you alright?"

"Honestly, Clara, I don't know. Look, can I share something with you?"

"Sure."

"I had this dream. This amazingly vivid dream. I went back in time to the early 1980s and I was a police officer with a special branch of the Met. I had this incredible partner and I was working on a case involving armed robberies. It was like all my fantasies were being realized, all at once. And now, I'm back here, *the last place in the world* I want to be."

Clara froze in her spot. He could tell that her kind brown eyes were trying to take everything in. "Graeme," she replied, slowly and matronly. "I'm not sure what's going on with you, but you really need to figure things out. I know you have it tough here at Winfield, and your frequent run-ins with Richards. I don't like him either, but you can't escape reality; you have to deal with what's in front of you."

As the lift began whirring its way upwards, Graeme thought about what she just said. *Was it just a dream? It* must *have been—my subconscious looking for a way to protect me. But it felt so good, being there in "that" world.*

"I'm sorry. Maybe I'm losing it."

"No, you aren't," Clara reassured him. "We all have challenges in our lives, but the trick is how you deal with them. I'm here for you Graeme, I really want you to know that." She grabbed his hand and squeezed it.

Graeme could feel the warmth and energy radiating from her palm. It felt *real*, as real as things had been in the "other" world. He was saddened, heartbroken—but as much as he did not like "this" reality, Clara and her touch were an olive branch, a lifeline of hope in a dreary and desperate world.

There were also questions about what happened in Porto's and earlier that same afternoon in Richards' office. He needed to find answers.

Suddenly, the lift stopped. Jamming the button for the fifteenth floor once again, he knew he had to ask.

As the lift started heading upwards once more, Clara stepped closer to him.

"Clara. Can I ask you something? Did I quit my job yesterday? I remember storming out on Richards, packing my things and asking you to join me for a drink. Did that really happen? I remember you telling me you couldn't join me because something happened to your mum—"

Graeme saw she was about to answer when the lights in the lift started to flicker. Then suddenly, they were plunged into darkness.

"Clara, are you alright?"

Her voice was soothing, reassuring even. "I'm okay Graeme. And don't worry, you're going to be all right."

The lights came back on and the lift started moving, only this time it was heading down, not up. Graeme held the button down for the fifteenth floor, but nothing seemed to happen. The more he pressed, the faster the lift descended. With a pit in his belly dropping down he turned to face Clara. She was radiating kindness, warmth and assurance—he could see it in her eyes and in the expression on her face. The lights turned off again. Graeme was surrounded by blackness and a sensation of falling down into the abyss...

Graeme nearly jumped off the couch. It was dark and he was sweating. He stood up and went to the big bay window at the front of the living room and opened it. The balmy night breeze was soothing. He stayed a while, looking at the street below. It was quiet. Leaves on the trees were in full bloom. Studying the parked cars, he noticed that the newest in view appeared to be a 1983 Toyota Carina and Volkswagen Golf GTI. He took a deep breath. In the distance, he could hear the sound of traffic on the A4, intermingled with the occasional siren and dog barking.

Who was he? What was going on? What was actually real? Graeme felt as if he was living in two different worlds, but what was the actual reality? Here, in this well-appointed flat, it seemed real enough, even though there was so much he didn't know. He could feel, touch and sense everything around him. But his job at Winfield—Richards, Clara, his small, unremarkable Shepherd's Bush flat in the twenty-first century—were they real? His head felt like it was tearing apart. There was one world he didn't like but where he appeared to understand everything that was going on. And there was *this place*—the one he increasingly wanted to be in but seemed to know very little of, at least regarding his own existence.

Graeme entered the bathroom, the same one where he'd briefly attempted to clean himself up earlier.

There was a corner shower with a glass door and chrome railing at one end, an adjacent bathtub, with a toilet and sink at the other. He walked towards the sink and looked in the mirror above it to examine himself.

Sure enough, he saw that same face, darker and leaner, staring back at him from before. He noticed that not only was his hair lighter, but it was slightly wavier and longer, covering the top of his ears. *I've even got a period haircut*, he chuckled to himself.

Graeme felt his chest and his arms. They were tauter, as if he worked out regularly. After washing his face in the sink and grabbing a towel, he started looking around the flat for clues to his identity. The place had three bedrooms: a master, a guest, and a third which had been turned into an office.

On the wall in the office was a framed certificate—graduation in flight training from the Royal Air Force College at Cranwell, 1972, with his name on it. A big, solid-looking desk with three drawers on either side dominated the room, complemented by a soft leather chair on casters. On the desk was a picture of him with somebody else he didn't recognize in British Army fatigues. He slid the photo out of the frame and turned it over. It was dated April 22, 1980.

He sat down at the desk. On one side were a bunch of papers—bills addressed to him: Graeme James, Flat 8, 75 Stanhope Gardens, South Kensington. There were also what looked like old-style DVLA vehicle registration documents and a pure paper driving license. He studied them carefully. The car listed in his name was a 1983 BMW 635CSi, in white, registration YLN 782 Y.

He sat back in the chair. The 635CSi had been one of his dream cars as a kid. He couldn't believe it. *I must be dreaming. Not more than forty-eight hours ago I didn't know anything about this place—nothing. Now it's almost as if all my dreams are coming true. It's like I'm starring in my own 80s TV show. I'm an undercover policeman, working for an elite branch of the Met; I've got a gorgeous female partner, the car and flat of my dreams, and I've never felt physically or emotionally better in my life.*

He headed into the kitchen, grabbing a bottle of Beck's from the fridge. Instinctively, he seemed to know where to find a bottle opener—in the top drawer to the left of the stove. Was this another clue? Had Em been right? Had he actually been suffering from some kind of amnesia? He popped the beer top and took a swig before heading back into the living room.

There was a large Bang & Olufsen Beovision TV on casters in front of the couch and a brushed silver Sony Studio Z-300 High-Fidelity system in the corner, along with a rack of LP records. He selected one, *Communiqué* from Dire Straits, and put it on the turntable before settling back onto the couch. He was fast asleep before the A-side ended.

This was no ordinary blag. It had been in the planning stages for months. As they stood around a makeshift table in an abandoned warehouse down by the docks in Millwall, each member contemplated what was going to happen in thirty-six hours. Outside, the sun was just starting to creep above the horizon.

On the table was a map of London. Highlighted on it in bright red pen was the primary route. In yellow: the diversion. There was no doubt they'd attract some serious heat for this job. After all, it was in broad daylight and Marylebone of all places.

The plan was to have one van approach the target from the east, the other from the west. The location of Dennison's on Edgware Road was almost perfect for a quick getaway. The western van would be used as a decoy, racing down the Bayswater Road; the eastern one used to block traffic and cause confusion—plus, if necessary, it'd be blown up. Meanwhile, amid the chaos, the actual loot would be taken to a third nondescript vehicle parked nearby. The lads assigned for this part of the job would wait until the dust settled before driving off, unsuspected, to the gang's lockup in White City.

Final arrangements were now being made, preparing the two Transit vans for the job. They'd be disguised as legitimate security vehicles, while each would carry a four-strong team for the blag.

The Boss studied his crew. Out of all the lads he'd hand-picked for this job, Charlie Downs and Robert Piper were the two he was most concerned about. They'd both done time and were known to both the local pigs and Scotland Yard. And, as he'd discovered, they weren't the brightest in this clan. But they were brutish and inconsequential of their actions, ideal thugs that could be easily disposed of if necessary.

The Dutch contact, on the other hand, was another matter. Since the Boss had met him eighteen months ago, he'd proved rather adept at getting what they needed. Thanks to his legwork, the team had security uniforms, guns (including a stash of West German Army Walthers) and so far, no questions had been asked. As suspicious and untrusting as he was, the Boss had no reason to believe that anybody, including the police, knew exactly what their plan was. And he intended to keep it that way.

He studied the map.

They'd gone over their plan a dozen times. Today, they would have one last practice run before the real thing.

"We'll meet at the demolition site off West Ferry Road this afternoon at 2:00 p.m.," he instructed. "And we had better get it right, down to the second, otherwise some of you won't be having a hot supper tonight, if you catch my drift."

"Understood." Even Piper, who stood 6'4" and weighed close to 300 lbs., knew not to question the man. *I still wish our old mate Mickey was around.*

Those sodding bastard pigs won't stand in our way this time.

He could hear it ringing. Had he been sleeping at his desk again? Was Richards not in today? He slowly opened his eyes. He was curled up on the couch in the front room.

Light beamed into the flat, transforming the white walls into a sea of gold. It was still ringing.

He shifted and grabbed the phone, pulling the cord so hard he almost knocked the base off the table.

"Do you know what time it is?" said the voice at the other end.

"No."

"It's almost *seven-thirty* in the morning. Remember Donaldson said he wanted us in the office by eight-thirty? And you've got my car." He could detect the irate tone in her voice.

"Oh, shit. Sorry. I'll be there in half an hour."

"You okay James? I'm still very worried about you."

"Oh, yes, yes," Graeme spat into the receiver.

"J-a-m-e-s?"

"See you in thirty," he rushed, and hung up.

Graeme was out the door not ten minutes later. Inside the Mercedes, he found his wallet, still resting on the passenger seat.

Pulling into the courtyard, he could see *her* waiting, clearly not impressed. *Wow, she looks absolutely stunning.* Her hair was tied back into a ponytail and she was wearing a short, above-knee summer dress, heeled shoes and a cardigan draped over her shoulders, plus she carried what appeared to be a designer handbag. *Hardly the look of a police officer.*

"Morning, Sergeant Braithwaite," he opened the door.

"Rough night again, was it Inspector?" she glared, sliding into the seat next to him. "We'd better get a move on."

As soon as they hit the King's Road, Em was on the mic. "Sierra 3 to control, we're heading in now."

"Roger, Sierra 3." It was Tim. "You two better get in here, pronto; Donaldson isn't happy. We're running out of time for any chance of foiling tomorrow's blag."

"Understood."

They drove in silence for a while, and Graeme found it hard to keep his eyes off Em. He desperately wanted to say something.

Finally, he bit the bullet. "Something tells me you've got something going on today. Am I right?"

"You mean something other than police work?"

"That's kind of what I was getting at."

"Meeting an old university friend for lunch, actually. Why? Do you want to join us?"

"Something perhaps tells me that I wouldn't be all that welcome."

"Oh James," she said with a sigh. "It's just Annabel from my days at Oxford, and besides, I'm not sure you'd really enjoy it anyway, she's hardly your type." She glanced at him, and for a second, Graeme sensed her smile from the corner of his eye.

Inside the office, Donaldson bellowed from his desk behind the glass door. "James! *Braithwaite*—in here."

The boss and Tim were poring over a pile of documents and some more photos. "Ballistics came back this morning," the superintendent rubbed his cheek. "Em, the bullet that killed your informant came from a 9mm Beretta."

"I think this case just went to another level," Graeme uttered instinctively. "I mean, a 9mm Beretta, that's standard issue for hit squads and security personnel in the Middle East. Perhaps the heists are just one aspect of something far deeper and more involved, something that traverses national borders. Why would somebody go to such trouble to take out a professional hit on a man like Del?"

They all stood silent for a minute. As they did, Graeme pondered how he could have known about the Beretta and possibly what else was actually going on.

"Good question," remarked Donaldson, finally breaking out of what seemed like an eternity of quietude. "There are just some things about this case that just don't make sense. A jewelry blag in broad daylight, a snout killed by a professional hit man? There's more to this than meets the eye.

"I need to get down to Scotland Yard," the superintendent added, with a hint of urgency in his voice. "We'll need the Special Patrol Group on this, but I'll need to get the *okay* on it, direct from the Met brass.

"Tim, stay here and hold the fort," Donaldson continued. "We're waiting for some telexes to come in about a Dutchman named Van Rooyen who could be connected to our jewelry robbers. Interpol says they've managed to trace him via an arms smuggling ring in Brussels, which has ties to criminal networks both here and in mainland Europe. Find out anything you can about tomorrow's hit, chase leads all over town if you have to and have the '*professionals*' here follow them up.

"You two," he swiveled with firm, still eyes towards Graeme and Em. "I want you to be at Scotland Yard no later than three o' clock this afternoon. You'll need to be kitted up ready for tomorrow and you're the best ones for briefing the SPG. And James, when I say three o' clock, I *mean* three o' clock."

The superintendent grabbed his jacket and marched out of the office. His car and driver were waiting outside.

"'*Professionals*'? What the hell was that about?" Graeme hissed under his breath as Donaldson skidded out the door.

His partner looked at him, smirking. "Because every time something blows up in this city or gunfire ensues—like Bodie and Doyle—you never seem to be far away from it. And I'm guilty by association."

They each sat down at their stations and went over the case files Tim had brought for them.

There didn't seem to be an awful lot to go on, especially with Del out of the picture, but as far as they knew, the hit on Dennison's was still going ahead tomorrow. Then Graeme thought of something.

"*Tim*, that driver who was nailed following the Blackwall job—Donaldson says he wasn't really connected to the gang. Are you sure about that?"

"As far as we know. He's still inside, at Pentonville. He got a five-year stretch."

"Just for being a getaway driver?"

"No. He was also linked to part of a stolen car racket we eventually broke up last year. They were stealing motors off forecourts, changing the serial numbers and number plates with crashed ones and selling them on. Why do you ask?"

"My bet is Chatsworth probably still has contacts on the outside. These thieves tend to stick together and given what we know about Mickey, he always relied on people close to him—family members, or guys that had done stretches together—that's how he got Piper and Downs, right?"

"I guess so," Tim considered.

"It might be a long shot, but I think it's time we paid Chatsworth a visit. I'm going to see if I can get the guv on the horn."

Em approached his desk. "I think you might be right on this one. Look, I've found something else here. Before he got nailed, Chatsworth was reportedly working out of a garage in Clapham; Carnforth Motors, which could have been a front."

"Is the garage still operational?" Graeme asked.

Em broke into a slight grin. "Let's call and find out." She picked up the receiver on Graeme's desk phone and dialed.

A gruff voice answered. "Carnforth Motors."

Em quickly hung up. "Yes, apparently it is."

"Tim," said Graeme, "see if you can dig anything on Carnforth Motors; look for bills, invoices, MOT tests, insurance repairs, anything. If this place is indeed a front, we'll be bound to find something that doesn't add up."

"Coming, Sergeant?"

"Yes—but first thing's first," said Em. "*Car keys*, Inspector? I'm sure you treat other people's cars like you treat your women, but I'm rather attached to my Mercedes."

They pulled out of SRI Headquarters and Graeme radioed his boss. "Sierra 1, this is Sierra 3. Come in, over."

"Sierra 1. What is it?"

"Guv, we think that *Chatsworth*—the driver, arrested from Mickey's last job—might have some information about tomorrow's heist. I think he was more than just a wheelman; he's been linked to that stolen car racket that was foiled in Balham last year. My bet is that if some of this gang are Mickey's boys, they're likely tapping the same sources—at least for using vehicles in their heists. Chatsworth's still in Pentonville serving out a five-year sentence, we're heading up there now. There's also a garage in Clapham that I've asked Tim to check out—could be a possible front for stolen cars and vans our gang have been using."

"Alright, but I don't want you chasing a dead end. Remember we're running out of time on this, we simply can't afford to be sent on a wild goose chase."

"Understood."

"So how do I treat other people's cars?" asked Graeme as he hung up the radio receiver.

"Rough," she replied, shooting him a quick glance before turning east onto the A40.

Fifteen minutes later, Em pulled the Mercedes into a spot adjacent to the prison.

Pentonville, located in the Borough of Islington, was one of London's oldest prisons. Originally opened in 1842, it was in need of some serious renovation. The place wasn't as ominous as say, Wormwood Scrubs or Wandsworth, but walking in, Graeme still had an uneasy feeling. Em was beside him and he felt glad she was, but neither of them said a word as the doors opened. A couple of prison guards gave her the old up and down, unaccustomed as they were to seeing such an attractive young woman in their midst. *Especially one of such pedigree*, Graeme added to himself—not that he'd ever tell her that to her face.

They were led into a rather drab, gray room and sat down at one of the long, canteen-style tables.

A small middle-aged man with balding hair was brought in, flanked by two guards.

"Who the bloody 'ell are you?" he sputtered, in a rather broad Lancashire accent as he took a seat.

"Police. Inspector James, Sergeant Braithwaite, SRI."

"What do you want from me?"

"Information."

"What kind of information?"

"In relation to stolen security vans in South London."

"Don't know what you're saying," said Chatsworth, nonchalantly.

"Look," Graeme exhaled, frustrated. "We both know you were involved with that South London stolen car ring that was busted last year. That's partly why you're in here. But I think you've still got ties on the outside; that you know where the gang responsible for a spate of recent jewelry robberies gets its hands on getaway vehicles."

"How would I know? I'm here, locked up, been since February '81."

Graeme could sense that it was Em's turn to chime in.

"Alright, have it your way, Chatsworth." Boredom was etched on her face. "If you don't cooperate, we can make your life a misery. How would another five-year stretch sound, for starters? Or how about we spread the word that you grassed on your mates? I'm sure they'd be interested in that."

"Think you're tough, don't you, darling?" Chatsworth sneered condescendingly. Em stiffened and pursed her lips, a look of disdain spreading across her face.

Graeme could see things were going nowhere and decided to interject. "Look, Sergeant," he said calmly, surprising himself, "why don't you grab us both a cup of coffee?" She drove her eyes into him like ice, but then they softened. He brought his face close to hers. "Give me a few minutes with this piece of pond life, alright?"

She left, shooting a glaring stare at the prisoner as she headed towards the exit.

Em could feel the anger inside her. Pompous, petty, little men like Chatsworth really got under her skin. Perhaps it was all those years at school and university, dealing with arrogant toffs who had such a sense of entitlement. As she walked down the corridor, the hallway proved a suitable outlet for those feelings to dissipate.

Back in the room, Graeme studied Chatsworth for a second. He was a defiant little prick; perhaps it was just a show, hiding fear.

"You can keep this up as long as you want," Graeme assured him, "but regardless, I'm going to find out what I need to know."

The inspector adjusted his posture, placing his elbows on the table and leaned forward, hardening his face and narrowing his eyes.

"What's your connection with the Carnforth Motors Garage in Clapham? If you don't tell me I'll put in a transfer request to have you moved to maximum security, perhaps somewhere up north? How does Wakefield sound? They'll love a little Lancashire runt like you. All it takes is a phone call."

"You're bluffing."

"Right," stated Graeme. He gestured to one of the prison guards. "Take Mr. Chatsworth back to his cell and get your guv'nor on the line, tell him SRI would like to put in a transfer request, with approval from the Met and Her Majesty's Government."

He turned to regard Chatsworth, who was starting to fidget and perspire. Graeme let a sly smile creep across his face, waiting for the man to respond.

"All right, *all right*." Chatsworth straightened his upper body, trying to hide his fear, but the heavy breathing gave it away. He continued, "But you have to understand that I want to make a deal before I say anything."

"What kind of deal? We might be able to cut your sentence down to three years from five. That means we can have you out of here in a few months."

"That's not enough, I need protection," the little man retorted. "If I tell you anything I want to know that for cooperating with the police I can be guaranteed that. They'll get to me. I need to be moved out of here."

"Hold on a second." Graeme rose and ventured outside to search for his partner. He discovered that she was walking towards him, a pair of foam teacups in her hands. "*Em*, call the guv, Chatsworth says he's willing to cooperate, but he wants a deal; he wants protection. I don't know what's going on but he quickly switched from being defiant to awfully afraid."

"Okay." She met his eyes with a hint of admiration.

Em often wondered how he did it—to get grown men to shake in their boots without so much as raising his voice. It was terrifying, but somehow sexy at the same time. But he was her partner, not her lover. *Half the time he's oblivious to me; to my feelings.* She tried to reassure herself that he meant nothing to her.

Graeme calmly sat down in front of Chatsworth back in the room. "Alright," he said, leaning back in a relaxed demeanor, tapping his hands on his thighs. "You have my word that SRI will protect you. My partner's on the horn right now, and we'll have you moved as soon as possible. Good enough? Now." He leaned forward intently. "Tell me what you know."

The little man gave him a twitchy squint of the brow and began. "I'm still in contact with a couple of my lads on the outside. When I got nicked, I instructed them to look after the garage while I was locked up. We helped provide cars for armed blags, but when the gang leader was shot, some other bloke took over; his name was Plank, or Porter, something like that. They said he was quite intimidating, but he paid cash up front."

"You mean Piper?"

"That's it."

"So exactly *what* did this Piper ask your lads to do?"

"Steal vans; Transits, usually brand-new ones, off forecourts or transporters. They take 'em to the garage and convert them into security carriers, legit looking, but the number plates are from other stolen cars. Then Piper and one of his guys pick 'em up."

"When?"

"They pick 'em up late at night or first thing in the morning."

"The night before a job?"

Chatsworth didn't say anything, but slowly lowered his head.

"How long does it take them to get the vans ready for a job?"

"Usually a week to ten days."

"And there were two vans stolen a couple of weeks ago?"

Again, Chatsworth didn't say anything. He just stared blankly at the copper.

"Alright Chatsworth, we'll be in touch." Graeme got up from his chair.

"I could lose my life for what I just said."

"I said we will be in touch," Graeme pushed his words into him. "Don't push your *luck*, sunshine."

The inspector pursed his lips together, raised his brow and lowered his head slightly, like a teacher disciplining a student. Inside however, he could feel a real sense of satisfaction, comfort even. He got up, heading towards the corridor without glancing back.

As he walked away, he tried to assess the situation and his feelings. *Bloody hell, how did I manage that? I've never been so assertive in my life. It was like I knew exactly how to get the information I wanted.* He was puzzled, but that satisfied feeling was still there and growing. Graeme broke into a smile. *I'm really starting to like where this "life" is taking me.*

Moving down the corridor, he saw Em, still holding the two foam cups.

"What did he say?"

"That we need to pay a visit to Carnforth Motors in Clapham. Sounds as if the place is being used as a front for preparing Transits for armed blags."

"Don't let your head swell too much, Inspector James, but good work," she said bluntly.

"How's the coffee?"

"It's bloody awful. Not sure why I bothered in the first place."

Graeme smiled again.

On the way to Clapham, as Em drove the Mercedes, Graeme pondered his actions over the last thirty hours. He felt stronger, fitter and more alert—that much he already knew. But the way he'd handled Chatsworth; the fact that he'd been able to detect the little weasel had a connection to tomorrow's bank job and acted on a hunch—it was both exciting and baffling at the same time. After all, he could still recall the night in Porto's, Richards, his grotty Shepherd's Bush flat and his lack of self-confidence, even though everything around him right now suggested that world didn't exist. After all, it was 1983, wasn't it?

Carnforth Motors occupied two arches under a grimy viaduct close to Clapham Junction, access to which was gained by a fairly narrow alleyway. The weathered Victorian-era brickwork and the forlorn remnants of several 50s and 60s cars, gave the place a slightly menacing and bleak aura, despite being smack dab in a big urban center. Graeme stole a look at Em as they pulled up. Pretty girl, flashy, expensive convertible, she looked as out of place in this environment as a wildebeest in Antarctica.

One of the viaduct doors to the garage was open. As they approached, out came a man in his late thirties, sporting a flat cap and a dark blue boiler suit. By the looks of things, he'd already spent much of the morning up to his elbows in grease and engines.

"Can I help you?" He surveyed the two of them and asked the question gruffly, while the two cops exited the Mercedes.

"We're looking for somebody who specializes in conversions," Graeme raised his voice over the short distance between them.

"What kind of conversions?"

"Armored security vans," Em answered.

"Who sent you?"

"A friend of Harry's."

"Harry who?"

She could tell the man knew exactly who she meant. "Harry Chatsworth. Word has it this garage is the best place around for getting transportation for specialized needs at short notice."

"Can't help you love, maybe try a limousine service in Marble Arch," he retorted with a snicker.

"Don't you '*love*' me," she exclaimed. "The people I represent are serious clients with serious connections. They have special requirements. We were told this was the best place for this kind of work. Looking at you, it's apparent that Harry was wrong."

"Mike," she addressed, referring to Graeme, "perhaps you can convince our friend here how serious we are."

Graeme deliberately brushed the man's shoulder and walked past him without saying a word. Heading directly into the garage, he started poking around, displaying the arrogance of a teenage public schoolboy.

The place was littered with car parts—mostly engine blocks, gearboxes, driveshafts, wheels and tires, seemingly at random. Based on a quick analysis and intuition, Graeme felt that perhaps this place was a chop shop.

Multiple engines, gearboxes and wheels, there's something fishy going on, he pondered. His curiosity was further compounded by a new Ford Sierra on a hoist, minus the front doors and bonnet—likely stolen. On the other side of the garage was a blue Datsun Sunny, in the process of what looked like an engine and gearbox overhaul. Nothing he could see indicated the presence of a Transit van or two, but something about the place just wasn't right.

A man working underneath the Datsun rolled out on a creeper. "Who the hell are you?" he asked angrily. "Get out of here."

Graeme kept on looking around, ignoring him.

"Did you hear me? I said, get out of here!"

"Up yours, mate," quipped Graeme, who turned his back and started making his way towards a small, dingy office at the back of the building.

The man got up and grabbed a crowbar. He was now directly behind Graeme, thinking the cop hadn't seen him, but Graeme caught a glimpse of him in the office window.

The man lunged forward but his attack was slow and clumsily orchestrated. Graeme swung around. Lifting his leg and pushing his foot forward, he struck the man's left kneecap—hard. The man lost balance and fell forward; as he did so, Graeme grabbed his shoulder, forcing him to the ground.

"Gerry, grab the bird!" he yelled to his mate outside. The man tried to wrestle free, but Graeme's grip was too strong. Then for a split second, Graeme thought about his partner. Loosening his hold momentarily gave the man a chance to turn over and make a swing at the cop, but Graeme's reflexes were too quick—he socked the man in the side of the head, knocking him out.

"James!" he could hear Em yelling from outside the garage. He grabbed the crowbar and rushed out. "Gerry" was dragging her towards a battered-looking Sherpa van parked at the end of the alley.

Graeme was running fast. They were already at the van. Gerry was opening the rear doors, but as he let go of Em's left arm, she saw the opportunity to elbow him in the ribcage. It was enough. He stumbled and she got free.

Just as she moved out of the way Graeme lunged at the man, dragging both of them into the back of the Sherpa. They slid across the floor and the punches started. The man hit Graeme in the temple, while the copper tried to hit back, using the crowbar for leverage, anchoring it into the right-side panel of the Sherpa. The man swung again, with enough force that it pushed Graeme against the side of the van, smacking his arm against the edge of a rusty toolbox. The man tried to grab the crowbar but Graeme was able to rotate his body, bend his knees and use his feet to kick the man's face hard. Gerry was stunned long enough for Graeme to grab the crowbar and press it against his neck, just hard enough that the man couldn't wriggle free. But he wasn't giving up just yet.

As Graeme tried to move to get a stronger grip, Gerry clenched his right fist and struck Graeme again, knocking him back. The mechanic grabbed the crowbar and tried to come at him, but the inspector darted out of the way, causing Gerry to smash against the other side panel of the van. As he did, Graeme pounced, grabbing the man's arm and twisting it. He could hear Gerry crying in pain as the wrist cracked.

"*You bastard*—you broke my fucking arm!" he barked. "Who the bloody hell are you two, anyway?"

"SRI," Graeme spat, trying to catch his breath. "And you're nicked."

They were counting the hours now. Piper and one of the younger lads, Gibbs, had picked up the two Transits the previous evening, all kitted up as security vans and ready to go.

One had been taken to the lockup in White City. The other—the decoy—was now inside the warehouse in Millwall.

Van Rooyen took a long drag of his cigarette. He'd been asked by the Boss to oversee the operation, and had arrived at the warehouse a little more than an hour ago. Not only had he proved a useful source in obtaining weapons, he was also a master at orchestrating professional heists. Two raids in Rotterdam, three in Antwerp, and nobody suspected a thing until it was too late. But he'd been careless. During a supposed arms deal in Brussels in preparation for another blag, he'd been made. He managed to evade local police, but soon became of prime interest to Interpol and one of the most wanted men in the Low Countries.

Electing to avoid attention and knowing he spoke English well enough, Van Rooyen decided to slip across the Channel on a ferry. He felt South London would be the perfect place to blend in, until he figured out a plan of action. Then one night, in late August of 1979, he'd bumped into Mickey Barnes at an underground boxing match.

Van Rooyen liked to bet on sports, legal or otherwise, and it didn't take him long to find his way into the South London underworld where such matches frequently took place. When Van Rooyen's fighter won that match and Mickey's boy didn't, the two of them exchanged words.

It wasn't amicable at first, but it turned out, they had a lot in common. Van Rooyen was looking for new ventures and Mickey, a good source for weapons. Van Rooyen was able to source guns for the Blackwall job, even though he didn't take part. When Mickey was shot, he'd essentially taken over his South London action and Piper, Downs and Barrymore had gone to work for him. While in the process of planning another raid, he'd met the Boss. The Boss had set him up with money, a decent flat and a nice, profitable protection racket to run.

Now, here he was, almost four years later, preparing to orchestrate one of the most ambitious blags in the history of London town.

In front of him, the eastern Transit was being rigged with explosive charges—one under the fuel tank, one by the rear door and one under the bonnet, all designed to be activated by remote control.

That should be enough to cause carnage in the heart of the West End, as well as giving the police plenty to do while we make our getaway.

Blowing up one of the Transits hadn't been part of the original plan. The eastern van had been intended purely as a diversion, designed to lead the police on a wild goose chase, with the other used to haul the loot away.

The sheer nature of the job would likely have attracted the attention of the cops anyway, even if there hadn't been a tip-off, but now, thanks to a snitch, modifications to the original plan had to be made.

The snitch killed at Embankment had likely told the fuzz exactly when and where it was going down before Van Rooyen had made sure he was permanently silenced.

The real problem was that girl. Pretty, intelligent...Van Rooyen had seen her talking to the snitch several times. But it was the second occasion, outside a bookmakers on the Old Kent Road that raised suspicion. It was a chance encounter. He'd been in there, placing a bet on the dogs and saw them as he exited; luckily the young lad hadn't recognized him.

Van Rooyen, on the other hand, instantly identified him and honestly, was a bit surprised. It was young Derek Robinson who worked at one of the dealers where they'd been getting the stolen vans.

Mickey had known the man's cousin, so Van Rooyen thought the young lad was trustworthy enough. He'd asked his boys to slip him a few notes each week for a spare set of keys when new vans came in on the transporter. But talking to her on the Old Kent Road—something about that just wasn't right. *Why would somebody like her be down here in the first place, especially with the likes of him?* She had to be police, or at the very least, government of some kind. That's when he'd called the Algerian and planned the hit on Del. *Maybe it's time to take the girl out, too...*

Van Rooyen went over the revised plan in his head. They would arrive at Dennison's with the two vans, blocking Edgware Road. Two four-man teams would raid the jewelers—it was a big shop, after all—and they needed to take care of the security guards and cameras.

Having raided the store, one team would jump into one of the armored Transits and make off as quickly as possible heading west, but this would be the decoy group, designed to ensure a police chase. The other four-man team would split into two groups. One pair would drive off in a stolen Jaguar saloon, while the other would jump into a bogus British Telecom van strategically parked around the corner from Dennison's, just after the second armored Transit was blown up. This team would wait until the dust settled before leaving the scene. These were the lads that would handle the diamonds—Brent and Smithson.

Williams, the explosives expert, would drive the second van to Dennison's and Van Rooyen would accompany him. While the robbery was taking place, he and Williams would carefully get out and Van Rooyen would walk to a phone box across the street. Nobody would suspect them wearing security uniforms. Just as the others were making their getaway, he'd set off the detonator and blow it sky high. *That should be enough to make a sizable distraction.*

Van Rooyen watched as Williams went over the Transit mobile bomb with the thoroughness of a quality control inspector at the Rolls Royce factory in Crewe. He was good—*really* good.

Van Rooyen lit another cigarette and smiled. In less than twenty-eight hours, it would all be over.

Graeme looked at Em. *A pretty English rose, soiled by South London grime.* Her cardigan was covered in oily prints. He thought about saying something, but better judgment prevailed.

They were still at the garage waiting for the Jam Sandwich Cavalry to arrive. Gerry and the other bloke were handcuffed to the hoist with the Sierra on it. Gerry was still moaning in agony over his broken arm.

"You know we could have done this the easy way, but you stupid bastards are now facing multiple charges for assaulting two police officers." Graeme glanced at his partner. He thought he could see a smile emerging, albeit a subtle one.

I'm starting to like this place quite a lot, he thought to himself.

As they stood there, they could hear sirens growing louder. Emerging from the door, they saw two Met Rover SD1 patrol cars round the corner and come thundering down the alley, followed by Tim Charles in his Ford Cortina.

"You both look like you've had your hands full. Did you find out anything?" asked Tim with a catlike grin on his face, jumping out of the car.

"Not yet," shouted Em over the whining sirens. "They just went for us—before we could ask any questions, James was lucky he didn't come a cropper."

"Slight exaggeration, I'd say, all things considered." Graeme was feeling a bit humbled, especially now that his adrenaline had largely dissipated.

Em turned her body and winked at him.

Tim and the uniformed officers began combing the garage, searching for anything that might tie in the operation with criminal activity, be it large or small. Tool chests, wall cabinets, the parts storage room and the office were all fair game.

"Sir, I think we've found something," said one of them, ushering Tim, Graeme and Em into the office at the back of the shop. The uniformed officer produced a folder, handing it to Tim who scanned through it quickly.

"James, you were likely right about this place being a front for stolen cars. Take a look at this." The young detective presented several pieces of paper to Graeme. "Here's a bunch of receipts for parts bought, but so far, we've found no corresponding labor charges billed for vehicle repairs."

"That's very interesting," Em chimed, picking up another folder and browsing through it, "there doesn't appear to be any income or profit and loss statements here, either." She peered into the back of the small office, noting what was probably a locked cabinet. "James, do you still have that crowbar?"

Graeme went back outside, grabbed the bar and handed it to the uniformed officer. Breaking the door revealed a small safe.

"Tim, we need to get this opened," Graeme affirmed. "Get a safe expert down here. I have a feeling we're going to find something very interesting inside here and oh, better inform the guv, too."

As Tim signaled another officer to call Headquarters, Graeme made his way towards the Sierra on the hoist. The two men that tried to assault him and Em had already been taken to the patrol cars.

After pressing the button to lower the lift, Graeme peeked inside. The car's steering column had been messed with and the dash pad loosened, obvious signs of VIN and odometer tampering.

"Tim, wasn't a car like this stolen from a Ford dealer in Croydon a couple of days ago?"

"We did get a report on a car fitting this description—give me the serial number and I'll contact the DVLA."

"Okay, we also need a forensics team to go over every inch of this place, Tim," Graeme instructed.

"They're already on their way."

The alley was becoming a hub of activity. As Em and Graeme made their way back to the Mercedes, they saw that a Ford Transit police meat wagon had arrived, along with another Rover patrol car.

Two male officers jumped out of the Rover and headed into the garage. Two more were standing close to the Transit. "Suspects secured ma'am," one of the officers announced as they moved nearer.

"Where are you taking them?"

"Straight to Scotland Yard, for interrogation."

"Contact DCI Donaldson at SRI. Tell him we've found two prime suspects linked to a spate of armed robberies. Ask him to call me at home in twenty minutes."

"Yes ma'am."

Graeme and Em climbed into the Mercedes.

"So, what now, Sergeant? I think at the very least, you need to get out of those dirty things," said Graeme cheekily.

"I think you got hit harder in the head than I first thought," she threw back.

They drove to Em's place. By the time they reached the King's Road, Graeme was starting to feel the pain. His temple was throbbing, his hands and arms sore from the grappling with Gerry. She glanced at him occasionally, but he was too wrapped up in dealing with his discomfort to notice.

Once they reached the flat, she exited the vehicle and opened the downstairs door to the complex.

"*Well*—aren't you coming?"

He slowly moved out of the Mercedes, following her. Once inside the flat, she led him to a chair in the kitchen.

"Sit down, here," she said. "I'll be just a minute."

Graeme took his first deep breath all day.

The kitchen had a very homey feel about it. He glanced around. The room was dominated by a substantial-looking breakfast bar with a bowl of fresh fruit in the center. There was also a wall-mounted high end SMEG oven, a separate stovetop on the counter, as well as neatly organized spice and baker's racks and a tall narrow bookshelf in the corner with a raft of recipe books. The kitchen was neat and clean—everything in it had a specific place and purpose.

He heard her pick up the phone to call Donaldson.

"Yes sir, I'm just at my flat. James was slightly injured, but he'll be all right." She paused. "Yes sir. I'll let him know."

Footsteps down the corridor followed.

Em soon returned with a first-aid kit. "Take off your shirt," she ordered.

Graeme complied readily and smiled to himself. *I'm really starting to enjoy this "second day" on the job!*

She opened the freezer to grab a bag of ice before wrapping it in a tea towel. Pulling out another kitchen chair, Em sat down beside him.

They were close now, he could smell her scent. Despite her face, clothes and arms covered in an oily mess, she still smelled fresh, clean and soft, enhanced by her perfume—Anais Anais by Cacharel. He knew the distinctive, flowery fragrance, remembering it from childhood in the *other world*. His dad had given his stepmother the same stuff as a Christmas present one year, or something like it. The aroma was rich and intoxicating. He closed his eyes, wishing the moment would never end...

The meat wagon trundled across Lambeth Bridge on its way to New Scotland Yard. The two men in the back sat in silence.

Gerry stared at the man across from him. "I'm going to fucking kill you," he mimed with his lips. The other man just spat back at him.

Twenty minutes later, the white Transit pulled into a secured car park near 10 Broadway. Things were about to get a whole lot worse for Gerald Doherty.

"*Ouch*, that hurts," he shot out as Em placed the ice over his bruises, her hair close to brushing against the side of his face. The initial pain was sharp, but her touch was gentle.

"You've got quite the bruise on your temple," she said softly. "Sit still, it only makes it worse if you flinch."

"Ouch."

"For somebody who plays tough you can be quite the baby sometimes," she giggled.

Em placed the ice on his shoulders for a few minutes, then his arms, before lightly massaging them—pleasure and pain in equal amounts. "You've quite a nasty cut on the back of your right arm," she noticed.

"Must be from when that idiot slammed me against that toolbox in the van. Bastard. I didn't think it was such a big one."

"Hang on." She got up to head towards the bathroom. "*In the meantime*, hold the ice to your forehead," she shouted from around the corner.

Graeme did as instructed. The ice was cold, but soothing.

Em emerged with a bottle of Dettol and sat down again on the chair, her arm virtually touching his. Taking a small dab, she placed it on a cotton bud. The Dettol stung, but it felt pure, cleansing Graeme's wound of South London grime. *A bit like SRI doing the same for this city*.

"Here." She placed a plaster over the cut as best as possible.

Then it was over.

"Okay, you can put your shirt back on. I'm going to freshen up now."

"Still have that lunch date with your college friend?" Graeme called out.

"You mean Annabel? *Absolutely*!" her reply drifted from down the corridor. "But *before that* we need to get you back to your flat. You're still a mess and I'm not your personal nurse! Plus we've only got a few hours before we have to reconvene at Scotland Yard."

He smiled to himself, wryly.

While Em got ready, Graeme engrossed himself in what appeared to be a "recent" copy of *Time* magazine on the lounge coffee table, the cover story of which "Maggie by a Mile" proved intriguing, to say the least.

Thirty-five minutes later they were ready to go. Em had changed into a fashionable blouse and brown trousers with matching heels and a belt, her hair freshly washed and styled. She looked every inch the young sophisticate. He still found it hard to believe she was a copper.

As they pulled out of Em's apartment complex and headed north on Chelsea Square, Graeme sensed an inner warmth. The way she'd doted on him in the kitchen, it had felt really special, sensual, intimate. There was something magical about the way she had brushed against him and the sensation of her fingers as they massaged his shoulders and his arms. *Why had she done that?* he pondered. *Could she be interested in my well-being other than just professionally?* He glanced over but she was just concentrating on the road ahead.

They drove for a while in silence. With the windows up, but the top down, the only noise was the slight rushing of the wind, the faint rumble of the SL's engine and the everyday sounds of traffic. As they headed up Onslow Gardens, Graeme decided to start a conversation.

"So, tell me more about this lunch date of yours?

Em turned to look at him briefly, a bit surprised at the comment.

"You mean Annabel? She's one of my closest friends, we've known each other for ten years. We stay in touch, but these days, don't get to meet up a lot. She still lives up near Oxford. Why do you ask?"

"Oh nothing, really, just curious to find out a little more about you, your friends, what you like to do. I figured that since we work together we should know a little more about each other."

"James, you've been full of surprises the last couple of days. That's hardly something I'd have expected from you."

"What would you expect then?"

"Not sure this is the time, nor the place to talk about it."

Okay then, Graeme thought.

A few minutes later they pulled up on Cromwell Road, across the road from his flat on Stanhope Gardens.

"So, I'll see you at three?" she said, raising her perfectly natural blonde brows.

Graeme nodded.

Once out of the car, he stood on the pavement. As the Mercedes roared off, his gaze lingered, watching the light blue car grow smaller in the distance.

Climbing the stairs to his flat, he felt stiff as a board.

CHAPTER 4

The interrogation room at Scotland Yard smelled of stale cigarettes. Donaldson reached into his pocket and offered a B&H to the man sitting across from him. He took it.

Behind him stood a Met Detective dressed in a brown leather jacket, gray shirt and trousers, who was keeping a firm eye on the proceedings.

After taking a couple of drags, the superintendent began. "Gerald Doherty." He brought his face close to the scum. "Why did you assault my officers?"

"Because I didn't think they were pigs," the man spat defiantly, "especially when one of them breaks your bleeding arm. He didn't tell me he was Old Bill until afterwards."

"But why did you and your mate Jones try and pull a fast one?"

"We don't take threats from nobody, especially some posh bird in a picnic dress. Plus we figured she'd be worth a bob or two in ransom money. It's not often we get people like her down in our neck of the woods."

Bloody Braithwaite, thought Donaldson. *She's one of my best detectives, but sometimes she still puts her foot in it.*

"So tell me about Harry Chatsworth. According to our sources, you've been keeping things running while he's on the inside. And if you're not willing to cooperate, DC Hungerford here can always break your other arm."

"That's police brutality," Doherty protested. "I've got rights you know."

"This is SRI, son," Donaldson growled, leaning across the table, his nose within inches of Doherty's face. "We're an undercover squad with special dispensations direct from Westminster. Your rights don't mean diddlysquat in here. Either you cooperate with us, or we're going to make your life miserable from this moment on. And there isn't a single thing you can do about it."

Donaldson was perhaps being a little economical with the truth, but up to this point in time, both the Home Office and the Met brass had given him surprisingly free reign over his "special" department. That being said, the antics of James and his partner had raised a few eyebrows at the Yard in recent months.

Nevertheless, the threat from the superintendent was enough for Doherty to spill the beans. He'd been keeping an eye on things while Chatsworth was on the inside. The garage had once been a legit operation, but Harry had been struggling, until he decided to take a last chance and hire an additional mechanic who happened to be quite skilled at paint and bodywork.

Doherty had criminal ties to South London gangs, including Mickey Barnes' operation, but Chatsworth had been desperate and they'd come to a deal. Doherty agreed to work for the man at a reduced rate. In return, Harry allowed him to do extra jobs on the side. He neglected to mention said work involved cutting and painting stolen cars.

It didn't take long for Doherty to figure out an opportunity was staring him in the face. Because the garage was located in the darkest corner of Clapham and down an alley at that, it represented the perfect location for hiding stolen motors. And Harry was broke—a man from the North who was about to see his London dream end in tatters. It didn't take long to persuade him. At first it was just small-time stuff; used cars off dealer forecourts, but then Doherty hit pay dirt. When Harry got busted, Gerry's "involvement" with stolen cars was conveniently overlooked.

That gave him free reign to do what he wanted and it was a few weeks later that the Dutchman first contacted him—a referral from one of Doherty's long-time South London hoods. The Dutchman said he was looking at procuring vehicles for specific jobs. And soon, Gerry was out stealing vans. The Dutchman paid a lot of money for each job and always in cash. That was how it started. In some respects, he was glad the two Transits had already been collected before the pigs showed up, otherwise he probably wouldn't be breathing. That big bloke, Piper, had done a stretch in Wandsworth for almost beating a man to death.

As the interview wrapped up, Donaldson gestured to Hungerford. "Get me Tim Charles on the phone. Tell him we've had a breakthrough in the case."

Graeme had just stepped out of the shower when the phone rang. It was Em.

"Thought you might like to know, we've had a major development in the case regarding our gang of merry men."

"Where are you?"

"I'm in a payphone in Covent Garden."

"Oh, *of course*, your lunch date."

"As I said before, Annie's just an old and dear uni friend. You can't tell me you're jealous at the thought of me spending time with somebody else besides you."

"Of course not. What could possibly give you that idea?" Graeme tried hard to contain his laughter.

"Anyway, I was just on the blower with Donaldson. Apparently Gerald Doherty, the man who tried to grab me at the garage, has just given one hell of a confession. He said that *he* was the one that got Chatsworth involved with the whole stolen car thing and that a Dutchman paid them big money to steal and prep vehicles for specialized jobs."

"Van Rooyen?" asked Graeme.

"Doherty didn't mention any names, but I'm betting it's probably him. Also, given that Chatsworth mentioned Piper, I don't think it's going to be too hard to put two and two together, especially since we've already got photos of Piper and Van Rooyen together, even if they are a few years old."

"You're brighter than you look sometimes, Sergeant."

"Are you giving me a compliment, Inspector?"

"Possibly. Anyway, enjoy your lunch. I'll see you at three."

Em hung up the receiver and walked across the square to a little café where her friend was waiting.

"Lovely to see you Annie," she smiled as they hugged.

"You're looking as gorgeous as ever, Em."

Annabel's eyes sparkled with enthusiasm. She was clearly very happy to see one of her best university friends. The two had stayed in touch regularly since their days at St. Catherine's College, even though they were often only able to get together in person a few times a year. With her long, raven locks and sultry green eyes, Annabel had been the yin to Em's yang at Oxford—at least as far as the boys were concerned. Since then, she'd established a very successful estate agency brokerage in Chipping Norton. For Annie, coming to London was a real treat, especially to meet with her best friend.

"Honestly, Em, I don't know how you do it—working in such a barbaric line of work, especially with all those men around. And that partner of yours, how do you cope with him?"

"He's not all bad, not all the time, anyway."

They both chuckled.

Especially over the last few days, Em mused. *In fact, I'm rather glad his injuries from the morning hadn't been worse, and in a way, he did save my bacon. And now that I think of it, I'm glad I had the opportunity to take care of him... It just somehow felt right nursing him back at my flat. Does this mean I'm falling for him? C'mon Emily Ruth Braithwaite, get a grip, don't go down that road, not now. Enjoy your time with Annie. Remember, it's been months since you've seen her!*

The Boss had it figured out. The raid on Dennison's flagship store was truly going to be the heist of the century. Yes, it was bold; yes, one of the primary reasons behind it was to secure enough funding for bigger things, but the prize itself was tremendous—almost £2.5 million in diamonds and other precious stones.

He'd gone into the shop several times, posing as a legit buyer. He'd inspected the wares on display, seen the security cameras and the four guards on duty. One day, when one of them was clocking off, he was sitting, parked across the street in his Jaguar Mk II. When the guard was about one hundred yards from the building, he ushered him over.

At first the guard wasn't receptive, but a little cash in the pocket can always be persuasive. All he wanted to know was the specs on the security doors, their thickness, weight, how they were activated. It took a couple of meetings to get the information out of him, and by then the guard was in his pocket—two hundred quid was all it took. But there was no going back. If he whispered to anybody, Van Rooyen would take care of him, just as he'd done with young Derek Robinson.

So now he knew the score. Precisely at 2:57 p.m. tomorrow, the guard, Jenkins, would deactivate the alarm system at Dennison's. At 3:00 p.m. exactly, the two Transits would be outside, blocking the entrance. By 3:10 p.m. the two four-man teams would be making their getaway. That's when the fun would really begin. A sly smile crept across his face, but then quickly faded. There was still one more practice run. *And there'd better not be any bleedin' mistakes.*

She was having an effect on him. He shaved and plucked, brushing his hair and cleaning his teeth with much more purpose than he could ever recall. But he still wondered why. After all, it was just a briefing this afternoon, wasn't it?

As he headed to the bedroom, Graeme took a second to figure out what he wanted to wear. He grabbed another striped Van Heusen shirt, a pair of slacks and leather shoes. He pulled out a sports jacket and tossed it on the bed. *I've never worn stuff like this before because I wanted to. But strangely, it feels good.* He glanced at the clock on the wall; it was 1:43 pm. Having gone into the kitchen and made a sandwich, he headed into the study, still munching away.

Time to look around and find more clues to my life here. How had he wound up as an inspector at the Met? What had his life been before that? Who was the man in the picture? What had he done in the Air Force?

He sat down at the desk and began routing through the drawers. He found more bills, a paper envelope with a sizeable stash of money—£300 in old-style notes (at least to his eyes), most of which appeared to date from the late 1970s.

Why would he have so much cash just sitting in a drawer? There were also postcards. One was from Cyprus. It read:

Hope you come back soon, missing you, love Trish.

An ex-girlfriend, perhaps from his days in the service? The postmark was dated August 14, 1981.

He also found a pair of RAF cufflinks, pilot's wings and rank shoulder bands. He knew enough about military ranks from reading about them as a schoolboy. Two large stripes—that indicated a flight lieutenant. He was still none the wiser. But why had he kept them? Souvenirs? Or for some other purpose entirely?

In the other side of the desk drawers, he found a key with a tag on it, which read "Property of SRI." He picked it up and walked towards the front door. Grabbing the rack of keys hanging on the little shelf by the coat stand, he pressed it onto the ring.

Time to leave, he thought. *It'll probably do good to get there early; Donaldson seems to think I'm never on time*. He grabbed his jacket and wallet and headed out the door.

Downstairs in the complex's private parking, Graeme found his car. It was under a heavy-duty, light gray cover. Pulling it back, the BMW glinted. It was brand new. *A chariot from the gods*, Graeme said to himself with wide eyes, *sparkling in white*. He must have spent a whole five minutes just gawping at the bloody thing. Folding up the cover, Graeme opencd the BMW's boot and placed it in before shutting the lid. Grabbing the key, he unlocked the door and sat inside. The leather smelled fresh, the tungsten, paint; it was unbelievable. All the controls angled to the driver and the steering wheel and gear lever felt solid—good to the touch and very natural. Graeme pinched himself a couple of times and then started the engine. Putting on his seat belt, he put the car in gear and pulled out onto the street.

Once he hit the A4 he turned on the radio, pushing the selector to 95.8 on the FM frequency. A song was just starting, A Flock of Seagulls, "Wishing." It was one of his favorite tunes from childhood. He could recall listening to it in his flat in Shepherd's Bush, on the cheap Sanyo stereo he'd bought from Currie's. The song was one of the few things that had kept him going through dark, difficult times. But here it was, playing on the Blaupunkt radio in a brand-new 1983 BMW...*his* BMW! He mashed the accelerator as he headed towards Westminster, reveling in the moment.

As the Boss wheeled his burgundy Jaguar Mk II into the demolition sight, he could already see his boys were about ready to start their final practice run for tomorrow's blag.

Once upon a time, the site had been the location for the Moorhead & Sons machine works. Like much of the surrounding area, however, this part of the Isle of Dogs had seen rapid decline over the last two decades. The factory had closed some twenty years ago and was literally falling apart. The Boss had bought the land for virtually nothing nearly a decade before and the dilapidated site had proved the perfect place for planning heists.

Inside, they'd constructed a mockup of the Dennison's store, with wooden boards representing the guards and old televisions posing as cameras. They were all dressed in fatigues, shotguns at the ready.

Parked out front were a Sherpa and a Bedford CF, the actual heist vehicles. One hundred yards away, on either side of the building, were a green Jaguar XJ6 and an ex-British Telecom Dodge Spacevan in their respective locations for the actual blag. A pile of bricks had been used to simulate the phone box where Williams would activate the detonator.

The men lined up, waiting for instruction. At a glance, they could have almost been ex-soldiers. Downs and Piper stood above the rest, with their big, beefy frames and military style crew cuts. Rafferty and Doyle were childhood friends from Northern Ireland and although smaller in stature, 5'10" and 5'8" respectively, were tough nuts who also happened to be seasoned bare-knuckle boxers with scars to prove. With his long hair and thick beard, Rafferty fancied himself a bit of a ladies' man, but his shifty looks and smug demeanor easily led to confrontation almost everywhere he went. Doyle was clean-shaven and arguably more respectable looking than his friend, but tended to talk too much, which frequently landed him in trouble. Williams, "the engineer" was perhaps the odd man out. Born in London to Trinidadian parents, he was fairly slight and slender compared with the others, but a keen mind and meticulous attention to detail made him perfect as the explosives expert.

The other lads, Barrymore, Brent, Gibbs and Smithson, were the youngest, lanky—small-time, petty criminals who'd been recruited primarily for their agility and to make up the numbers. They were also considered the most expendable, should things go wrong.

"Right," Van Rooyen's words parted from his lips in his nasally, guttural, accented English, "time to do your stuff. Williams, Rafferty, get your teams ready and put them in the vans. Piper, Downs, I want you two to synchronize your watches with my clock. Take one of the two-way radios. When the driver of each van reaches the start line around the corner on West Ferry, I will give the signal 'go.' You have exactly *fifteen* minutes to get back here, neutralize the guards and make off with the loot."

Just as the lads were getting ready to set off, the Boss got out of his car and walked over to the Dutchman. Even in this environment, he was dressed in a smart, beige, Nutter's of Savile Row three-piece suit.

"I trust everything's in order?"

"Yes, Chief."

Em was enjoying her lunch with Annie, savoring every minute, especially considering that these days they rarely had time to get together like this. And for the first time in a long while, she actually felt relaxed, despite knowing what lay ahead.

Although this was the first time they had been able to get together since New Year's, this particular occasion was proving a real treat—and they were hell bent on making the most of it.

"So, how's your family and life at Beaufort Hall?" asked Annie. "It must be at least five years since I was last there."

"Good, actually," Em nodded, trying not to be too distracted. "I haven't gotten up there much in the last year, but Daddy's still enjoying his retirement. The horses and pheasants keep him busy. Mummy's in Holland at the moment visiting her sister; she said she might stop by next week on her way back to Suffolk. Which reminds me, I'm sure she'd like to catch up. If you're able to, perhaps we can make a day of it—the three of us—shopping, a few drinks, a show, perhaps?"

"Sounds great," Annie beamed with her viridescent eyes.

Secretly, however, Em wondered if it would actually be possible. After all, she was about to face one of the biggest challenges of her career and if her partner wasn't completely on the ball, things had the potential to go disastrously wrong. She smiled, putting on a brave face to hide the turmoil beneath.

CHAPTER 5

The two vans came tearing into the yard, screeching to a halt amid the dust and rubble. Out they jumped and ran to the entrance. Piper and Downs were first, throwing smoke canisters into the building, their teams following closely behind.

Out went the televisions, the "guards" quickly neutralized. As they exited, the teams broke up. Rafferty and Doyle headed for the Jag, while Piper and Downs led one team to the Sherpa. Williams had already walked across the road to the "phone box." *Boom*—he yelled over the mic—at that instant Brent and Smithson walked casually over to the Spacevan as the Jag and Sherpa tore off. But they were too slow. It took seventeen minutes and thirty-three seconds.

"Stop," yelled Van Rooyen.

He glanced at the Boss, who didn't look amused. Things, it appeared, were going backwards. The chief pursed his lips, his hazel eyes scanning the situation.

"*What the bleedin' hell was that?*" he yelled. "We've practiced this heist five times already, and that's probably the worst rehearsal in a week."

"We're trying our best, Boss," Doyle murmured.

"Really?" The chief was generally not one to show much emotion, but Doyle's comments unleashed a barrage of fury inside him. "I think I'll be the judge of that."

He turned to face the Dutchman. "Niels, perhaps Mr. Doyle here needs a bit of a reality check."

Van Rooyen picked up one of the shotguns and fired, hitting Doyle in the chest. He dropped to the floor, screaming in pain.

Everybody else was silent.

The Boss walked towards Doyle and stood over him. The bullet was rubber, but it still hurt.

"Keep your mouth shut and do your fucking job." He was seething. "Next time I shan't be as forgiving. Got it?"

Graeme had never been to New Scotland Yard before, but he found it soon enough. The big glass tower at 10 Broadway was imposing. At the gate he was directed to special parking for SRI and pulled into a bay beside a gold, Y registration Ford Granada Ghia.

He stood in awe, looking up. *I can't believe I'm actually here... This is incredible.*

Entering the building, he found a hub of activity. Detective Constable Mark Hungerford met him at the door.

"Ah, *Inspector*," he issued with a hint of sarcasm. "Your boss is on the fifth floor just finishing up a meeting with the Deputy Commissioner. He asked me to meet you here. To be honest, I didn't think you'd show up so soon. Follow me."

Graeme could sense that Hungerford was a bit insecure and this was his way of trying to one-up a superior officer. Nevertheless, he chose to ignore it and simply engaged in the conversation as they headed down the corridor towards a lift.

"I heard Doherty, the bloke that tried to kidnap my partner, spilled his guts."

Hungerford nodded. "Pretty much. I barely had to do anything. The super had him squealing like a pig. Apparently the vans were collected early this morning. Your boy Charles has forensics working on items collected from the garage. They've found welding apparatuses and spray guns that appear to have been used recently... Dark blue paint."

Exiting the lift, Hungerford led Graeme into a large conference room with rows of long, staggered benches and minimalist seating. Uniformed officers and others in plain clothes, along with admin staff were standing around talking. At the front of the room was a wide projector screen. Much like the building at 10 Broadway itself, this space was clearly a product of the 60s, part university lecture hall, part amphitheater and one hundred percent built for function. Like the SRI offices, Graeme noticed that official government building scent, though here it appeared slightly stuffier and less seasoned.

Hungerford introduced him to a tall, fair and fit middle-aged uniformed senior officer who was standing at the front of the room talking with a couple of colleagues. "Chief Inspector Peter King, Special Patrol Group," he announced, extending his arm.

"Inspector Graeme James, SRI," Graeme offered a firm handshake.

"We've heard a lot about you, Inspector James," said King enthusiastically. "My men and I are looking forward to your briefing this afternoon. We heard you did some incredible stuff in Belize."

Belize? Graeme tried not to let his expression get away from him. *Never been there.*

Then it hit him. *That photo on the desk in my flat. Yes, of course!*

A WPC approached him. "Sir, would you like tea or a coffee? I'm Constable Kathy Griffin; I'll be taking notes from your presentation."

"A tea would be great, thank you Constable. Milk but no sugar please. Also, can you make sure the full notes from the presentation are provided to SRI and also the Special Patrol Group?"

The WPC nodded and left to fetch the tea.

Their second attempt was a huge improvement. They were in and out of the building in ten minutes, five seconds.

The Boss looked at Van Rooyen.

"Now that's more like it," the Dutchman said as the Sherpa and the Jag sped off. "Let's try it two more times. I want this blag to be as *finely tuned* as possible. We've got a lot riding on this."

The SPG officers and a few detectives were just taking their seats when Em walked in the door. A few wolf whistles ensued, but she shrugged it off.

"Have a nice lunch, did we, Sergeant?" Graeme asked.

"As a matter of fact, I *did* actually; it was nice to chat to somebody with proper table manners. Are we ready yet?"

"Almost. We're just waiting for Donaldson and a few others."

"Who's giving the briefing?"

"Me, apparently. Though I'm sure you could set me straight on a few pointers, what with your extensive knowledge and connections."

She looked at him as-a-matter-of-factly, with the hint of a smile.

"Ah, you're both here. Good, good." Donaldson entered the conference room, hastily followed by a shorter, slim, bespectacled man who appeared to be in his late fifties. From his looks, well-dressed appearance and precise movements, Graeme guessed the other man had to be one of the top Met brass.

"Is Tim coming?" Graeme asked.

"No. I instructed him to go back to SRI HQ and work on more of the evidence collected at the garage this morning. I want him to brief you on it after we're done here. In the meantime, I've got somebody who wants to say a few words.

"Inspector James, Sergeant Braithwaite, I'd like you to meet Sir Alfred Morrison, Deputy Commissioner, Metropolitan Police."

"Pleasure to meet you, sir," Graeme and Em said, almost simultaneously.

"I've heard a lot about you two; your boss says good things. I just hope we can foil these bastards once and for all tomorrow."

"We'll do our best, sir," Em replied.

The gang's third attempt was their best yet—just under ten minutes. It seemed as if everything was coming together.

As they wrapped up, the Boss gestured. "Piper, Charlie, over here, lads."

Downs and his mate sauntered over. "What is it?"

"You boys did better that time. We're done here. I want you two to take the

Sherpa over to the lockup in White City. Niels will meet you there in three hours with rounds of ammunition, smoke canisters, uniforms and masks. I want you to make sure we've got everything locked down for tomorrow's blag. Check everything twice if you have to. I'll meet you there at 10:00 a.m. tomorrow."

"Understood Boss," Piper said automatically. "Come on, let's get a move on."

The Boss turned to Van Rooyen. "Get the rest of them together. We're heading back to the warehouse. Let's go over the escape route one more time."

The room was full now, with everybody seated and attentive, ready for the briefing to get under way. With all eyes fixated upon him, Graeme felt nervous; but, sensing he'd done it before, his anxiety quickly melted.

Clearing his throat a little, he began, "As many of you are aware, one of the biggest heists in the history of the city is scheduled to happen tomorrow at Dennison's Jewelers on Edgware Road in Marylebone. According to our best intel, the gang will use two Transits, likely one as a decoy for a diversion. We have it on good word that there will be two teams of four, heavily armed and dangerous.

"There are links to suggest that two members of Mickey Barnes' South London Grafton Gang are part of this crew—do we have their pictures?" He directed the projection officer, who placed a pair of black-and-white photos of two robust men with buzz cuts and broad shoulders on the screen.

"Charlie Downs and Robert Piper are hardened criminals and veterans at smash and grab robberies. We also believe a Dutchman known as Van Rooyen is also involved," continued Graeme, gesturing to the officer to place another photo on the screen, which although fuzzy, showed a stocky, bald man with a round head.

"However, we still haven't determined exactly what part Van Rooyen will play in this operation. Interpol has him on their most wanted list for arms trafficking and jewelry heists in Holland and Belgium, so I wouldn't be surprised if he's orchestrating this thing.

"As far as we know, the robbery is scheduled to happen at exactly 3:00 p.m. tomorrow. As I said previously, this gang will likely be heavily armed and very dangerous, so we need to be prepared, especially in view of recent robberies north of the river. I'm sure some of you remember the heist in St. Paul's where they shot their own getaway driver."

Some faces in the crowd nodded wearily.

"...I propose that we have two teams of the Special Patrol Group to counter the two vans of armed gang members. Chief Inspector King, do you have any suggestions?"

King got up and went to the platform.

"Edgware's a busy street, but we've got reasonable vantage points. There's one, here, across the street, in this block of flats," he pointed to an aerial photo on the projection screen. "We can place two snipers—one on the fifth floor here and one on the third here at the other end of the building. Approximately fifty yards south of the jewelers on the eastbound side, there's a hidden entrance between two buildings, which has a good view of the Dennison's store. We can place another man here at street level.

"Because we're still uncertain that this robbery will *actually* happen, we can't block off the road completely, since, if they *are* planning to hit Dennison's tomorrow, doing so will alert them to our presence. But," King emphasized, "we *can*, at least, make their getaway difficult. I propose placing two unmarked units parked on either side of the street, to the north and south. In addition, we'll have six armed plainclothes officers from our team on either side of the street, ready and waiting."

"Do you think that will be sufficient?" asked a senior uniformed officer with a raised hand, who was sitting in the front row.

Other heads in the room nodded in agreement.

"To be honest, sir, it is really difficult to gauge at this point," King responded. "What we do know is that this lot are dangerous and based on past experiences we need to tread carefully. As a result, we don't want uniforms or marked patrol vehicles on this one. It will draw too much attention and the last thing we need is a hostage situation or a standoff like the Blackwall raid."

"Duly noted. Thank you, Chief Inspector King," Graeme spoke. "In addition, SRI will have two vehicles to act as backup to the SPG units. I will be positioned in one of them, along with Sergeant Braithwaite, while a second will be located just off the roundabout on Bayswater Road. It's likely they'll probably make their escape route this way."

"How can you be certain?" quipped an officer sitting four rows from the front.

"Because we've been closely following this gang's modus operandi," added Em, getting up.

Unapologetically, the whole room's eyes landed on her as she walked towards where King and Graeme were standing. "So far the concept has been a smash and grab, with a fast getaway. Because the jeweler is located close to the Bayswater Road, here," she pointed to the map on the projection screen, "this is the quickest and most direct exit route. It's likely they will try and head out of town, or at the very least, out of the immediate area."

King chimed in once more, "We believe, that in conjunction with SRI, we have a very good chance of stopping the thieves quickly, but I must emphasize that for everybody directly involved with this operation, our efforts must be as coordinated as possible."

"Agreed," added Graeme, surprised at his decisive use of language and apparent confidence during the presentation. *How the hell did I manage all that?*

"Thank you Chief Inspector King, Inspector James, Sergeant Braithwaite." Donaldson stood up and headed to the front, indicating the briefing was over. "I want everybody that has a direct role in tomorrow's operation to stay behind afterwards for a few minutes."

"Good work, Sergeant," Graeme whispered as they left the stage.

"Don't mention it. I just hope we're really on our game tomorrow."

"You two," Donaldson yelled. "That's been some good detective work you've done over the last twenty-four hours; as Sir Alfred mentioned, I just hope that we can catch these bastards."

"What did you get out of Gerry Doherty, Guv?" asked Graeme, slightly changing the subject. "Hungerford says you had him squealing like a stuck pig."

The super cleared his throat. "Basically, he'd been using the garage as a front for stealing motors. Chatsworth originally hired him, but he knew the old man was desperate and used the garage as a way to fund criminal activity. He told me that once Chatsworth was on the inside, a Dutchman had paid princely sums to have new vehicles stolen, painted, and converted, particularly Transit vans. DC Charles and a team of forensics are now working on items collected from the garage this morning. We'll soon find out if any evidence from those stolen vans from a couple of weeks ago turns up."

He gave Em a hard stare. "Sergeant. You were lucky things didn't go worse down in Clapham this morning. You could have ended up on a slab. I expect better from my top detectives."

"Sorry, sir."

As the super nodded, Em lowered her head slightly, pursed her lips and glanced at Graeme. He gave her a quick, sympathetic smile as an indication of support.

"Right," the super continued, rubbing his hands as if to declare something juicy was about to come. "You two need weapons. And I strongly suggest bulletproof vests for tomorrow just in case. The fifth floor has granted SRI approval to carry weapons from this moment on. But," he emphasized again, "I need both of you to tread carefully. That incident down at Southwark back in April is still on the minds of some upstairs, if you know what I mean. If word gets out about too many gunfights in the city related to SRI, all of our heads will be on the chopping block, understood?"

Graeme and Em quickly glanced at each other before saying, "Yes, Guv," in almost perfect unison.

"Good. Now follow Chief Inspector King, he'll make sure you get kitted up." Donaldson turned on his heel and headed back to talk with Sir Alfred and a couple of senior Met brass.

Southwark? Graeme was still trying to figure out why there were repeated references to it, both from Em and the super. *Must have been some kind of gunfight or a bomb exploding,* he mused. *That probably explains why we've both been referred to as the 'professionals'!* He continued, attempting to piece things together in his mind as they followed King out of the room and along the corridor.

The SPG head, along with three members of his team, led them up a couple of flights of stairs into another corridor. *More security*, Graeme scoffed. *This place is like bloody Fort Knox, and it's "1983." Why all the precautions?*

He soon found out why. Having been let through and shown their badges to the on-duty officers, a large room appeared before them. There were two big tables, each littered with guns of varying description, all tagged and labeled.

"Jesus Christ," said Graeme.

"This must be heaven to you," Em remarked sarcastically. Her arms were folded. "So many weapons and all in one place. Please excuse my partner, Chief Inspector King, he has a thing for guns."

King said nothing, but went over to one of the cabinets at the far end of the room.

"Donaldson has given me specific instructions," he then said pointedly, and paused. "You're to have these." He reached for a pair of pistols hanging on the rack. "These are brand new," he stated, handing one to Graeme and the other to Em. "They've been developed for the Austrian Army and the Met has been given some for trial use. They're Glock 17 Safe Action Pistols that use standard 9mm rounds. Donaldson requested they be given to members of SRI, with specific reference to you two."

"Not bad." Graeme carefully examined the Glock given to him. He checked the safety and clicked the slide. Inside though, he was quite uneasy. It was if he knew exactly what to do with this weapon and feeling the firearm in his hands, knew he would have no trouble using it under stress. At the same time he wasn't sure how, as he'd never knowingly fired a gun before. He felt as if he was changing as a person, and somebody else was taking over. *Just what the hell is going on here?*

The memories of Porto's, Winfield, Karen and the text about his son were still there. He remembered drinking the port with Paolo, but were the memories fading? Was this his real life? Then he was brought back.

"Looks like you've found your new best friend," Em was saying.

"Think you can handle yours, Sergeant?"

"It's not me I'm worried about."

"Very funny." *She could sure come up with the one-liners, and frequently too. Perhaps she does care about me.* No; it wasn't possible, surely. Given her looks and status, she could have any man she wanted wrapped around her finger. He promised himself it wouldn't be him. *Just think of the job at hand,* he thought. *After all, she is my partner and I am professionally responsible for her, whether she has feelings for me or not. And feelings can get in the way...*

"You'll need these, too," he heard King say. One of the SPG officers had opened up another cabinet and handed each of them a bulletproof vest. "These should fit."

It took Piper and Downs almost two hours to get to White City; the traffic was murder. Piper wheeled the Sherpa into a back alley towards a row of nondescript lockup garages.

Parking nearby, the two men got out of the van and walked to the second unit from the end. Piper removed the lock and opened the door. Inside, the 1983 Ford Transit looked every inch a legitimate security vehicle, its dark blue livery, reinforced windows and front bullbar lending a purposeful yet somewhat menacing appearance.

"Looks like we've got a bit of time to kill," observed Downs. "Where's that set of cards you have? If I'm going to waste time waiting for a bloody Dutchman, let's at least have a bit of fun."

They pulled up a pair of boxes to sit on, along with a third as a makeshift table. "Fancy a bit of blackjack?"

"Thought you'd never ask," replied Piper, sitting down.

They were just signing the acquisition forms for their latest items of police equipment when a uniformed officer appeared through the door.

"Sergeant Braithwaite, Inspector James, you've been requested for another meeting downstairs."

Graeme looked at King, who gestured to the officer.

"Don't worry, Inspector; here, take your guns and these holsters. I've already arranged with Donaldson to make sure you'll have extra rounds and your vests shipped to SRI HQ; I'll take care of this little lot and see you down there."

As they holstered their guns and walked into the corridor, Graeme grew inquisitive. "What do you suppose this one's about?"

"Not certain, really, but considering our boss is here, it probably has to do with SRI procedure tomorrow."

"Makes sense. That's probably why King will be in on it."

Em and Graeme glanced at each other as they walked. He could sense that pit-in-the-stomach feeling, and knew she could, too. The hours and minutes were counting down. They'd gone over the mission numerous times in their heads but no matter how much planning, nor preparation, there was always a chance something could go wrong...

Em glanced at Graeme again as they headed to the meeting. She took a deep breath, briefly closed her eyes and rolled her shoulders. As she did, the inspector turned and did his best to give a reassuring smile. If he was being honest with himself, Graeme didn't like the thought that she could get injured or killed. Was this a sign of growing feelings for her? He tried to block it out of his mind and concentrate on the task at hand.

Yes he can be reckless at times, Em thought, *but so far he's never let me down. And, let's be honest, I do feel kind of safe when he's around, though I'd never tell that to his face. Perhaps we could grab a drink tonight after the meeting. I know it would help calm my nerves and probably his, too.*

Piper was winning. They'd played three rounds and he was sure the odds were stacked in his favor. The Dutchman was late—more than twenty minutes now—but the Boss had given them strict instructions to wait for him at the lockup.

Back to the game, Piper had four cards left in his hand. "Come *on*, mate, let's get on with it."

Downs placed his next card, an ace, signaling the start of a new suit. Just then, they heard the sound of a car entering the alley. Piper folded his array of cards and walked outside the lockup to see a brown Mk2 Vauxhall Cavalier heading towards them. It was Van Rooyen.

"What the bloody hell?" he exclaimed, as Van Rooyen shifted to get out of the car. "I thought we were supposed to be getting our weapons and uniforms."

"You are," the Dutchman said, somewhat annoyed, cocking his head to look back down the alley. Sure enough, a green Bedford CF plumber's van appeared from around the corner and pulled up behind the Cavalier.

Out jumped two men. Van Rooyen motioned for them to open the rear doors of the van. "This should be everything you need."

Piper and Downs surveyed the cargo. Eight sawn-off shotguns and shells, three Walther P1 pistols and rounds, five boxes filled with smoke bombs along with a fistful of balaclavas and four security uniforms.

"Good enough?" the Dutchman glanced upwards and sternly with his keen eyes.

"Yeah, Boss," replied Downs disappointedly.

Van Rooyen walked to an adjacent lockup, pulled a key out of his pocket and unfastened the padlock.

"Put the stuff in here," he ordered. "All of it. I'll do an inventory check first thing in the morning at eight. It had all better be there. The Boss will be here by ten at the latest. At that time I'll give each of you your guns and rounds. Make sure you're in uniform." He covered Piper and Downs with a full stare. "We'll be kitted up and ready to leave by twelve, understood? Now, let's get to work."

"Got your weapons?" asked Donaldson.

Graeme and Em opened their jackets to show their holstered Glocks.

"Good, good. Did Chief Inspector King already mention about having the rest of the gear shipped to our offices?"

"Yes he did sir." Em put on a brave face, perhaps sensing bad news was to come.

"Excellent. Now, the reason why I called you here," Donaldson changed to a more serious note, "is that there's been a slight change of plan. I've just been speaking with the deputy commissioner. Since SRI is now permitted to carry weapons, and this is a high-profile robbery, he's asked me personally to make sure my best officers take a more '*active*' role—and by that I mean you two will actually enter the jewelry store as paying customers. I want you to be inside, in case anything goes wrong and we end up with a hostage situation. Having eyes and ears in there will give us the advantage.

"We've also worked it out with Dennison's so that two of the regular guards will also be replaced by Special Patrol officers. You'll have your vests and we'll set wires and mics up. If something goes wrong I want either or both of you to say '*Susan.*' That will be the call for us to storm the jewelers."

The super changed gears once more, and continued loudly, "We've come to the conclusion that we need to nail this lot on sight. If they make the getaway, it's going to be a lot harder to catch them and the last thing the brass wants is a car chase all over the city and additional fatalities or injuries."

Graeme and Em passed along worried looks.

"I'll brief King and the Special Patrol Group. I'll be onsite tomorrow, just down the street in a surveillance van with Tim. And, I can't stress this enough: *DO NOT shoot unless I give the order*, do you understand?"

"Yes Guv," they complied with solemnness.

"Right, you two, head back to SRI. Tim's got some interesting information dug up from this morning's incident at the garage; he'll also provide you with your vests and rounds—the packages from Scotland Yard should've arrived by the time you get back to the office. Meet me there tomorrow, by 9:00 a.m. at the latest. And try and get some sleep, the pair of you; I need you to be on your best form tomorrow. Let's catch these bastards once and for all!"

"Yes, sir."

As they exited the room, Graeme could feel a lump in his throat.

"I don't know about you, Inspector James, but I need a rather big drink," Em commented as they walked down the corridor. "...Fancy joining me?"

"Thought you'd never ask, but first, we need to get our gear and find out what Tim's uncovered. See you at SRI in twenty?"

"Are there other things you're devoted to as much as your job?"

Graeme could see Em was irritated, no doubt fueled by what Donaldson had just said.

"Perhaps. See you back there, Sergeant."

She gave him a slight frown before heading down the stairs towards the exit. As soon as she was gone, Graeme stopped for a second, leaned against the wall, took a deep breath and closed his eyes.

Once outside the building and walking towards his car, Graeme pondered Em's last comment and reviewed it again and again. It felt like his "partner" here in this world was really starting to get under his skin. *Just two days I've spent with her,* he realized. She'd been short with him, almost frosty at times, but back at Em's flat this morning following the Clapham arrest, he knew that there was chemistry there. He recalled once again the way she nursed his wounds. Delicate, tender; sensual, even, in the way she went about it. Still, Graeme couldn't figure out if she was trying to be suggestive or just simply taunting him. This girl was truly an enigma. Nevertheless, it had felt wonderful and stirred in him feelings and thoughts he'd not experienced before. His wife in the other "*life*," Karen, had never given him a gentle touch like that, even when Graeme had first met her and he'd convinced himself he was in love. *No, it can't be*, he assured himself. *You can't let her get to you, least of all now. She has to count on you now more than ever, especially since we're both going to be right in the firing line tomorrow.*

He opened the door to the BMW. Taking his seat, Graeme turned the key and started the engine. The silky inline-six purred like a kitten. Fastening his seat belt and closing the door, he put the car in gear and headed out. As he turned right from Broadway onto Victoria Street, he blipped the throttle just enough to feel the BMW's rear end come around slightly, the back tires chirping for a second as they regained traction.

Graeme grinned from ear to ear as he rowed into third gear and sped down the road. In fact, he was smiling all the way back to the office.

CHAPTER 6

At SRI Headquarters, the forensics team had been going over the evidence collected from the garage with a fine-toothed comb. The welding apparatus was one item of interest. According to the paper trail, there hadn't been any evidence of major welding repairs in over a week, yet the equipment collected from the scene had obviously been used within the last few days.

There were some other interesting discoveries. Going through the bins at the back of the garage, the team had found masking paper with fresh residue, evidence of blue and white paint, as well as some recently used spray guns. A pair of vehicle registration plates had also been uncovered, one of them belonging to a Transit reported stolen around two weeks ago.

Doherty hadn't mentioned any specifics, but it wasn't hard to put two and two together. A van had been stolen and obviously modified and painted at the garage, likely for heist work.

Tim studied in detail some of the evidence collected, including additional photographs and reports. Turning to look up, he saw a pair of plainclothes officers walking in carrying a pair of boxes.

"I'm looking for Detective Constable Charles?" one of them questioned, looking around.

"Over here," said the thin young man with dark, bushy hair.

"These are for you, courtesy from the Special Patrol Group at New Scotland Yard."

Tim got up and grabbed the boxes from the two men, placing them on the floor near the big central table. Opening them up to check the contents, he found Glock 17 rounds and a pair of bulletproof vests. Having signed the requisition forms for the items, he headed back to his desk, just as the two men were leaving.

No sooner had the officers departed than Em walked through the door. "Hi, Tim. How's the evidence from the garage?" she asked, taking off her jacket and sitting down at her desk.

"There's some stuff that's interesting. Here, take a look at this." He got up and handed her a photo of one of the registration plates. "This was found in one of the bins at the back of the garage. It belongs to a Transit that was stolen a couple of weeks ago."

"Likely one of the vans that Chatsworth was talking about when we visited him in prison this morning," she added.

"Did he give you any specifics?"

"No, but he was very afraid of something, or *somebody*, as was my former informant, Del, before he was killed. Donaldson is right, there's something sinister about this whole thing—I feel it's nastier than just an armed robbery."

"I think you're probably right," Tim replied slowly. "Oh and by the way, this just came. I presume it's for you." He lifted one of the boxes and handed it to her.

Em placed the box on the big table in the center of the room before opening it. Within it were two bulletproof vests. She held them up before placing one of them on her partner's desk.

"Any more word on tomorrow's operation?" the young DC asked.

"Actually, there is. Donaldson wants James and me to go into the jewelers posing as customers. He thinks that by having people on the inside, it will help contain this thing, stopping the gang from trying to make a getaway and causing mayhem on the streets of Westminster."

"Good God," Tim's eyes widened and his brow creased. "He didn't mention anything to me about that. Do you think you're up for it?"

Em's tone was somber. "We need to catch them and this is likely the best shot we'll have."

"It looks like we've all been given the right to bear arms," the constable commented quickly, trying to change the topic, perhaps as a way to ease her thoughts. "Mind you I'm a bit rusty; haven't been really out in the field in some time, not entirely sure it's my thing."

Em looked up at him. Tim was young, but since joining the SRI team six months prior he had proven himself competent, dependable and always there when needed. She smiled. "Thanks Tim. And, I just want you to know that even though the others might not say it, we really value having you as part of our team."

"I really appreciate that." There was genuine warmth in his response. "It's not often anybody says that around here. Thank you Em."

She winked at him.

Just then, Graeme walked through the door. Still on a high from the briefing and the trip back to the office in his BMW, he appeared alert and quite chipper. With his striped Van Heusen shirt, beige slacks and gray sports jacket, he also looked the part of an elite Met Detective.

"Ah, James," said Tim. "Em has been filling me in on a few details."

"Can you fill me in?" asked Graeme as he removed his jacket and placed it over the back of his chair.

"Just told him that Donaldson wants us to be at the jewelers tomorrow," Em explained, "and that Chatsworth seemed *very afraid* when we visited him."

"On a slightly different topic—Tim, how did you make out with the forensics boys from the garage?"

"It looks like your hunch this morning paid off. There's evidence to suggest that a Transit was modified and painted at the garage recently. We're still going over the material. I'll let you know if I come up with anything. In the meantime I think you two should get some rest, especially considering what's in store tomorrow."

"Thanks Tim, appreciate the info and the gesture." Graeme frowned at Em. "Are you all right, partner?"

"Oh yes, fine. Look, I've put your vest on your desk."

Seeing the bulletproof jacket draped across his table, Graeme's heart began to race, driven by a combination of both exhilaration and fear. He had no clue how things would pan out at the jewelers, yet despite the uncertainty, there was also a measure of comfort, too. *This is strange*, he thought to himself, *I feel like I'm changing inside again. I'd never have imagined this could be happening when I was at Winfield...*

Then Graeme was back in the moment again.

"Great," he said. "I guess we should probably get going, then. Are you ready, Sergeant?"

"Just a sec."

"Night, Tim, see you in the morning."

"Right you are; have a good evening."

As they were leaving, Tim got back to going over the evidence. It was going to be another long night.

"I know a little bistro on New Bond Street," Em suggested as they walked to the front door of the façade. "Fancy a drink?"

You bet I do. He couldn't think of anything better than spending one-on-one time with this most incredible woman. "Good idea, I think we both need it," Graeme replied, wanting to accept the invitation without appearing overly eager.

It was another fairly balmy evening, so they decided to walk, partly to alleviate the stress of what was to come. Strolling down Maddox Street towards New Bond Street, Graeme was trying to soak in as much of the world around him as he could. He still found it hard to believe he was in 1983...especially when it came to the way people were dressed, the store fronts and "To Let" signs with their 01 numbers. A black and then a burgundy FX4 taxi trundled past, followed by a British Gas Morris Marina van, a Renault 18 and a Maserati Khamsin. As they turned left onto New Bond Street, Graeme glanced at the old Midland Bank across the road. In his twenty-first century life he recalled walking this way, only the bank was an HSBC branch. He wondered when he'd find himself back in "that world" again and where things would lead. Could he perhaps use "the future" to make better decisions here? He tried not think much more of it.

"There we are." Em had an excited tone in her voice, as if she'd found something that had long been thought lost. "Let's cross the road."

As they entered through the glass door, Graeme scanned the surroundings. The bistro was charming and intimate, with tiled floors, white walls, blue accents and square wooden tables. By the looks of things, it had been recently renovated. It was also popular—only a few of the tables were vacant.

A waiter with a French accent greeted them. Settled at a small table by the window, Graeme ordered a pilsner, Em a glass of sauvignon blanc.

For a while neither of them said anything, they just stared blankly into space. It was a lot to take in. A tricky situation had become even more dangerous.

Finally, Graeme broke the silence. "What's the expression, '*Out of the frying pan, and into the fire?*'"

"You're actually right for once, Inspector," she retorted.

"Do you ever give up?"

"Me? No, never."

"Here we are, trying to get ready for this thing and you're just jabbing."

"No I'm not."

"Look, can we just enjoy this bloody drink? I shouldn't be saying this, but the fact that Donaldson sprung that on us this afternoon bothers me too, you know."

She sighed. "*Yes*, I know. I'm sorry, it's just I don't really like surprises, and I don't particularly like to see people get shot."

"Neither do I. Look, let's have a toast. To *James* and *Braithwaite*, the Met's real life '*Professionals*.' Bodie and Doyle have got nothing on us." Graeme saw a smile and what he thought was about to become a chuckle. "I could be wrong, but it looks like you're actually enjoying this, Sergeant."

"Don't push your luck James, remember this is serious business but right now, I need this drink just as much as you do."

"Cheers."

They ended up staying a couple of hours. By then Graeme still hadn't found out a great deal more about his partner. Instead, their conversation had been more or less idle chatter, politics, and trying to decide on what to eat. But then, she'd said something he soon wouldn't forget.

"Look, I could use some company tonight, at least for a couple of hours," she issued. "But this doesn't mean..."

"Okay, but we've got a big day and an early start," said Graeme assertively. "What exactly did you have in mind?"

"You can follow me back to my place. I've got a nice bottle of Château Lafite Daddy gave me on his last visit into town. If there's any time to have a glass, tonight is it, and it's just too bloody good to drink alone. Since I've got nobody else to share it with right now, I might as well do it with you."

That's quite the offer, he thought. This girl really was an enigma. *Is this her way of enticing me, or does she just need comfort?* After all, Graeme suspected that as strong as his partner was, now and then she still needed reassurance from him. He tried to brush aside any romantic thoughts. *Just provide her with some professional support, don't try to take advantage of her because she's vulnerable.* That said, he could still think of few other people he'd rather share an expensive glass of wine with other than her.

Graeme summoned the waiter, instinctively pulling out the Access card from his wallet and settled the bill. He could sense she was appreciative. So was he, not only in paying the bill, but that he actually had a "*Flexible Friend*," with which to do it. For a split second, he recalled the 80s TV ads from Access in his twenty-first century existence, by which time the card he was paying this bill with had long been defunct.

After leaving the bistro, they strolled back to SRI and got in their cars. Traffic was still fairly busy as they turned onto the King's Road and Graeme had to remember how to get to her flat in case he lost her. He'd only driven the route "once" before.

At a traffic light, she went through, while he was too late. A Leyland Terrier delivery truck and a FX4 black cab turned onto the King's Road at the junction of Sloane Street, followed by a couple of Routemaster buses and a gaggle of other vehicles before the light turned green again.

Great, he whinged, *I'll never find her place now.* Then intuition took over. He was rushing a bit now, but the BMW felt like an Arabian horse, power throbbing from its 3.4-liter straight-six engine. He started recognizing a few landmarks and before long had turned right and into Chelsea Square.

He could see Em's car as he pulled into the courtyard. Parking up, Graeme got out of his car and rung the bell.

"Come in, the door's open," her voice buzzed over the intercom.

He could hear music playing as he walked in. Jazz, but old school. *Charlie Parker*, he remembered.

There was also a sound of chopping emanating from the kitchen. Walking, Graeme saw Em busy at work slicing some celery and cucumbers on the big white counter. He could sense she enjoyed cooking and the kitchen, dominated by the breakfast bar in the middle, had just the right combination of coziness and functionality.

"Just making a few nibbles and then we can get to that wine."

"About that."

Em turned to face Graeme with a look of surprise.

"Look," he started, "I know this situation is stressful, but we really need to be on our game. I was thinking on the way over here, that perhaps, as much as I'd like to, we should save the wine for another night."

Em's eyes widened and her brow furrowed. He could see she was disappointed, perhaps even a little angry.

"Do you ever think about anything else, other than your bloody job?" she snapped.

"Actually, I do." He was quickly becoming irritated, but tried to defuse by stiffening up and clenching his hands. He didn't want to start an argument.

"And what might that be? *Your gun* that you got issued today?"

I've not seen her so upset, at least that I can recall. Is it just the anxiety for tomorrow's blag, or something else? I need to try and defuse this situation, it's not doing either of us any good. Graeme took a deep breath and tried to compose himself. She was obviously nervous, and within he felt just the same. The inspector knew that come sunrise tomorrow she'd be relying on him; that they'd both be putting their lives in each other's hands. In an effort to lower the tension, he tried to change the subject.

"Can't we just have tonic water, or a coffee, or something?"

"You really put a damper on things, don't you?" She turned away from him and started busying herself by putting food back in the fridge.

"Sorry, I didn't mean to," said Graeme.

Em turned her head and glared at him. "Why don't you just go?"

"Em, *Em*," he said in an almost fatherly tone, "I don't like this any more than you do, but we need to be focused, otherwise we're both in deep shit. Don't do this, not now."

"Go."

"Look," he held his hands up in surrender. "If you need to, call me tonight. I'm your partner and I do worry about you. I'll see you in the morning." Graeme turned and walked out the kitchen towards the front entrance, choosing not to look back.

Christ, he thought after he snapped the door shut. *She can be emotional at times.* This was the worst he'd seen her so far. *What's going on? Why did she get so irate over a glass of wine? Is it just stress about tomorrow's tasks, or is there more to it?* Graeme stood for a minute by her front door and took another deep breath, trying to piece things together. He knew she was a good copper—had to be in order to reach her position, especially in *this world*. But what would cause her to react like that over something so trivial? *It's just got to be anticipation about tomorrow. Has to be.*

Trying to convince himself it was, Graeme unlocked the door and climbed into the BMW. As he drove back to South Kensington, he tried not to think any more about it.

CHAPTER 7

On the drive back to his flat, as much as he tried to ignore it, the spat with Em was still bothering him. *Why had she been so snappy when we'd got to her place?* Although he tried not to show it, he was nervous; he didn't want to eat or drink anything.

After parking his car and putting the cover on, Graeme walked up to his flat and opened the door. He found the silence comforting. He turned on the light and walked into the kitchen, sat down at the table and flicked through a magazine.

This is shit, he thought. *I'm going to have to call her.* It was then that he remembered he didn't have her number. At that moment, the phone rang. Graeme ran to the living room and picked up the receiver.

"Hello?"

"James, it's me." Em's voice was calmer and more composed. "I'm really sorry I snapped at you like that. You're probably right—we *should* save the wine for another night. I'll see you in the morning."

"Get some sleep," Graeme answered, the tension in his shoulders leaving as he finally exhaled. "Try not to think about it." He hung up the phone.

Although Graeme was trying to project an image of toughness, he was pretty scared. *I've never been in this kind of potential danger before. Yet somehow, I don't feel as nervous or anxious as I did in my "other life" in the twenty-first century. Come to think of it, if this kind of situation had happened there I'd have shat a brick by now!* Graeme recalled how it had taken every last ounce of courage he had to tell Richards to take a walk. He shook his head and sighed. Deciding to get up and open the fridge, he glanced at the bottles of Beck's in the door. *It doesn't really seem fair to be having a beer, especially after I told her not to have a drink, does it?* His gaze lingered on the beer bottles for a few seconds. *Nah, I'll just grab a glass of water; really need to be on my game tomorrow.* With that he closed the fridge door, grabbed a glass off the counter and placed it under the tap before heading into the bedroom. Within thirty minutes he was fast asleep.

Chatsworth had taken a phone call late in the evening. After that, things just weren't the same.

It was the final straw. He'd regretted getting involved from the very beginning and it had just gone from bad to worse.

The guards hadn't noticed it as he was escorted back to his cell. Those cops had told him they'd get him out, but he'd warned them about what could happen. Now it was as if his worst fears were coming true.

He laid on the bed for a while, contemplating a way out, but there wasn't one—not now. At approximately 3:30 a.m. he made his last decision. He removed his shirt, rolling the fabric and tightening it into a noose. Placing it around his neck, then pulled the bed to the center of the room so he could feed the noose through the ducting on the ceiling. He counted to five, kicked the bed away as hard as he could and closed his eyes. He was dead within minutes.

Em had been trying to sleep but she was just too restless. She'd done as he said and reserved the wine for another night.

A nice drink after a hard day's work was one of her favorite pleasures, but the hardest day of all was tomorrow.

She rose from her bed, having decided to take a shower. The running water proved to be a soothing surge, helping rinse away *some* of the stress, at least. She must have stayed bathing in the hot steam for almost a full half-hour. After finally stepping out, she dried herself off, staring at her frame in the mirror.

It was early morning in the West End and traffic, even in this part of London, was still fairly light. Nobody really paid attention to the yellow Dodge Spacevan, nor the green Jaguar as they traveled along Wigmore Street.

Turning onto Edgware Road, the van pulled up a few hundred yards from Dennison's Jewelers. The Jag drove past and turned onto the corner of Burwood Place, further up the road. The driver in the Spacevan got out and headed southeast towards Kendall Street. The man in the Jag stayed awhile longer before getting out and walking towards Norfolk Crescent and Oxford Square.

Em managed to sleep a few hours; the shower had done wonders. That said, she was still up by 5:00 a.m. and elected to go for a jog.

She ran a mile and a half loop. It wasn't much, but it helped to quell the nerves a bit. She'd barely got in through the front door to her flat when the phone rang. It was Donaldson.

"Em," he crackled over the line, "glad you're awake."

"What is it, sir?"

"It's Chatsworth. They found him hanged in his cell this morning. ...Looks like it happened in the wee hours. Perhaps you'd better get that partner of yours on the phone. He's probably still sleeping, anyway."

The sun was just coming up as Van Rooyen parked the green Bedford van in front of the warehouse in Millwall. He could already see a brown Ford Cortina Mk IV, a red Triumph 2500 and a beige Mk I VW Golf in front of the building.

The lads are already here.

As soon as he got out, Williams, Brent, Doyle, and Smithson silently exited their cars and entered through the front door.

"Alright," he stared at everyone through glazed eyes. "Grab your gear from the back of the van. Brent, Smithson, here's your uniforms. Put these on."

Each man grabbed a shotgun and extra shells.

"The Boss will be here in a couple of hours, around eight o'clock. I suggest you get some sleep before we go over the plan one last time. We move out at eleven, and nothing had better go wrong."

CHAPTER 8

Graeme was standing in the middle of Blackheath Common. It was a dreary, gray December day, and the trees were barren, adding to the feeling of exposure and bleakness. He held his Blackberry in his right hand. A lady and a boy were walking away from him. As they did, he saw a text message appear on the phone:

"I don't want to see you; I don't want to see you; I don't want to see you ever again."

The message kept repeating, then the Blackberry started ringing, the tone getting louder and louder; but somehow, the ringtone just didn't seem right...

"Jesus!" Graeme shot up out of bed, sweating. He rolled to the other side and grabbed the beige BT Viscount telephone receiver off the nightstand.

"I should have known you'd be sleeping," he could hear Em's voice on the other end of the line. "Thought you'd want to know, Chatsworth hung himself this morning. Donaldson just called me."

"Christ," Graeme reacted. "That's all we bloody need. I'll tell you, Sergeant, there's something fishy about this whole case. When did they discover the body?"

"One of the guards found him, doing the rounds at about four this morning... He used his shirt to make a noose."

"What did the boss say?"

"Coroner has taken the body; uniforms are already questioning the guards and other inmates to see if they saw anything last night. In the meantime, he wants us in the office by 8:00 a.m. Dress smart, it's our big day. We're supposed to be buying jewels, remember?"

"How could I forget, darling?" Graeme said cheekily.

"Just bloody be there, will you."

As the call ended, Graeme pondered, *Had I been asleep when she called me? Was it simply a dream this time, or was it part of my other life in the twenty-first century? I've never been to Blackheath Common and just who were the lady and the boy? The* message on the Blackberry indicated that the woman was Karen, but he hadn't seen her face. *And the boy? It can't be my son, surely; it looks as if that boy was at least six years old. The last I recalled, Karen had said she was pregnant. So how could I jump six years into the future?*

What he could definitely still remember, however, was the message Karen had sent him while at Porto's on that fateful Tuesday. That's when Graeme's world had literally collapsed, or so he thought. *And that's how I ended up here—a different person, a different life, one that I enjoy and feels so real to me. I'm really starting to like who I am here. That's something I could never have even imagined in the twenty-first century.* Sitting up on the side of the bed, Graeme drew a deep breath. His thoughts were spinning and the only way to cure it right now was to take a shower. He got up and headed to the bathroom.

As Em hung up the receiver following Graeme's last comment, she shook her head. *You'd better bloody be there for me today, James. This is one time I need you more than ever.*

Heading to the bathroom, Em took off her running clothes and jumped in the shower. Ten minus later, having dried off and wrapped herself in a big comfy towel, she made for the corridor and picked out a smart trouser suit from her favorite wardrobe. After styling her hair and putting on her makeup, she got dressed and went into the kitchen, pouring a cup from the freshly brewed pot of tea. Sitting down at the table, Em nibbled on a piece of toast as she read last night's *Evening Standard*. "Murder on the Tube in Rush Hour," she noticed on the bottom of the front page. The thought of Del's untimely demise still made her stomach churn.

The Boss was early. He walked into the warehouse and found the lads sleeping in the Transit. Letting off a blast from his Walther P1 pistol, the sound reverberating around the warehouse was more than enough to startle them. The Boss knew he had a sadistic streak, something that went right back to his childhood. *Nothing like a bit of shock and fear to get things going!*

Though the gunshot had caused the lads to jump and scramble out of the back of the Transit in a disoriented and disorganized fashion, Van Rooyen wasn't fazed one bit. Hiding in the murky shadows at the back of the warehouse, cigarette in hand, he didn't even flinch when the gun went off.

As they gathered around a table, the Boss went over the plan with them one last time.

They wrapped up, and Williams walked over to the Transit for a final inspection. He crawled underneath it to make sure the two incendiary devices were secure before popping the bonnet to check the scuttle below the windscreen for the third. "Mr. Holland," he announced, gesturing to Van Rooyen, "can you check the remote for me to see if it is working?"

The Dutchman switched it on and gave a thumbs up. "Goot," he said in his distinctive accent. "Now let's check the tire pressures and make sure we have enough fuel to get us there, the vapors will add to the explosion. Smithson, start the engine and make sure everything is okay."

The Transit fired up on the button. "We've got just over half a tank of fuel," the young lad yelled.

"Uitstekend." Van Rooyen was pleased.

The mobile bomb was now ready to cause havoc on the streets of Marylebone. A couple more hours and they'd all be ready to leave. But the mood, even among a bunch of hardened criminals, was uneasy.

The Boss glanced at Van Rooyen before addressing his crew. "Looks like we're all set," he said coldly. "Play your cards right gentlemen, and by tomorrow you'll all be rich men." Then turned and left the warehouse, nodding at Van Rooyen on the way out.

Graeme was out the door less than thirty minutes after waking up. He carried a bag he found in his study and placed his Glock in it. He was dressed the part of a well-heeled London businessman. It was just another aspect of his 1983 life that surprised him.

In the spare bedroom, he'd found a freshly dry-cleaned suit, a pinstripe, and it was tailored to fit him. The apartment, his clothes, the car—how could he afford all this on a copper's salary? Government issued, or earned on his own? *Just one more mystery to solve,* he thought, but it could wait. An arduous day lay ahead; he could feel it. Graeme got in his BMW and headed out to SRI HQ.

Traffic was busy this Friday morning, and he didn't reach Maddox Street for over an hour. As he turned into the cul-de-sac, he glanced in his rearview mirror and saw Em a few cars behind. He was just getting out of the car when she pulled in.

"Morning Sergeant."

"Ah, Inspector. Dare I say it, but you're looking rather dapper this morning. You really are full of surprises."

"Sometimes I surprise myself," he grinned. "Bring your gun and your vest with you?"

She nodded, and they headed into the four-story Georgian-era brick building.

Donaldson sat at his desk. With a veteran copper's instinct, he knew the second Graeme and Em walked into the office.

"James, Braithwaite, in here," he bellowed.

"What is it, Guv?" asked Graeme.

"I've been on the phone all morning about that murder at Pentonville. You mentioned that Chatsworth seemed scared after you broke him, so to speak."

"Yes sir, it seems to be a pattern. Same with Em's contact, Del. Both men looked like they were scared for their lives—it's not something I'd expect, especially if we're just dealing with blaggers."

"But this lot aren't just blaggers, are they?" Donaldson gave Graeme a direct, stern look and raised his brow, indicating that the inspector ought to know better.

"It would appear that way, sir," Em chimed in, "but still, none of us have a whole lot of information to go on, apart from what we've got from interrogation, and some of the items that turned up at the garage yesterday. Has Tim found anything else?"

The super scratched his crew cut. "Not really. We know a van was modified and painted there in the last few days, and the number plates were changed, but that's really it. We've still got to wait on fingerprints, though I doubt we'll find any other dabs except those of Doherty and Jones. We've got a couple hours before we need to get ready, I suggest the two of you dig up anything else you can find about this afternoon's blag, even though we're running out of time. I'll see if we get anything else regarding Chatsworth's death."

The lads inspected their kit and got ready. By 11:00 a.m. they were all set to go. Williams started the Transit, while Doyle jumped in the passenger seat. Brent and Smithson climbed in back.

Van Rooyen tossed Williams a two-way radio. "Follow me," he ushered. "We'll head to Piccadilly Circus. When I tell you, pull up and wait. There's a parking space just off Jermyn Street. I'll change vehicles, and we'll lie low for a few hours. When the Boss gives me the signal, we'll head west towards the target. There's a drop-off point near Marble Arch. Stop there for a few minutes, and Williams, make sure you arm the detonator. When I say 'diamonds,' we hit the store."

Williams nodded, waited for Van Rooyen to climb into the green Bedford CF, and pulled out of the old machine works and onto West Ferry Road, followed by the Dutchman in the second van.

As the eastern crew headed out towards Marble Arch, the Boss was at the lockup in White City, going over a few final details with the lads that would be using the western Transit.

Despite having pulled countless armed blags before, Downs and Piper were nervous, though they didn't show it. They'd be riding up front, dressed as security guards, with Barrymore and Gibbs riding in back. Gibbs was barely nineteen, and Downs and Piper had reservations about using him on this job. Mind you, the Boss didn't exactly care as long as the job was done. Casualties were to be expected; after all, the Old Bill likely knew something was going down at this point. There was no reward without sacrifice.

At 12:45 p.m., the western Transit pulled out of the lockup and headed for Marble Arch. The Boss watched it disappear around the corner before casually strolling to his burgundy Jag. Climbing into the driver's seat, he reached into the glovebox for a cigar. A guileful smile crept across his face as he lit the stogie. Zero hour had begun.

"James, come have a look at this." Em had just finished going through a file handed to her by Detective Constable Warren, an officer from downstairs. "I think we've found another clue to this puzzle."

"What is it?" asked Graeme, coming over to inspect.

"Some bloke called Jenkins. He works as a security guard at the Dennison's location on Edgware Road. He made two £100 deposits in the space of a week to his bank account at a Barclays branch, down the street from the jewelers. A clerk at the bank noticed that the notes were new and the deposits were out of character from what he usually puts into his account every month."

"Guv," Graeme called. "Did you hear about this?"

"What?"

"It looks like our blaggers might have a man on the inside, at the jewelers."

"Bollocks. It's too late to arrest him." The super rubbed his forehead. "Look, I'll pull up his profile so our lads will know which one he is. It also means we can't put our SPG boys on the inside now, it'll raise too much suspicion. I'll call King and let him know. I'm afraid you two are on your own. I'm sorry to put you into this, but we don't have any other options. Put your vests on."

Em and Graeme didn't say anything as they headed for the changing rooms. Though they were gone only a few minutes, getting ready and placing the vests on underneath their clothes felt like it took hours. Donaldson was on the microphone as they returned to the office.

"Sierra 1, Foxtrot 2." It was King from the SPG. "Our lads are ready to move in. We're taking up positions."

"Right, understood," Donaldson said firmly into the mic. "You two," he then turned to face a solemn-looking Graeme and Em, "take James' car. If there *is* a chase, both he and his motor can handle it. Have you got your guns and ammo?"

They nodded.

"Good, good. Now head downstairs. Tim and Ralph are waiting for you and will set up your wires and test them. I'll see you there in a minute."

Bloody perfect. Graeme's mind was flaring up as they headed downstairs. *Maybe this is all a dream and it's about to end—with me "dying."*

CHAPTER 9

The vans were edging closer now. There was less than two hours to go. The mobile bomb was parked just off Piccadilly. Williams and Doyle sat quietly, awaiting orders from the Dutchman.

Doyle glanced at his watch—it was painful to watch the seconds pass. Despite his tough guy persona, deep down he could feel nervousness building from within. He looked at Williams. The explosives expert was staring straight ahead, clearly engrossed in the music emanating from the headphones of his personal portable stereo. Watching him bob his head back and forth, Doyle sighed.

Twenty miles to the west, the second Transit was heading along the A4. Inside, the tension was such that you could cut it with a knife. Piper, Downs, Gibbs and Barrymore all sat there, silent. Like Watson and Doyle, they were counting the minutes.

Although they'd undergone multiple practice runs, none of their training could quite match the real thing.

As they walked into the downstairs room at SRI Headquarters, Graeme and Em saw plainclothes staff busy at work, making the place appear like a human beehive.

"James, Em, these are for you," Tim appeared with a beaming face, clearly excited and keeping whatever nervousness he had at bay. He presented the pair with two covert listening devices just as soon as they'd walked through the door.

"These are for attaching under your clothes," remarked the young detective constable in a manner that was evidently beyond his years. He beckoned to a middle-aged man at the far corner of the room. "Ralph, can you assist Inspector James?"

"Sergeant Braithwaite, please go and see WPC Calder in the room next door," Tim instructed. "She'll make sure you're all set up. We'll test each wire here to make sure they're working properly before you both head out to Dennison's."

Em nodded and headed to the room next door.

The green Bedford CF could have been mistaken for any typical plumber's van; that was one reason why Van Rooyen had chosen it for this part of the plan. Driving west, the Dutchman glanced at his Tag Heuer. Although he was not one to get emotional, Van Rooyen could nevertheless feel the tension building. A meticulous planner, he firmly believed nothing had been left to chance—yet past experience had taught him that no matter how perfect the plan, something could always go wrong. He turned his thoughts to the next task at hand, changing vehicles.

A few minutes later, Van Rooyen curved into a small car park off of Bayswater Road. Parking the Bedford van, he sat quietly for a minute before getting out, quickly scanning his surroundings and donning a flat cap.

Not somebody prone to smiling, he nevertheless could feel a grin creeping across his face as he strolled across the car park. Directly in front of him, on the far side of the lot, sat his favorite ride. It was a little dusty, perhaps from sitting there for several days, but there was no mistaking the distinctive silhouette of his 1982 Ford Capri 2.8 Injection. Sporting two-tone metallic gray and silver paint and distinctive pepper pot alloy wheels, the Capri looked purposeful and sleek.

Opening the driver's door, Van Rooyen slid down in behind the wheel. Turning the key, the V-6 engine rumbled to life, bellowing through the dual exhaust. He sat there for a minute to inhale.

Engaging first gear, the Dutchman stomped on the accelerator, causing the Capri to come alive. Holding the brake for a second, he smoked the rear tires before releasing it. The thrust of forward motion was enough to cause the car to slide sideways as the short, wide rear tires fought for traction.

Van Rooyen smiled again as he raced to the exit of the car park before applying the brakes and turning gingerly onto Bayswater Road. *Fun and antics can come later.*

For now, it was time to focus on the task at hand—orchestrating the perfect robbery in ol' London town, and the Capri was the perfect vehicle with which to do it.

With their police wires properly fitted, Graeme and Em both reconvened in the busy main room on the lower level at SRI Headquarters. They could see that Donaldson had now joined the activity and was busy talking with DC Charles.

"Okay. Ready to test?" asked Tim as they came up beside him. He beckoned them to the back of the room where another young plainclothes officer was fiddling with some recording equipment.

"Just start talking and we'll let you know if we can hear you clearly. It's important that the audio is as clear as possible."

The officer donned some headphones as Graeme and Em started a casual conversation. After a few seconds, he gave the thumbs up.

"Right, that should do it," Tim nodded sharply. "Looks like you're both all set."

"Now you two," Donaldson interjected, "we'll be in a surveillance van just down the street listening in. The minute you think something goes awry or you need assistance, yell the word 'Susan' and we'll storm the building. *Got it?*"

"Yes, sir." Graeme and Em's voices held in the air somberly as they did their best to focus on the task at hand.

"Just remember." The superintendent stopped. He lit a fresh B&H. "This is our big opportunity to nail these bastards once and for all. Good luck, Inspector, Sergeant—and I want you both to know that we're right behind you and will back you to the hilt on this."

As they left, Donaldson gestured to the others remaining in the room. "Right, everybody! It's time. Get yourselves ready and let's move out!"

The drive to the jewelers seemed to take an age. Neither Graeme nor Em could think of anything to say. He concentrated on the road ahead, trying to stay focused while she glanced out the window. In a sense, they looked like the archetypal affluent couple, successful in their own paths yet distant and detached from one another.

Eventually, Em broke the silence. "So...what do you like to do?"

"*Like to do?*"

"Outside of work, I mean. Do you have any hobbies?"

Graeme's eyes widened. Unsure of what to say, he came up with what he thought was a suitable answer. "I like to tinker with things."

"What kind of things?"

"Cars, motorcycles, mechanical things; I've always been fascinated by them. Why do you ask?"

"Well," she mused, "it has just occurred to me that since we first started working together, I've never asked you."

He tried to pretend that it wasn't a big deal, but deep down he appreciated her asking the question. *Is this her way of trying to feel close to me, to reassure me?* Graeme wasn't quite sure what to make of it.

He turned off the Bayswater roundabout and saw the jewelers ahead, on the left side. A silver Peugeot 604 was just pulling out of a parking spot as they drew up. Graeme drove into the now vacant bay and switched off the engine.

The pristine white Beamer fit right into this part of London and the pair of them looked every inch members of the established elite, Graeme in his pinstripe, and Em sporting her smart ladies' trouser suit.

"Ready?" asked Graeme.

"As ready as we can be, I guess," his partner responded as she opened the car door. "Let's just get this over with, shall we?"

They each grabbed a bag from the back seat, Graeme his small leather carrying case and Em a designer handbag.

Walking into the sizable store, Graeme counted four security guards. It was tough to tell which was Jenkins as they had left HQ before details of the guard came in, though he had a hunch it was the man closest to the wall on the far side. They headed for the right-side counter and started looking at diamonds.

"What do you think of this one, darling?" quizzed Em.

If anybody could carry off the old money act it was her. *After all,* Graeme thought, *she's the real deal, anyway. Well, sort of.*

"Can I help you sir? Madam?" asked the man behind the counter.

Em studied him. He had to be in his mid-sixties, but had an elegant manner and was fairly short and slim. In fact, he reminded her of Daddy's butler, Wilson, back at Beaufort Hall.

There were already half a dozen customers in the store as they entered. A seventh—a middle-aged, well-dressed woman—walked in shortly after they did. Em thought she looked vaguely familiar.

"I'd like to have a look at that one," Em said, pointing to a 2-karat stone.

"Certainly, madam," the man replied.

The mobile bomb was now en route. Van Rooyen, in his gray Ford Capri, followed a few cars behind. As instructed, Williams pulled into the layby and waited for the signal. The Dutchman drove past and pulled up. There was less than twenty minutes to go.

Peter King's men were already in their positions when the white BMW parked up not far from Dennison's. The SPG head had regretted not being able to post two of his men on the inside, but it was too late. The snipers had a good vantage point and would pick off the thieves if things got ugly.

King sat in a beige Ford Cortina in radio communication with his lads. One lingered at a nearby bus stop reading a newspaper. Two were inside adjacent shops, their eyes firmly on the windows while three others were on the street in plain clothes, keeping a close watch.

As promised, he had two cars parked north of the jewelers and two close to the junction with Bayswater Road. *These bastards aren't going to get away—not if I can help it.*

He saw a white Mercedes 308 panel van approaching from the south. As it went past him, the driver gave a thumbs up out the window before parking further up the street. It was Donaldson and DC Tim Charles.

"Diamonds. *Go, go, go,*" Van Rooyen spat into the radio. It was time. Doyle tapped Williams on the shoulder, signaling. His comrade nodded before switching on the detonator and pulling out of the layby, heading towards the jewelers.

"He just proposed and I want to find a nice wedding ring," she said to the familiar-looking thin man. "How about something like this?"

"Well… Madam, this is a nice stone, but I think we've got something that might be more to your taste. Hold on a moment. I'll be right back."

Graeme was scanning the store. He counted three security cameras. Two of the guards were near the entrance and the others were at each side, close to the back.

He looked at his watch. It was 2:47 p.m. The air was so heavy. Glancing quickly at Em, Graeme put his right hand on the counter. He was taken aback when she then put hers on his.

"Here we go, madam… I think you might like some of these." The clerk opened the steel box he'd brought from the back of the store and let Em take a look.

Just that second, Graeme saw one of the guards turn and head for the back of the store. *Jenkins*, he deduced. He turned towards his partner.

"Excuse me, darling," he said, "I'm going to take a look at some of those over there. Be right back."

"Okay, but don't be long." She squeezed his wrist before letting go.

Graeme slowly raised his right hand and reached into the small leather bag with his left. He turned to face the wall as he moved in order to avoid the security cameras and raise suspicion with the guards. He could see Jenkins heading down the back corridor, beyond the main room. Discreetly grabbing his Glock, the inspector carefully followed the guard.

It didn't take long for Graeme to figure out what was going on. The real valuables were kept back here in a Chatwood-Milner Monarch safe. Jenkins was going to disable the alarm system and unlock it.

The inspector waited patiently while the guard inched closer to the safe room. Graeme's intuition was so strong now he knew exactly when and where he would strike Jenkins. It was as if he'd been trained in clandestine operations. *Another clue*, he thought, *obviously from when "I" was still in the service in this world.* Nonetheless, he could feel the adrenaline pumping as he moved with the focus of a jungle cat stalking its prey.

Jenkins reached into his pocket for the keys and turned the lock. Entering the rectangular room with multiple cabinets on each side, he headed straight for the control panel to try and deactivate the alarm system so he could access the dark gray safe on the far side. Jenkins was about to start the sequence on the panel when

Graeme struck him on the chin with the butt of his Glock.

Jenkins tried to fight back, but Graeme was too fast and smacked him on the side of the head. The guard went down like a sack of potatoes.

Graeme looked around. He found a small storage room off to the side of the corridor and dragged Jenkins into it, surprised at his strength. *Quickly, quickly; time is running out.*

The inspector stole the guard's keys and locked the door to the storage room before swiveling around and heading back to the main area of the store.

Customers were still browsing and inquiring with staff. The place was large, with rich gold and red decor, plus an impressive array of jewels and watches neatly on display—a symbol of order in a chaotic world...

As Graeme entered the room, Em caught him in the corner of her eye and quickly flashed her badge at the man.

"Police; SRI," she said with trepidation. "We have it on good word that your shop will be hit by armed robbers, probably within the next few minutes. *You!*" she looked at one of the customers. "Get the others and find a way out. Is there a back exit?" She stared at the salesman.

The well-dressed man froze for a moment, not knowing what to say. Finally, the words came out. "Yes... Around and to the left."

"Come on." Graeme appeared by the counter. "Get moving."

The middle-aged woman who'd been browsing stones on the far side of the room was startled. "I beg your pardon, young man!" she shook. "I have every right to be here. You can't just shoo me out of here like some peasant! Do you have any idea who I am?"

"Now, look," Graeme said to her forcefully. "If you don't get a move on right now there's a good chance you could be shot—even killed by armed thugs and they certainly don't care who you are. Understand? Now *move it*, madam."

"Well I never!" she snorted indignantly, but did as instructed.

Donaldson and Tim had barely set up their audio gear when the two "security" Transit vans motored down Edgware Road and came to a halt outside the jewelers.

"It's on. It's happening right now," the chief superintendent said into the mic. "James, Braithwaite, we're counting on you."

Smoke bombs flew through the entrance, quickly engulfing the room in a thick haze. Em dove behind the main counter, Graeme crouched off to the side. He caught a glance of two men coming through the door, shotguns at the ready. The first one smacked one of the guards so hard he almost went flying across the floor. The second masked raider dropped the other by the front door. The third guard put his hands up before being pushed to the floor.

Although they wore masks, Graeme knew it was Piper and Downs. *Jesus they're big bastards.* One of them began making his way towards the back of the shop.

He's going for the safe. He doesn't know the alarm's still active. Graeme's mind flared. He tried to crawl as quickly as he could across the floor, hoping he'd trip the man.

But it was too late; he'd seen him. The big fella raised his shotgun and fired, shattering one of the glass cabinets.

Graeme twisted around and fired his Glock. He missed his target, the bullet hitting the far wall. Then another blast from the shotgun; this time the slug almost hit the copper's leg.

Shit, don't miss this one you bastard! He struggled with himself.

It was a split second, but it felt like minutes. The slide clicked and Graeme fired again, this time hitting the man in the shoulder. Piper stumbled. Shocked at the hit, he pressed the trigger on the shotgun again but his aim was off.

Graeme fired a third shot, this time getting him in the left knee. It was enough for the big fella to lose his balance—down to the floor he went.

"Braithwaite, *cover me!*" he yelled to his partner.

She sprung up from behind the main counter and started shooting, just as the other hoods were coming through the door.

The shots caught the armed gang by surprise. They'd expected some kind of police presence but not this; the smoke was only adding to the confusion. Downs, seeing his mate go down, stiffened his body and screamed with rage; it was like Blackwall all over again. *You're gonna pay for this!* he thought, as he took aim at the pretty blonde girl behind the cabinet.

He fired a couple of rounds in the direction of the main counter, shattering another glass cabinet. The force knocked Em back, cutting her face and arms with shards, but she was a tough girl. Rotating her body, she slid into a corner. Even though it was their tactic, the smoke was working to her advantage.

Downs was confused. *Where the hell did she go?* He edged closer towards the far side of the room, determined to find out if the girl was still there.

Having crippled Piper, Graeme leapt towards Downs, grabbing the shotgun. The second man was preoccupied on the other side of the store, but there were more thugs coming in. He fired in the direction of the door, trying to slow their progress. Swinging Piper's shotgun around, the inspector took aim at the other big man in an effort to distract him.

Things were going badly. One man was down and the others were drawing fire. The smoke bombs had been a bad idea—visibility inside the shop was now limited. Doyle and Rafferty were behind Downs, but the Boss had given them orders: *Get the loot or else.*

The bullet grazed Downs in his side just below the armpit, knocking him sideways, but it was then that he caught a glimpse of the girl trying to reload in the corner. He steadied himself and lunged over the counter towards her.

But he didn't see Graeme coming at him from the other side.

"Braithwaite, *over here*!" Graeme shouted.

She turned to the right, but so did Downs, just in time to see Graeme fire his Glock straight towards him. The bullet hit him in the face, shattered his nose and he collapsed in a haze of blood.

"*James, look out!*"

Graeme turned to see Doyle pointing a pistol right at him. He tried to move, but he wasn't fast enough. The bullet hit him in the shoulder.

It was all happening in slow motion now; he was falling.

"*Susan!*"

He could hear Em yelling.

"*Susan*, get those bloody SPG officers down here, *now*!"

It was falling apart. *Pop, pop,* the shots seemed to come out of nowhere—but the Transits were now disabled, the tires flat. Brent and Smithson, not even in the door, decided to make a run for it.

"Fuck this!" they said to each other. But they didn't see the plainclothes SPG men, nor the snipers watching their every move.

"*Police*! Drop your weapons! *Drop them now or we'll shoot!*"

Graeme was in agony but he grit his teeth to best hide the pain. Luckily his right arm was still okay. He propped himself up and tried to reload the Glock, but then he felt somebody standing over him.

"This is fur my friends, you bastard pig," he could hear the man's Belfast accent.

Then—*boom*. Graeme closed his eyes. *This is it, I'm finally going to meet my maker*. But then, nothing came.

He slowly opened his eyes again to see the man slumped on the floor. His partner was staring at him, her gun still smoking.

A fourth man was now in the building. He took aim at Sergeant Braithwaite but he didn't see the guard by the door. Having regained consciousness, the guard swung his body around and tripped him up.

"Grab his gun!" Graeme yelled. "Don't let the bastard move!"

At that second, four more men entered the building. Em could tell they were

SPG.

"Don't shoot, *don't shoot*! *SRI*!" she put her hands up, breathing a sigh of relief.

Williams had seen it unfold firsthand. Four of them had gone in, and Brent and Smithson were now in custody. That left him, Gibbs and Barrymore.

Screw it. I'll blow up the van anyway! He could see there was nowhere to go; police were closing in from all sides and he could hear sirens coming from down the street.

"James, *James*! Are you alright?" Em walked over and knelt beside him. The SPG officers and the security guard had the fourth man pinned down. There was no sign of life from Piper.

"You saved my life," Graeme breathed heavily and tried to ignore the pain.

"That's what partners do and to be honest, you saved my bacon back there too." She was out of breath and frantic.

At that second, they noticed Chief Inspector King coming through the door, gun at the ready. "We count six—including the four in here. You told me they'd be eight. Where are the others?"

"We don't know." Em had now caught her breath and was looking up. "Perhaps they decided to make a run for it?"

She'd barely finished her sentence when the blast hit, shattering the shop windows and the rest of the cabinets, knocking everybody inside to the floor.

Gibbs and Barrymore were about to exit the western van when the bomb went off. The explosion blew parts of the other Transit more than thirty feet in the air and shattered windows on both sides of the street, knocking pedestrians to the ground and damaging several cars.

"*What the bloody hell is going on out there?*" All the air left his lungs as Donaldson bellowed. He slid open the side door of the Mercedes surveillance van. "*Oh Christ*—it's like World War bloody III out there! Tim, call uniform, fire and ambulance; get them down here right away, and I mean NOW! Where the hell is King? And what about my officers inside? *The brass are going to have a shit with this!*"

The superintendent got out and hobbled down the now hazy street towards the jewelers, his own Glock in hand. A pair of unmarked police Rover SD1s pulled up and blocked the north side of Edgware Road to traffic. In the distance, he could hear the wail of more sirens growing steadily louder. One of the Transits was still burning merrily; the other sported flat tires and broken windows, immobile as well; debris littered the immediate vicinity.

A Dodge Commando Fire Engine pulled up on the south side of the street. The crew quickly got out and attended to the burning van. A police Transit meat wagon then pulled up, followed a few seconds later by a Bedford ambulance that screeched to a halt not ten yards from the jewelers. The ambulance team immediately began taking care of pedestrians injured by the blast.

"*Oi*, you!" yelled Donaldson to a plainclothes officer. "*Get on the blower* and get me some more ambulances, now!"

What a bloody mess, thought the super. *A real fucking mess! Never in all my years as a copper have I seen something like this.*

Dennison's was by far the hardest hit building; all the windows had been blown in and the bomb had left charred residue on the face of it. The prominent sign out front was now nothing but a shell, the letters having shattered into a thousand pieces by the blast. Donaldson navigated through the rubble and made his way to what was left of the entrance.

Gibbs and Barrymore knew something was off. They were going to be the last two in the door, but then Gibbs lost his bottle. When they heard multiple gunshots they decided to hesitate and stayed in the other Transit. Now that the bomb had exploded, their only choice was to make a run for it. Barrymore had the spare keys to the Jag parked up the street on Burwood Place. On the count of three, they'd make their exit.

With so many distractions, if they were going to run for it, *now* was the time. Opening the rear doors, Barrymore and Gibbs jumped out of the now battered Transit, walking briskly towards the Jag parked on the far side of the police blockade.

"*Oi*, you two, *stop*!" An SPG officer saw them and started running, but the two young lads were already past the blockade and far enough up the road that they might still be able to make a clean getaway.

Barrymore and Gibbs broke into a sprint. Making it to the Jag, they jumped in and Barrymore turned the key. The straight-six engine rumbled to life and the old XJ6 peeled off down the road, just as the officer reached the parking spot. "Bastards!" he exclaimed, bending forward and catching his breath.

Graeme was trying to concentrate. The pain was excruciating, and the blast had just made it worse. Yet he was comforted to have his partner sitting right beside him.

Even with cuts and bruises, she was still beautiful. She'd torn part of the sleeve off her jacket and wrapped it tightly around his shoulder to help with the pressure. More SPG officers had arrived in the building, along with a team of medics who placed the unconscious Piper onto a stretcher and hauled him away. The other man had been cuffed by the SPG officers and was being led to the meat wagon. Downs and Doyle still lay lifeless on the floor, surrounded by the shattered glass, waiting for the coroner to arrive.

"What's your name?" Graeme asked the security guard, his voice growing weak from the bullet wound.

"Dodson. Elliot Dodson."

"You did a fine thing back there, Elliot... You saved our arses. ...Have you ever considered police work?"

Just then, Donaldson walked through the door. "*What the bloody hell happened to you?*"

"We got them sir," Em interrupted, "we fucking got them."

The super shot his head back and his eyes popped, clearly surprised at her use of language.

Tim was about to exit the surveillance van when the breathless SPG copper cornered him.

"Get on the horn as soon as you can," the officer said, panting. "I think two more of that lot just took off. Green Jag, registration DWG 226 N."

"Roger."

Chief Inspector Peter King had been knocked outside by the blast, but aside from being a little stiff and some cuts and bruises, felt reasonably okay. Once his lads had taken the two surviving thieves away, he slowly walked back inside the building.

"I think your lot did an outstanding job today." His lean, chiseled face broke into a smile. "Sorry we couldn't get our lads on the inside in time."

"Just as well we had Dodson here," garbled Em, her words tripping over one another. "Perhaps you should consider him for SPG... A fat lot of good your boys did for us today... We almost bought it and my partner's injured."

King's expression quickly changed to a frown. "Now, look here."

The SPG head was about to challenge her when Donaldson stopped him. "*Leave it,* Chief Inspector; now's not the time." He gave him an official-style nod.

King turned around and walked out.

"James, can you stand?" asked Em.

"I think so."

With his boss supporting him on one side and his partner on the other, Graeme was able to make his way to the door. It had been the roughest day of his life, but he'd never felt such a sense of belonging as he did right now. They were a team, and they'd live and die by each other; that much he knew for certain. Things would never be the same again.

They led him towards an ambulance where the crew was waiting with a stretcher.

"Where are you taking him?" he heard Em question.

"Saint Mary's," the ambulance technician answered.

"I'll be seeing you around, partner." Em leaned forward and gave him a peck on the cheek. It was the last thing Graeme remembered before he blacked out.

CHAPTER 10

Graeme could hear the rain lashing down. He fumbled for his Oyster card—the rechargeable, electronic travel pass for London's transportation network. Standing at the entrance to Tottenham Court Road tube station, people rushed by him, many glued to their mobile phones. He was soaked through. Looking through his wallet, Graeme found just a couple of £5 notes and a few coins.

He was bewildered and lost. Turning around, Graeme saw Richards glaring at him. Consumed with anger, Graeme clenched his fist and struck out, hitting the overweight, bearded man in the jaw.

"I'll sue you, *you worthless worm*!" Richards sniveled. "I'll sue you for every last miserable thing you have!" You're FINISHED!"

Graeme heard other voices. They were faint at first, but started getting louder. He counted three—two female, one male.

Then he heard one above the others, a feminine one. "It's time," it said. He could hear the echo bouncing around inside his head.

Graeme slowly opened his eyes to see a nurse in a traditional-style uniform standing over him. Quickly scanning his surroundings, he saw he was lying in a hospital bed in an old-style room with gray walls, hooked up to a drip and a very angular-looking blood pressure monitor. His left shoulder and the top of his arm were bandaged.

"Time for your food," she directed.

"What's going on?" Graeme was completely dazed.

"You're in recovery. You've been asleep for more than four hours." The nurse talked to him quickly, under her breath in soft whispers. "They got the bullet out and stopped the bleeding. Lucky for you. It could have been worse."

"I know," Graeme sighed, relieved now that things were coming into focus. "I owe the staff at this hospital a big thank you."

The nurse smiled at him and briefly placed her hand on the lower part of his arm. "How are you feeling?"

"It still hurts," he grimaced, raising his eyebrows. "Wish it didn't bloody ache so much, but as you said, it could have been worse, right?"

Although the pain was significant, Graeme tried as hard as he could to be grateful, one that he was "alive" and two, he was in "1983" and still excited about where things would lead.

"Dr. Roth will be by shortly to give you an update on your diagnosis," the nurse added. But, other than that and a few bruises, you're not bad off considering what's happened to you. We heard about the jewelry store robbery on the six o'clock news."

Graeme lay back and drew a deep breath. *If the incident was on the news, there's a chance that some more unsavory characters knew what happened. Oh, shit!! That means Em and I could be targets!*

"Where's my partner; where's my belongings?" he asked, turning his head again.

"Don't worry," the nurse reassured him. "Just try and get some rest."

He studied her. She was about forty-five, he guessed, with dark brown hair that was starting to gray. Her face was kind and sympathetic.

"Now, eat up. You need your strength."

Van Rooyen had never been in this situation before. It was planned meticulously. *How could it have gone so wrong?* The Boss would be livid. He hadn't tried to contact him yet, and he wasn't even sure if he should. That man was a sadistic bastard, even more than he was.

He'd seen the bomb go off, even from the far side of Bayswater Road. He chose to drive up Edgware, but when he saw the amount of police presence, he turned around, fully knowing that things had gone south. There'd been no communication from the lads once they had got to Dennison's. As far as he knew, everybody was either dead or in custody, along with all the weapons he'd supplied for the job.

"*Godverdomme,*" he said in disgust. With a cigarette in hand, he paced up and down the concrete in the underground parking garage. Fairly dark and with only a handful of cars, it was a good place to plan the next move. After a few minutes and the last drags of his butt, he got into the gray Ford Capri 2.8 Injection, just as a middle-aged lady driving a red Vauxhall Chevette pulled into the garage.

Leaning over to the passenger side of the Capri, Van Rooyen opened the glovebox. Inside was a nickel-finished Smith & Wesson Model 10. *If the Boss comes for me, I'll be ready for that klootzak,* he thought.

It was almost 9:30 p.m. Donaldson was in his office. The robbery had been foiled, but still, the brass at Scotland Yard were screaming for blood. The ensuing explosion had caused a five-car pileup on Edgware Road and the damage likely totaled hundreds of thousands of pounds. Downs and Doyle were dead, Piper had been taken to hospital but was in critical condition. Rafferty, Brent and Smithson were in custody and under close watch by SRI at Bow Street Police Station, while Barrymore and Gibbs were still on the run.

The super took a long drag of his cigarette, trying to get his head around what had happened earlier that day. Suddenly there was a knock on the door.

"What is it?"

Tim poked his head in. "Guv. Scotland Yard fifth floor want to know when you plan to interrogate the gang members we caught this afternoon."

Donaldson sighed. "As soon as I get around to it. It's a Friday night and I should be home with the missus and you should be somewhere else, too. Instead we've got one huge mess to clean up. Tell Sir Alfred personally that I'll be down at Bow Street as soon as possible. There's just no rest for the wicked. And where the bloody hell is Braithwaite?"

"She's on her way in, Guv. Remember you asked her to go to hospital for a checkup?"

"...Oh, yes, I do, now, come to think of it. Thank you, Tim." The super softened his tone. "Good, good. When she gets in ask her to come in here, will you?"

Van Rooyen wasn't one to back away from anything. The Boss likely already knew. Driving west along Goldhawk Road, passing the rows of low-rise nineteenth and early twentieth century flats and small business storefronts, he pondered a plan of action. *Screw it, I'll call him.* Pulling the Capri off to the side of the road a few hundred yards down from the Metropolitan Line tube station, he sat in the car for a few minutes. He could feel the tension and his head was starting to throb.

Reluctantly, he got out of the car and walked to a nearby phone box. It was raining by the time he reached it.

Thin with gray hair and a slightly hawkish appearance, Dr. Roth had a strictly business look about him and certainly wasn't a man to mince words.

"You lost quite a bit of blood but your arm will heal. To be honest, you're very lucky. A bullet from a Walther pistol like that can make a hell of a mess. In this case it was a fairly clean wound and the bullet was essentially intact, meaning we could remove it and patch you up pretty well. I firmly suggest that you stay here for at least another forty-eight hours. At that point we'll review your progress. In the meantime, if there's anybody you'd like us to contact, notify Nurse Davenport. Try and get some sleep."

With that the doctor did an about-turn and marched off in military-like precision. Graeme was still very sore and didn't want to move, though deep down he felt quite relieved. Amid all the confusion he barely remembered how things went down at Dennison's. *Must be the trauma*, he reckoned. He tried to fight the fatigue but it was no good; he started drifting off into sleep.

Sitting in a big oak-paneled room at his favorite West End gentleman's club, the Boss was engaged in idle social chatter with some prominent barristers, bankers, and managing directors. He enjoyed settings like this and through some influential connections, had been able to join the club several years earlier. To the establishment, he was seen as a hardworking East End lad that had pulled himself up by his bootstraps and become a successful businessman.

"Sir, a telephone call for you," said the steward as he approached. "It's on the private line. You're welcome to take it in the next room."

"Excuse me, gentlemen." The Boss got up, extinguished his cigar and walked through the big oak door.

Inside the small room, he quickly snatched the phone off the desk and pressed the flashing button.

"What is it?" he snarled into the receiver.

"It's me," said the voice in that distinctive Dutch accent. "I take it you already know what happened."

Silence followed.

"You know that we cannot tolerate failure," the Boss uttered without emotion. "This has been a major setback in our plans, Niels. How did the police know precisely what time we would be there, and how the bloody hell did they manage to get men on the inside?"

Van Rooyen didn't have an answer.

The Boss went on. "Somebody knew about the whole thing. I want you to find out who orchestrated it and eliminate them, understand? Do not contact me again until the job is done."

Then he hung up.

Van Rooyen's head was already turning. He thought back to the bookmakers on the Old Kent Road. *That snitch, Robinson, talking to that girl.* He was sure she was involved, that she'd known something about the robbery. He'd find her. A wry smile crept across his face. The Dutchman got back in the Capri and took off, spinning the tires down a now rain-sodden Goldhawk Road.

"Braithwaite!" She could hear Donaldson's voice blast like the sound of a trumpet as she walked through the door.

"I want to speak to you. Now."

The super studied his protégé as she entered his office. She had a few cuts on her face and looked weary, but he could also sense a feeling of relief.

"Yes, sir?"

"That was a hell of a job you did today. Didn't want to say it in front of King and the others, but I'm proud of what we accomplished as a unit—but keep it to yourself, alright? Don't want anybody to think I'm going soft in my old age."

"Yes sir, and thank you." She gave a curt nod. Despite all she'd been through during the last twenty-four hours, Em was still every inch the quintessential lady, copper or not.

"Right," continued Donaldson. "Now, as far as we know our gang has effectively been neutralized. Piper is a vegetable, and Downs was killed during the robbery along with another henchman. We have three others: Brent, Rafferty, and Smithson in custody, and we'll be interrogating them shortly... But apparently two more got away in a Jag. We're still trying to track them down, but no luck so far."

"What about Van Rooyen?" asked Em. "I'm absolutely certain he actually planned the job, and he's still at large. We need to find him. Are there any leads at all?"

"Nothing's come up so far," Donaldson grunted. "He seems to be keeping a very low profile, but we already have Special Branch and MI5 out looking for him, with assistance from Interpol. Do you think he might be planning something else?"

"Difficult to say, but there's something in my gut that tells me this isn't over yet."

"You sure about that, Sergeant?"

There was a pause. "I've always trusted my instincts, sir, and I feel he'll have at least one more card to play. I think it's even more likely now that my partner's in hospital."

"Have you seen him?"

"Not yet. They whisked him off into surgery to remove the bullet. By the time I got there he was already in the operating theater. I should probably call the hospital and find out. For whatever it's worth, he's a big reason I'm here talking to you."

"Alright, Sergeant, but before you go and visit him, I'd like you to sit in on the Rafferty, Brent, and Smithson interviews with me down at Bow Street. We need to find out everything we can about this gang. I think you're right about this not being over yet. I want to make sure we do all we can to catch the remaining members. Are you up for it?"

"Of course," she said with conviction, trying to appear strong.

Within her, though, Em felt a bit irritated at that last remark from her boss. *I really don't like it when he does that. It makes me feel like he thinks I can't handle interrogations like this. I know I can do it. Steady, Emily Braithwaite, keep in mind that you've endured the longest day of your life and you're also very tired. Remember that James likely saved your life today, be thankful.* As her thoughts turned, Em also reminded herself of how grateful she was to work in her position. *I know I'm the exception rather than the rule in this line of work, and I know it's taken me guts and determination to get here. Most of these men have no idea, plus they probably couldn't handle it if they were in my shoes anyway!* She smiled to herself.

Even though he tried to put on a brave face, the Boss sat among some prominent members of London's business community—few of whom knew the extent of his criminal activities—and he was still angry. Van Rooyen was one of his best operatives—a man with an excellent track record in orchestrating successful armed heists. But perhaps he'd outlived his usefulness. Puffing on his cigar, he contemplated what to do next.

Van Rooyen had arranged for a shipment of grenades and US M16 assault rifles—some *real* weapons—to be sent across the Channel from Belgium by truck for the next operation.

Brussels was a major center for firearms trafficking in Europe and the man had known how to get his hands on the stuff required and get it transported to Britain. Slowly, he'd been expanding his network into France and Spain. He'd even managed to bribe a couple of HM Customs officers along the way. Nevertheless, the Boss still felt he was becoming a liability.

He'd give Van Rooyen five days to track down those coppers that had foiled the robbery. If it wasn't successful, the next job would be the Dutchman's last—he'd make sure of it. He smiled and took another puff of his cigar before easing back into the big leather Chesterfield chair.

"Gentlemen, can I invite anybody else to another glass of brandy?" The Boss smiled and leaned forward, grabbing the decanter.

CHAPTER 11

*B*ang! Graeme could hear the sound resonate as the bullet left the barrel. He was falling back...falling down.

Then he was awake. It was raining. Walking down Chancery Lane, Graeme ducked under shop awnings to avoid the drops. Not knowing his destination, he nonetheless kept walking.

Anger permeated his every pore. His knuckles ached from punching Richards. *Why had that bastard been there, at the tube station? Would he really sue me? I don't have anything to begin with!* Graeme felt immersed in his environment. Suddenly, he heard a sound from his coat pocket. He reached in and grabbed his mobile. It was ringing.

"Hello?"

"You're in dangerous territory, you need to tread carefully," declared the voice.

"Who the bloody hell are you?"

"Your guardian angel." The caller hung up before Graeme could reply.

Tired and hungry, Graeme yearned for a sandwich. He saw a Pret a Manger and headed towards it. As he was about to walk through the door, somebody tapped him on the shoulder. Graeme spun around.

It was Clara.

"I've been looking for you."

"How did you find me?" Graeme asked, stunned.

"I've been following you ever since you left the office."

How could that be? He tried to process. Didn't I go straight to Porto's after I told Richards to stuff it? I remember her calling me on my mobile telling me she couldn't make it, but then just before I passed out I do recall seeing her come towards me. Nah, couldn't be. Get a grip Graeme James, just try and deal with what's in front of you.

He glanced down at his watch. It was 10:20 a.m.

"What day is it?" he asked.

"Wednesday." Clara pursed her lips as if deep in thought and looked into his eyes. "There's something you don't know Graeme, something I forgot to tell you before you left."

"What, what is it?"

"I..."

It was at that second when he felt himself spinning, almost as if he was being lifted. He opened his eyes. The white ceiling, the smell—he was still in hospital and still in pain. He pressed the call button by the side of the bed.

Van Rooyen pulled up outside his flat in Holland Park. He was on the phone as soon as he had busted through the front door. He heard it ring several times.

Finally, a voice answered.

"We have unfinished business," the Dutchman seethed. "There's somebody I need you to find for me."

"Who is it?"

"She's a blonde woman. Maybe early thirties. Police officer, I think. Works for the Met."

"I think I know exactly who you mean," said the voice. "I'll be in touch."

Van Rooyen placed the phone receiver back on the base. He wondered where she might be and who else had helped her. There had to be others involved and they'd need to be taken care of, too. Nobody was immune, not even Met Police officers. Lighting a JPS Superkings cigarette, he took a seat on the couch.

It was going to be different this time. The Algerian would find her, no question, but it was he who'd carry out the final act. *Nobody makes me look like a fool!*

They were on their way to Bow Street in the super's Granada Ghia. Donaldson drove. The rain was coming down quite hard now, making the road ahead seem ominous and murky. In the passenger seat, Em thought about her partner. She was in dire need of sleep, but he'd saved her life. Once these interviews were done she'd go and visit him, stopping home on the way to get cleaned up, no matter what the hour. If there was ever a time to show him support, now was it, especially with some of the gang's members still at large and likely planning something else.

But it was more than that. Did she actually care about him?

She'd definitely felt something just prior to the robbery going down. *Maybe I just needed reassurance,* Em pondered to herself. *If I'm being honest, I was terrified, getting out of the car and walking into the jewelry store yesterday. That being said, I honestly felt that I genuinely wanted to know more about him as we drove to Dennison's. Could I really be falling for him?* She tried to brush such thoughts away.

Twenty-five minutes later, Em and Donaldson sat in an interrogation room at Bow Street Police Station. Chief Inspector King and another plainclothes officer had joined them. From the look on his face, Em could see that her boss was not impressed. He sat, jacket off, cigarette in hand, glaring at Rafferty. She was seated beside her boss, noticing that the thief could barely keep his eyes off her.

"So," Donaldson began. "You're up to your neck in it, sunshine. You're looking at a fifteen year stretch minimum for assault, robbery and possession of an illegal weapon. What we want to know is: who were the two that escaped and who else is still at large?"

Rafferty said nothing. He was still staring at the Sergeant. Then he winked at her.

"Alright, last chance to cooperate." Donaldson, raising his voice, clenched his fists and slammed them on the table. "Tell us what you know."

Again, nothing.

Donaldson got up and backed away, slowly turning to face King. "Pete, get this bastard out of here. I've got no time for him; take him back to the cells and have him processed. I want this arsehole kept under watch."

As he was led away, Rafferty looked over his shoulder at Em. "Take care, Sergeant," he said snidely, "wouldn't want anything to happen to that lovely bod of yours." He pursed his lips together to simulate a kiss.

"*Screw you*!" She was livid.

"*Sergeant*!" roared Donaldson. "Try to control your temper! He's not worth it."

"Sorry, sir."

King and the other officer looked at each other, eyes wide, almost as if in shock. Her boss sighed. "King and I will interview Brent and Smithson. It's almost three o'clock in the morning. Why don't you get some rest and then go see that partner of yours? I'll drop by the hospital later on."

Em rose and walked out of the room. She was angry, but also drained. All she wanted was a soft mattress to lie on and a big glass of wine.

"Call me a taxi, will you?" she asked one of the front desk officers. Fifteen minutes later she was in a black FX4 heading back to her flat in Chelsea.

"Nurse," pleaded Graeme, "I need you to do me a favor. Can you contact my partner, Detective Sergeant Emily Braithwaite of the SRI? I need to find out if there's been any development in our case since the robbery. I can't stand being kept in the dark, it's driving me insane."

"I'll do my best. We were given a contact number when you arrived at the hospital."

"One more thing," Graeme added, trying to sit up in the bed bravely, albeit with difficulty. "When on Earth do I get out of here?"

"Not yet, I'm afraid; you're still in pain." Nurse Davenport was firm, but Graeme could see from her facial expression that she was also sympathetic. Her eyes softened. "We've been told to keep an eye on you until otherwise instructed. I'll definitely let you know as soon as we have any more news or anything changes, Love. Now, as I said before, try to get some rest, okay?"

As she left, Graeme leaned back and sighed. It was driving him crazy. He knew his partner was out there, without him. He was worried about her. She was tough but also vulnerable, as he'd seen both the night before the heist and this afternoon, but under fire she'd been calm and collected. And that peck on the cheek—what was that about? *There are times when she barely tolerates me*, he remembered, *but others when she seems to have genuine affection for me.* Graeme was certainly physically attracted to her; she was the most gorgeous and sophisticated woman he'd ever laid eyes on. But he tried not to let any feelings get the best of him. *The nurse is right*, he surrendered. *I should try and get some rest.*

Em walked through the front door to her flat at almost a quarter to four in the morning. It had been the longest day of her life. She went into the kitchen and grabbed a glass of water, sitting down at the counter.

The incident in the interrogation room had really touched a nerve. *That bastard Rafferty knows something. I'll have a talk with the super when we meet at the hospital. I'll find out what he's hiding.*

Having finished the glass, she got undressed and took another shower. Just like the long day before, it proved to be soothing, washing away the grime and filth that seemed to be lurking around nearly every corner every day she was on the job.

I wonder how James is holding up? she wondered, as the water cascaded onto her face, hair and down over her shoulders, back and chest. *It's got to be driving him crazy, being stuck in a hospital like that and without a weapon by his side. For all it's worth, he is a gun-happy control freak!*

Having finished showering and drying herself off, Em brushed her teeth and went straight to bed. She was asleep in less than fifteen minutes.

Brent was the first into the room.

Donaldson, now having been up for almost a full twenty-four hours, was far from amused, but pressed on with the task at hand. He'd developed rather good skills at interrogation over the years. As a special ops commander in the Royal Marines, he'd learned the art of extracting the information he needed. It had stood him well when he'd joined the police force, almost fifteen years ago. Small-time bank robbers like Brent were easy prey.

"So, you and your friend Smithson were supposed to make off with the loot yesterday," he commented, savoring each drag of his B&H.

Brent didn't say anything.

"You'd better start speaking, son, or I promise that I will break you, personally. Where's King?" he asked the other officer in the room, Detective Constable

Templar. "Go find him, will you?"

As soon as Templar closed the door, the super fixated once again on Brent. "Now, I want you to tell me everything you know. How did you get involved with this robbery? Who planned it?"

Brent looked at the super in defiance. He could see the older man was clearly running on reserve energy. He said nothing.

"Tell me," Donaldson repeated angrily.

Again, Brent didn't say a word, but a dark smirk appeared on his face.

For Donaldson, it was the last straw. He got up and walked towards the corner of the room. Picking up a chair, he turned around to face Brent and threw it at him.

The young man was stunned. The chair passed inches from Brent's face before hitting the gray, featureless wall with a crash.

Donaldson marched towards the man, clenching his fists like he was about to take a swing at the young, fresh-faced criminal.

"You wouldn't," the man retorted with a scrunched, upturned nose.

"Oh yes, I bloody would and I can assure you, sunshine, I'd enjoy every last second of it. Tell me what you know. NOW!"

Realizing that his options were diminishing by the second, Brent put his hands up and pushed his body back.

"Alright, *alright*!" he exclaimed, his tone a mixture of fear and anger. "I'll tell you what I fucking know, but I want a deal before I say anything."

Donaldson grabbed the chair again, set it down in its original place and went back to the desk. He leaned forward, right into Brent's face. "And what kind of deal would that be, my son?"

The younger man started to sweat. "I want money. I've got gambling debts, you know. That's why I fucking did this. I'm into a loan shark for ten thousand quid."

The super smiled. "And I suppose you want us to bribe you with money in order for you to spill the beans. So you can service your debts, so to speak." Donaldson leaned further forward until his nose was just millimeters from Brent's. "Let me tell you something, son. *There is absolutely no chance* we'd do *anything* like that for the likes of you. We'll start spreading word across London that you're a known police informant; I'm sure it won't take too long for that to reach the less-savory citizens of this fair city. Either way, you're going to jail; all you need to decide is how badly you want to be somebody's bitch on the inside."

"What if I give you some names and addresses?"

"It's a start."

Brent paused for a second. He glanced right, then left before turning to face the super.

Donaldson was fixated on him, eyes locked.

The suspect cleared his throat and continued, "The robbery that happened at Dennison's, it was planned weeks ago."

"Go on," the super instructed.

"Me and Smithson were both recruited by that big bloke, Piper. We met him at a pub down in Wandsworth, the Ship."

"What else?" asked Donaldson intently as he lit up a fresh cigarette.

"We met up with some others and there was this Dutch bloke, they called him Niels. Another man, who he just called Boss, was also there. A sadistic bastard he was, everybody was terrified of him, even more so with each passing week. Just before the robbery, he instructed the Dutchman to shoot one of the guys, Doyle, in the chest, for complaining."

"So what did this Niels and the Boss ask you to do for the Dennison's job?" Donaldson took another drag.

"To ride in the back of one of the Transits. Once we'd all forced our way into the shop, Smithson and I would be handed the loot. We'd wait until the bomb went off before exiting. We were instructed to get into an ex-BT van that had been left just down the road and then, once things had calmed down a bit, we'd drive off, casual-like."

"Where were you supposed to go?"

"A lockup in White City, just off Wood Lane."

"What was going to happen there?"

"The Boss and Niels would meet with the rest of us. We were told we'd be given our share of the prize and then head off in our separate ways."

"Anything else? We'll need the address of that lockup."

Brent nodded.

"Is that it?" continued Donaldson.

"That's all I was told."

"What about your mate out there?"

"He just knows the same as I do."

"Really?" snarled Donaldson. "I think we'll be the judge of that."

Just that second, the door opened and King walked in, with Templar following behind him.

"Pete." Donaldson's tone changed ever so slightly. "Get a party down to a lockup in White City, just off Wood Lane. I'd send a couple of your SPG boys, just in case there's anybody there who's armed. Templar, go grab me a pen and note pad will you? And find Hungerford; drag him out of bed if you have to. I want him in here before we interview Smithson."

Clara? He looked around but couldn't seem to find her. The sandwich store was busy, the din of multiple conversations and the sound of registers ringing in money adding to the hustle and bustle. People lined up to get their sandwiches, salads and drinks from the self-service refrigerated shelves. Graeme grabbed a BMT and a bottle of Ribena and headed for the cashier.

Six quid fifty for that? He couldn't believe it. Although the store was packed, he managed to find a spot to sit down at one of the tall, skinny tables.

The Blackberry rang again. Graeme pulled it out of his coat pocket and put it on the table. He didn't recognize the number. It kept ringing and ringing but he didn't answer. People around him were starting to give him irate looks. After what seemed like the thousandth ring, he finally picked it up and pressed the button.

"It's me, Clara. Sorry I had to leave."

"What's going on?" Graeme asked.

"Something happened to you," she said. "You're not who you think you are."

"Who am I supposed to be?"

"You're special, Graeme. I knew that from the moment I first met you. Richards—he doesn't matter. None of what you see matters."

"I don't understand, Clara. What is important and what isn't?"

"You're on your way to finding the answers," she said. "You're also in danger, but you're not alone."

"I need to see you. Where can I find you?"

"Don't worry. I'll find you."

The line went dead.

Graeme took a swig of his sugar-free Ribena. He tried to walk back out onto the street. Absolutely nothing was clear, though at least it was no longer raining.

Graeme ran to a nearby bus stop and jumped on an Arriva B7TL that was boarding passengers. He found a seat on the lower deck and soon fell asleep.

Clara's words were in his ears. He could feel a hand touching his face. It was soft, warm, and soothing. He knew the scent. It was then that he found himself at home at Christmas, like he remembered as a boy. There was the tree, the presents; he could hear music, Shakin' Stevens' "Merry Christmas Everyone" playing on the record player.

It was reassuring, but where *was* everybody? Where was his father and his stepmother? He could smell her perfume. He headed towards the kitchen, where he could see light radiating from the far side of the door. Graeme turned the lock and as he opened it, he was dazzled; it was so bright, so brilliant. A voice called out to him.

Opening his eyes, Graeme found it took him a while to focus. The voice was persistent.

"James? James? Are you alright?" Em was sitting in a chair at the side of his bed.

Graeme drew a deep breath and exhaled, feeling his body relaxing. Had he been dreaming again? It had seemed so real at times, but so did *here*. Could *she* be real? It was as though she'd been the voice of angel, reaching to him down in the depths of his own misery and confusion. Then, he was back.

"I was wondering when you'd get here," he said, attempting to stretch as he woke up. He studied her. It was daylight now and she looked a lot better than the last time he'd seen her. Most of the cuts on her face seemed barely visible. Her hair was brushed and her eyes sparkled. Her makeup and clothes—a short blue skirt, a white, fairly low-cut blouse and a big belt—made her look more relaxed than he'd so far seen, even off-duty.

"What time is it?" Graeme asked, sitting up and adjusting his posture.

"It's almost ten on Saturday morning, James; July 16."

"How long have you been here?"

"Since about half past nine this morning... Donaldson said he'd be in to see you in about an hour."

"What's happened to the case?" Graeme pressed.

"Not a huge amount, I'm afraid." Her Bedales English was proving utterly seductive to his ears, even in hospital. "In the small hours of this morning, Donaldson and I drove down to Bow Street Police Station, where the surviving gang members were taken. It was like the bloody Fort Knox when we got there."

"What happened? Were you able to learn anything?" As Graeme spoke, he tried to summon what strength he had.

"Not much, really. I sat in with Donaldson for an interview with Rafferty. Remember the one that security guard overpowered?"

"Yes, vaguely." Graeme's head pounded as he tried to piece together the violence and confusion from the Marylebone heist.

"The bastard said nothing," Em continued, "except some leering, actually threatening remarks aimed at me. He made me so angry that after he was taken back to the cells, Donaldson suggested I get some rest, so I called a taxi and headed home. I slept for a few hours, took a cab back to the office, then drove here."

After hearing that, Graeme did his best to inject some humor into the conversation. "I have to say Sergeant, that considering what we went through, you don't look half bad right now."

"Are you trying to be charming?" she countered. "Because if you are, it is most definitely not working."

"That's the problem with posh birds," said Graeme under his breath. "No bloody sense of humor."

He could tell that she heard him. No sooner had he finished muttering that Em got up off the chair and came closer to him, bending down to whisper in his ear.

"It's just as well you're in this vulnerable condition," she said softly and seductively before withdrawing back to sit in the chair.

Graeme didn't know whether to laugh or cry.

Em returned to the topic of conversation, as if the last few moments hadn't happened at all. "On the way here this morning, Tim radioed me and said that one of the others in custody, Brent, had told them about a lockup in White City where the gang was supposed to meet after the robbery to divvy up the spoils. There's some SPG officers going over it now. As far as we know, nothing much has turned up yet."

"Did Tim come up with anything else?" Graeme was striving not to feel helpless and out of the loop, despite being banged up and in hospital.

Em pressed on. "He also said that Donaldson and Hungerford were in the process of interviewing the other one they captured with Brent—Smithson. But I haven't got word on anything so far. By the way, you look terrible."

"Thanks. I presume that was a compliment, Sergeant?"

"Don't flatter yourself Inspector James." She was looking at him as-a-matter-of-factly again.

As Brent was led out of the interrogation room, Donaldson walked to its far side. He clenched his fist and was about to punch a hole in the wall when Hungerford walked in.

"About bloody time you got here," the super exhaled. "Where's Smithson?"

"They're just bringing him in now."

"Alright."

Donaldson grabbed his pack of B&Hs on the desk and pulled one out. Hungerford gave him a light.

"So," the detective stated, "did you find out much?"

Donaldson cast a glance at Hungerford, angered a little that the detective forgot to call him "Sir."

"They were apparently going to rendezvous at a lockup in White City and divide up the loot after the job. We've got some people heading down there now. Brent said we weren't likely to get anything more out of Smithson, but I still want to try, anyway. ...Why don't you start on him and I'll go and stand on the other side of the wall?"

The super put his jacket on and walked out the door.

Smithson had made a career out of being a petty criminal. A few stolen cars here, a couple of newsagent robberies there—he was the archetypal opportunist, always looking for an easy score. For him, meeting up with Piper had been like graduating to the next level and a chance to do some real stuff, robbing banks and the like.

Brent was down on his luck but also easily led. He'd be a good scapegoat should things go south. Now they had Smithson, who was also in the same predicament as his "friend."

Hungerford studied the man closely. Short, mousey-blonde spiky hair, brown eyes and a round, cheeky face—a pathological liar. This one was going to be interesting.

"Cigarette?" asked the detective, opening his packet of Embassy Number 1.

Smithson took one without hesitation.

"Your mate Brent has just wet his pants, pretty much told us everything he knew. Question is: what do *you* know?"

"Same as he told ya, I've got nothing more to add."

"Really? Well, he said you were the one that roped him into this gang in the first place. Ship Inn ring any bells?"

Donaldson and a couple of other officers peered curiously through the glass as

Hungerford got on with the task.

"He didn't 'ave to go, he could've backed out any time he wanted. Besides, I didn't give a toss either way if he came or not," said Smithson arrogantly.

"You know what?" Hungerford leaned forward across the table, breaking into an actual smile. "I think you're a conniving little twat. I think that you were going to use Brent as a scapegoat. That Piper was a big, intimidating bloke and if that meeting had gone wrong, he'd have taken the fall, right? Well, now, it looks like you're shit out of luck too. Piper's a cabbage, Brent's in custody and so are you."

"I've got nothing else to say. I want my brief."

Donaldson knew that was his cue to get back into the room and interrogate the suspect.

"Then I guess we're at loggerheads," Hungerford shook his head. "You're not getting anything until you've told us *everything you know*!" The detective's face reddened and he pursed his lips, raising his shoulders, clearly showing his patience was running out. Hungerford, not one to suffer fools, was known for having quite a temper when pushed.

At that moment, the super walked into the room.

"Here, sir," Hungerford gave him a stare. "Perhaps you'll have more luck with him."

Donaldson shot the suspect a confident glance.

"Mark, go get us some of that wretched coffee they have here, will you? If I can't beat a confession out of him at least I'll have him throwing up in the corner."

Smithson's brow creased as his eyes widened.

As Hungerford closed the door, the room fell into an eerie silence.

"I've got just one word for you, Smithson," said Donaldson coldly. "Dutchman."

"Don't know what you mean."

"I'll say it again," said the super. "Dutchman."

"Sorry, no idea who you're talking about."

"Alright, sunshine, you've had your chance."

At that moment, Hungerford re-entered the room.

"Mark, forget the coffee, this one's more interested in a knuckle sandwich. I hear you make some of the tastiest in town."

Hungerford dropped the coffee cups, letting the hot liquid spill on the floor before taking off his jacket. He grabbed Smithson by the scruff of his collar, yanking him to his feet.

The super started again. "One last time, Smithson. I want to know about the Dutchman. Your colleague said him and another bloke called the 'Boss' were the masterminds behind the Dennison's job yesterday afternoon, and probably those other robberies north of the river in the last few months, including that job at St. Paul's."

Smithson said nothing.

"You stupid bastard," chuckled Hungerford, before socking him in the mouth. The suspect slipped and fell to the floor.

"Get up you miserable piece of pond life," the super yelled. "I've been up for more than a full day. I've witnessed half of Marble Arch blown to pieces and had one of my best officers injured in the line of fire. You tell me what you know about the Dutchman now or you'll be floating with the jetsam down the Thames this time tomorrow."

Hungerford clenched his fist again, ready for the second strike when Smithson broke down.

"So what was that peck on the cheek about, then?" asked Graeme.

"What are you talking about?" Em replied.

"You know, before they put me in the ambulance. I'm growing on you, aren't I?"

"If you're meaning like a cyst, then I suppose you are," she said haughtily.

"That was harsh."

"But fair," she sideswiped, faking a smile.

"I just want to get out of here, Braithwaite, this is driving me insane. I've been told that they'll probably keep me under observation for another forty-eight hours."

"As well as they bloody should," was her answer. "You were *shot*, James, in the arm by a pistol. There's no way they'll be letting you out anytime soon. For God's sake, you can't move your arm."

"I know, but I hate not being able to do anything. I feel powerless and the bad guys are still out there."

"Well whining is not going to solve anything, is it?" she replied tartly.

"I guess you're right," he sighed. "So what do we do now?"

"There's not much we *can* do, really," she said flatly. "But we're waiting to see if Donaldson gets anywhere with the suspects we bagged from the robbery."

"And what do you think, Sergeant?"

"To be honest, I don't think we're in the clear yet. Van Rooyen is still at large, as are two others from the robbery. I told Donaldson that I think they're going to plan one more move."

Graeme could sense it; he could recall his vision from the twenty-first century, whether it was real or not—the voice on the phone saying he was in danger. *Could this be it? Could we be the targets?*

"You've got to get me out of here, Braithwaite."

"But you're in no fit state to be walking and I don't need a cripple for a partner."

"Look, after Donaldson has been here, find a way to get me out, can you? If Van Rooyen knows we were the ones inside the store that foiled the robbery, then he knows how to get to me in here and probably you, too. The only way we can beat this is by sticking together and that means getting the hell out of here."

"His name is Van Rooyen, first name Niels I think," said Smithson. He could taste the blood from his lips and nose and feel his face aching.

"What do you know about him?" the super snarled.

"He was the one that supplied weapons for the blag. The shotguns, the smoke canisters. He was the one that shot Doyle in the chest for questioning the Boss. He's a sadistic bastard if you ask me."

"When was the last time you saw him?" Donaldson took another drag of his cigarette.

"Yesterday morning. We met at an old warehouse down by the East India Dock. He instructed us to follow him to a spot near Piccadilly where we'd wait and then on to another one just off Bayswater Road. I was in one of the Transits, the one that was blown up. It was rigged with explosives. This bloke called Williams was driving, he was the one instructed to blow it up. Doyle was in the passenger seat. Me and Brent were riding in the back."

"So, where was Van Rooyen?"

"He was in another vehicle. A green van I think which we followed, but then he said he was going to switch cars at Piccadilly over the radio."

"Did you see him after that?"

"No, it was just radio. I was riding in the back, so I had no clue."

Clever bastard, thought the super. *He switched vehicles so he knew we wouldn't be able to find him, even if the mob had been caught and we'd gotten confessions, like now, really. He could be anywhere.*

"Can you give us an accurate description of Van Rooyen?" asked Donaldson.

Smithson drew back for a second, but saw Hungerford clench his fist. "Look, I've told you a lot already, give me something."

"*Tell us about Van Rooyen*!!" Hungerford was about to grab the suspect once again.

"Five foot eleven, bald, round face, maybe thirty-five years old; he was wearing a black leather jacket—good enough?"

"Mark," said Donaldson, gesturing to Hungerford. "Get Tim Charles on the blower right now. I want to have another look at the photos of Van Rooyen we have on file."

"Yes, sir." The detective shrugged on his jacket and left the room.

"Now, Smithson," said the super. "What do you want from us? Immunity or protection, I assume? It seems to be an emerging pattern on every suspect we've interviewed regarding this case."

"I want safe passage out of the country. I was thinking maybe Spain?"

The super burst out laughing. "You expect me to pull some strings and send you abroad at the taxpayer's expense, because we almost had to beat a confession out of you about information from a botched robbery? You've got to be joking, son."

"You don't understand," said Smithson. "There's more to this. Van Rooyen's got ties to some major heavies on the continent. He and the Boss were really serious about the Dennison's robbery. I don't know for certain but I think it was just a step, maybe, towards something bigger."

"You think? Who the hell is this '*Boss*' you're talking about?"

"I don't know his name, but he scared the shit out of all us, including Piper and Downs. He talked posh, but the way he said things sometimes, he was fucking psychotic."

"What does he look like?"

Smithson shuddered.

At that moment, the door opened and Hungerford walked in. He beckoned Donaldson over and whispered in his ear. The detective smiled at Smithson before removing his jacket and placing it on one of the chairs.

The superintendent turned to face Smithson with a clever grin. He sat down at the table. "Let's start again," he ordered, taking another drag of his cigarette. "Tell us what this '*Boss*' looks like."

Smithson didn't speak. Instead, he darted his eyes from Donaldson to Hungerford and back.

The SRI chief growled, his brows creasing inwards. "Let's just get on with it shall we? The way I see it, you're pretty much done. Telling us a little bit more isn't going to make a shred of difference. We can make a deal but first you have to tell me anything you know about this '*Boss*.' I'm not one to have psychos running around on the streets of this fair city, no matter how well-connected they might be. Protecting Londoners from filth like that comes before anything else, including your poxy existence, if you catch my drift." Donaldson leaned across the table and stared right into Smithson's eyes.

"...About forty-five to fifty, maybe, dresses well, dark hair, graying at the temples, kind of dark-skinned."

"And you said he was posh? Like, how?"

"Public school, I think, no obvious accent as far as I could tell, just Queen's English."

"Mark?" The super turned to face Hungerford. "Get in touch with Pete King and also contact the senior boys at Scotland Yard about this '*Boss*.' We need to have his description sent out to as many as possible. Also, get a couple of the local lads to take Smithson to the cells, will you?"

"Right sir," the detective agreed, who donned his jacket and headed out the door.

"I thought we had a deal!" exclaimed Smithson.

"We do," said Donaldson, getting up. "I'll be in touch." He got up and left the room, just as two uniformed officers walked in.

CHAPTER 12

The task had already begun. He knew he'd find her soon, that much was certain. A reputation like his hadn't been earned by being second best. Instincts—they were everything. She wouldn't know what was coming, though he was a bit disconcerted at the Dutchman's tone. It was as if things weren't as solid as before. All he knew was that he'd better get paid. If asked to do a job, he always kept his end up. That's how he'd become the best. And finishing the job meant compensation—always.

He sat in the room, fiddling with a Rubik's Cube. He'd enjoyed playing with them ever since they came out. The challenge in getting all the squares on each side back to the same color was a journey, much like how he saw a contract. From being assigned the job, to gathering information and stalking his prey—it was a complex task, just like figuring out this square, rotating piece of plastic.

On the desk beside him was a Nikon F2 camera, a Vivitar zoom lens and a few rolls of Kodak film. In a couple of hours, he'd start the search for his target. In the meantime, he was determined to solve the cube.

"Tim, what's the latest word on that evidence collected yesterday morning?" Donaldson was on the police radio in his Granada. Hungerford drove. "We've got three of the bastards still at large."

"There's some more fingerprints we've found, Guv, from a set of keys left at the garage in the small office in the back. I asked a couple of officers from C-Division to go back down there this morning. They discovered them about an hour ago. We've sent them off to the lab. I've asked them to put a priority rush on it, so we should have it back by first thing Monday."

"Good. I'm glad you didn't trust the task to uniforms. The last thing I need right now is for my blood pressure to spike, especially after interrogating those three we've got in custody. Let me know of any further developments, will you? I'm on the way to the hospital to see how our injured John Wayne is holding up. Sierra 1, out."

"So, what do you propose we do?" Em asked.

"I'm still thinking up a plan." Graeme was a bit annoyed at her remark. *I don't think she's taking me seriously!*

"Here we go again, another one of the famous James plans. I just hope it doesn't involve shooting this time."

"Why should it? The sooner I can get out of this bloody bed, the better." He looked at her and smiled.

Em just shook her head.

"Since you're here, Sergeant... Fancy getting me some more water?"

She exhaled loudly and got up. "Sometimes I really wonder why I put up with you."

"Come on—admit it, you love having me around."

Em shook her head again and walked off exasperatedly.

Graeme studied her as she left. *Wow! You're looking great today, partner!* He could hear the sound of her heels tapping down the corridor, growing progressively fainter. Lying back on the pillow, he closed his eyes, trying to think up a plan that wouldn't draw attention to him, Em, or the hospital staff, but he was still sore and tired. He found himself craving sleep.

Leaving the hotel, the man put on his sunglasses and walked outside. He carried a small Samsonite bag. Inside it was the Nikon camera and his Beretta. He walked across the street and got into a light green, X registration C2 Audi 100. It was time to find the target.

"End of the line, mate. It's time for you to get off," said the driver.

Graeme stirred, opening his eyes to see the distinctive yellow curved handrails and oval blue-gray seats of a London Arriva B7TL double-decker. He was back in the twenty-first century again.

"Where am I?"

"Victoria Station. This service has ended and so has my shift. C'mon, off you go."

He got up and walked off the bus. Graeme really had no idea where he was going. In Victoria Station he headed for a WHSmith on the concourse, just for something to do. The phone in his pocket started ringing again.

"Hello?"

"You're running out of time."

"Clara?"

"Listen to me. Get on the tube. Take the circle line to Notting Hill Gate. I'll meet you there at 2:30 p.m." She hung up.

Graeme glanced at the clock on the Blackberry. Two hours to kill.

Having grabbed a bottle of water from the newsagents, he slowly began making his way to the tube station. He looked around him. Nobody appeared to be paying any attention—people were just getting on with their lives. He felt groggy. His Next suit and overcoat were still damp, suffering from the aftereffects of the morning's rain.

Down on the platform he waited for the train to come. As it pulled into the station, he cracked the cap on his water bottle, taking a swig. The doors opened and he stepped forward and into the light.

"This should keep you going for a while." He heard the sound of plastic beakers landing on a shelf.

"Nod off again, did we?" She was just about leaning over him, placing cups of water on the shelf by his bed. She was close now, her scent proving an aphrodisiac. It was taunting his emotions. He could feel his pulse quicken, heightening his senses. He wanted to kiss her more than anything, he thought, as her hair brushed lightly against his face.

She smiled and drew back, sitting on the chair beside his bed. "There's somebody else to see you." She gestured over her shoulder.

Donaldson walked in, followed by Hungerford, chewing gum.

Graeme took a good look at his boss. He appeared as though he hadn't properly slept in weeks, yet he was still trying to carry on as dignified as possible. Despite the deep bags under his eyes, he still looked dapper in a three-piece dark blue pinstripe and white shirt. His navy blue and red-striped tie was remarkably straight.

"So, how are they treating you in here?" Donaldson inquired without expression on his face.

"Not bad, sir. As you can see, Sergeant Braithwaite is keeping a close eye on me."

"Good to know that at least somebody from our department's got tabs on you." His partner shook her head again.

"What's the latest on the case?" Graeme asked, his head throbbing.

"Still trying to put the puzzle together. We got nothing out of Rafferty, the bastard is as tight as a drum and I don't think he'll give up the game easily. We'll just let him stew in the cells for a while. Since he's the only hard case in custody, I will do my very best to make sure he stays locked up. Brent and Smithson tried to put up a front, but we eventually got them to squeal...with a little persuasion, of course." The super gave Graeme a wink.

"What did you find out from them? Em has told me that apparently there's a lockup in White City that has something to do with the whole job."

"That's right. King sent some of the SPG lads down there to check it out. We're still waiting on any results, but there are a few developments."

"I'd love to hear them."

"Smithson said that the Dutchman is tied in with some pretty heavy criminals on the other side of the Channel. He also gave us a fairly good description of him, which somewhat matches the photos we have. Tim Charles also said that some more fingerprints were found at the garage, on a set of keys. They're being examined right now. But there's one other thing that bothers me."

Donaldson scratched his crew cut for a brief second.

"What's that?"

"Smithson said that Van Rooyen reported to somebody who was simply called the '*Boss*.' A sadistic bastard, apparently."

"I'm guessing he didn't give a name?"

"No. In fact, he seemed quite terrified of him. Even said that Piper and Downs were, too."

"Do you think he's the one behind all this?" Graeme propped his elbows up in an attempt to sit up in the bed. "Perhaps the one responsible for killing Em's star informant, and that bloke Chatsworth?"

"It looks like it," the super replied, "but we've got no name, only a description. Olive-skinned, dark hair with graying temples, and a snappy dresser. Oh, and apparently he talks Queen's English."

"By all accounts a toff, then," barked Graeme.

His partner rolled her eyes, but then something sparked. "Did he say how old he was?"

"Probably in his fifties," Donaldson answered. "Why? Is there something else, Sergeant?"

"I'm probably just speculating, but to me there seems something familiar about him. I could have sworn that a man fitting that description had dealings with my father at some point. I think I remember seeing him at Beaufort a couple of years ago. Though I can't, for the *life* of me, remember his name."

"Guv." Graeme gestured to his boss to move closer to him, in an attempt to keep his voice down. "*You've got to get me out of here*. I've got a hunch that the gang members at large—or more specifically, Van Rooyen and this '*Boss*'—have probably got a contract out on both me and Braithwaite. I'm sure they'll want to tie up any loose ends, especially in view of the fact that this robbery—from their standpoint—was a disaster. And I'm doing nobody any good sitting in this bed like a lame duck."

The super didn't remark, but looked Graeme straight in the eye before gesturing to his partner.

"Sergeant Braithwaite. Keep a good eye on him, won't you?"

"Yes, sir," she sighed.

"Right. We'll be off. I'll be in touch. Em. Stay close to your radio."

"Ta, da." Hungerford made a little signal as he followed Donaldson out the door. Em swiveled back to look at Graeme.

"So, what was that about?"

"Sit tight," she said confidently. "I'll be back shortly."

"Okay."

As she headed out the room and into the corridor, Graeme lay back down again, his eyes fixed on the ceiling. *I really hope I can get out of this place soon. I really don't want to end up dying in this world, I feel there's just too much to live for now.* He took a deep breath and tried to relax.

"Mark, I'll meet you downstairs by the car in a few minutes. I've got a phone call to make," said Donaldson.

"Right, sir." Hungerford nodded as he turned and headed for the stairs.

Once the detective was out of sight, Donaldson turned around and walked back down the corridor. Approaching him from the opposite direction was Em.

"Ah Sergeant, I knew I could count on you."

Em cocked her head inquisitively. "What do you have in mind, sir?"

"When you've been in this game as long as I have, you learn to trust your instincts. And what you said to me back at SRI last night got me thinking. I had a feeling James would be getting antsy and along with you I have a sneaking suspicion that if we don't get him out of here, pronto, somebody will try and take him out. Follow me."

Turning a corner, he led her into a hospital staff room. Inside, two nurses and hospital porters were waiting, along with a hospital bed on casters.

"Alright people, time to move," the super instructed. "Our man is in the recovery ward. You know what to do."

"Yes, sir," said the older of the two porters. "C'mon, everybody, let's go."

As soon as the hospital staff made their way down the corridor to Graeme's ward, Donaldson pulled Em aside.

"Look. We're getting your partner out of here. There's an ambulance waiting at the back entrance, ready to transport him to Charing Cross Hospital in Hammersmith. I want you to follow it. Once it arrives, they'll put James in recovery. And we'll post officers outside his room to keep an eye on him. Staff at the hospital will be given strict orders to wait for you. When you get there, I want you to meet a man named Thompson at the emergency entrance—he's fairly short, about five foot five with a beard and a balding head. Have him call me the instant you get there. Thompson will then direct you to the room where James will be kept under observation. I've instructed Doctor Roth to transfer the patient records to Thompson and his team at Charing Cross. There's a Doctor Porritt that will be observing him. In forty-eight hours, if James is well enough, I want you to have him transferred to your place."

"What? Sir?" exclaimed Em distraughtly. "Why my place?"

"To be honest, it's the best place for both of you once he's been given the green light to be discharged. If this 'Boss' is as dangerous and calculating as I believe he is, there's every chance James could be targeted, even at Charing Cross. Plus, if he's at your place, there's only one way in or out. We can have up to three unmarked units watching everybody that comes into your building, day or night, plus if our gang of merry men *do* show up, we have a much better chance of catching them there than at a big, multi-story hospital."

Em's eyes widened and her body stiffened as she pursed her lips. Clasping her hands together, she did her best at trying to avoid anger and maintain composure.

"I know you're not thrilled with the idea, Sergeant," Donaldson added when he saw her facial expression change. "But right now it's the best option we have. Even if they *do* shoot the place up, your special SRI insurance policy will more than cover the damage." The super broke into a grin.

Em looked at him frankly. Although unhappy at the thought, she was beginning to get the picture. *No matter what I think, he is right. It's not too far from Charing Cross Hospital to my place, which would make getting James out and to the flat easier than trying to do it from here at Saint Mary's.*

"Alright sir, I'll do it," resigned Em with a sighing tone, well aware that Donaldson could sense the reluctance in her voice. "One more thing, though."

"What is it, Sergeant?"

"Can you have somebody stop by at James' place for some clothes and his personal effects? I don't exactly like the idea of him being naked in my home."

Donaldson smiled. "Very well."

To find the girl, he needed answers. He'd start at the crime scene and use one of his many fake identities to ask the right questions. As he drove up Edgware Road, he could see the area surrounding the jewelry store was cautioned off. Several police cars and numerous uniformed officers were on the scene. After parking the Audi just down the street, he placed his Beretta in the glove box.

Getting out of the car, he started walking up the road towards the section the police had roped off. Looking beyond the barricade, he could see signs of significant damage on both sides of Edgware.

"Jim Hanson, *Evening Standard*," he said as he presented his ID to an officer.

"We've already had a bunch of you lot here earlier," retorted the copper. "What's *your* angle, then?"

"I've been covering those armed robberies in the city. Looks like you've got a regular crime wave going on."

The officer shook his head. "Alright, you can go on, but we'll be keeping an eye on you and don't touch anything. Got it?"

With his Nikon F2 in hand, he walked towards the crime scene. A white BMW 6 Series was being loaded onto a Met Police Ford D Series flatbed recovery truck. The car was covered in dust and debris from the blast, but otherwise appeared intact.

There was something about the car that drew his attention. He turned around and quickly snapped a picture of it, making sure to grab the registration number just in case it might lead anywhere.

As he snuck closer to the store, a couple more police officers asked him for his ID again. Waved through, he scanned the premises looking for any evidence.

As part of his training, he'd learned to look for clues, no matter how small they might seem. He could see that a clean-up operation was already well under way, so if he was going to find anything he had to do it quickly. He headed towards the back of the store.

"What's going on?" Graeme turned his head.

"You're being transferred," commented the man in the white coat, plainly.

"Where the hell to?"

"You'll find out soon enough."

"*I'm not going anywhere* until you give me some bloody answers! Who the hell are you?"

The man and another in a white coat, along with two nurses, tried to pick him up and move him onto the stretcher bed they'd brought in.

"Get the hell off me," he said under his breath, but he knew he was a sitting duck. Then he heard *Em's* voice.

"It's alright, James; they've been instructed by Donaldson to get you out of here. Just do what they tell you. I'll see you in a bit."

"That makes me feel a whole lot better," he shot her way sarcastically.

She walked right up to him and leaned towards him, her face just inches from his. "Remember your plan of escape? Well this is it, only *I'm* instigating it. You're going to have to trust me. Can you handle it?"

"What choice do I have?"

"Right now, none," she whispered into his right ear.

He could see that the safe had already been locked and was being guarded; two uniformed officers were on the door.

"You're not supposed to be here," barked one. "Go, on, off you go."

"Sorry, my mistake."

He headed back towards the front of the store, taking pictures seemingly at random, all the while on the lookout for anything to lead him to the target. Examining a couple of the glass cabinets, he saw that all the stones had been taken away and secured. But then, out of the corner of his eye, he saw it.

Of course. The closed-circuit TV cameras. They'd have footage of the store and its customers just before the raid. If the girl had been involved, she'd show up on the tapes, surely.

He sauntered up to one of the officers who was helping clear up the mess.

"Jim Hanson, *Evening Standard*. I'm doing a story on armed heists in the city. Is there any chance we could use some stills from the cameras for our tonight's story on the Dennison's botched robbery?"

"You'll have to talk to Chief Inspector Wade of the Forensic Unit and there's no guarantees I'm afraid. We're not even supposed to do this under normal circumstances."

"But these aren't normal, are they? Look, the whole city is buzzing about this robbery. If I can get an exclusive and show the Met in the best light possible, it could do wonders for your PR. Don't you think?"

Graeme found it hard to just sit there, but cooperated with the hospital staff as his partner suggested. He was still on a drip, so moving wasn't as straightforward as it perhaps might have been. Nonetheless, the staff quickly loaded him onto the hospital trolley and moved him out the door and down the corridor. Graeme figured it took the staff less than twenty minutes to get him from lying in his bed in the ward to being loaded onto the Ford Transit ambulance at the rear entrance of St. Mary's.

Safe and secure, with the ambulance technician watching over him, Graeme's "1983 emergency ride" to Charing Cross began. He lay back on the stretcher, glancing at the interior walls and roof of the ambulance. The Transit appeared to be almost brand new.

Across the street, Em sat in her Mercedes. As the ambulance pulled away she followed it, remaining a few cars back. She wasn't particularly pleased at Donaldson's suggestion to babysit her partner—and at her own flat, as well—but it was an order, and she respected her boss enough to follow protocol. She still had career ambitions, and so far her tactics had served her well in the police force.

But deep down, was she *really* unhappy at the thought? The notion of Graeme being with her gave her some kind of security; it was comforting, even if he was still not quite at full strength. She was about to break into a smile but then wondered if Van Rooyen or the "Boss" *did* come looking for them, could he protect her and, ultimately, could she do the same for him?

Em tried not to ponder on the thought, choosing instead to focus on the task at hand, following the ambulance to Charing Cross.

"Somebody tells me you want to see the CCTV footage," said Chief Inspector Wade, clearly irritated at being bothered by another beat reporter.

"I just think it would really add some sizzle to the piece," he said gruffly.

"Alright, Hanson. Here's what I can do. You can sit and watch, supervised by us, but you're not to take any pictures of the footage, alright? You can base your story using information from what you see, but I need the paper's word that it will show the London Metropolitan Police in a good light. We've been working for months trying to bring this gang to justice."

"Agreed, you have my word." He shook Wade's hand.

"Okay then, follow me."

"Sierra 3, come in."

"Roger, this is Sierra 3," Em spoke clearly into her microphone, trying to keep pace with the ambulance as she turned from Craven Hill Road onto the A40.

"It's Donaldson. Where are you?"

"Still en route, a few cars behind him."

"Good, good. Now, listen. I've had word from the C-Division boys who went down to White City this morning. They've found a Sherpa van that was reported stolen almost three weeks ago. Forensics are already going over it. They've also been inspecting the lockups nearby, trying to figure out which one our boys were using. So far nothing's really turned up, but I'll let you know as soon as we hear anything. When you arrive at the destination, contact me as soon as possible, understood?"

"Yes sir."

Wade pointed him into a room off the back corridor. Two uniformed police officers followed.

"Right, have a seat." The chief inspector gestured to a drab, plastic chair.

As soon as the tape started rolling, he scanned the footage intensely. At first there were just a number of customers in the store, nothing out of the ordinary. Then two more came in. He tried to study them as close as he could. There was a sharply dressed man and a woman with shoulder-length hair, which looked to be blonde. A satisfied smile glinted across his face. *It's definitely her—the one Van Rooyen asked me to find. I'm certain.*

On the video, the man was by her side briefly before heading towards the back of the store. There was something familiar about him, the way he moved; it was if he'd been trained to do so. He was gone for a few minutes while she looked at stones. Then she must have said something, because the other customers in the store were being ushered out.

Then the man was back, talking to one of the customers. Then it all went blurry. He could just about see him dive to one side while the woman went the other way.

"That's all you get, I'm afraid," Wade grunted.

"Good enough. Thank you for your cooperation, Chief Inspector. It should help us make one killer of a story. I'll let you know when it goes to press. I'll be off now."

Barely a minute after the man left, Wade gestured to one of the other officers.

"Call the *Standard*, will you? Find out more about Jim Hanson and this story he's supposedly running."

"May I ask why, sir?"

"There's just something about him that doesn't add up somehow. He seems a bit too polished for just a beat reporter."

Graeme wasn't particularly enjoying his 1983 ambulance ride. The Transit was primitive in his eyes and the journey from St. Mary's to Charing Cross was taking what seemed like an eternity.

"How much longer?" he asked, with a slight shake in his voice.

"About half an hour," replied the ambulance technician. "Depends on traffic and getting down to the Fulham Palace Road isn't always easy, even during an emergency."

I feel like an invalid, Graeme thought, *and I don't know what the hell's actually going on*. He tried to lie back and clear his mind.

"*Hanson*? He hasn't worked at the *Standard* for almost three years," the voice on the other end of the line crackled dimly. "And, according to you, he was just at the scene of yesterday's botched jewelry robbery in Marble Arch, claiming to get an exclusive for us? As far as I know he's still at the *Mirror*, following the gossip trail; seemed to be more of his thing, anyway."

The copper hung up the portable phone and went back into the store, searching for Wade.

"Sir, I just got off the phone with somebody at the *Evening Standard*. Apparently Hanson hasn't worked for them for three years."

"So who the bloody hell was that? I knew something wasn't right. Get his description out right away; tell everybody you can that if they come across him, to get in touch with the police ASAP. We need to bring him in for questioning. And oh, contact George Donaldson at the SRI, they should be interested to hear about this."

Van Rooyen was still contemplating how to finish things off. Time was marching on and the Boss had given him a deadline. He knew the shipment of arms was coming in early next week, but there was still no word from the Algerian on that lady copper and her accomplice.

He was at the bookies again, this time on Portobello Road, placing some more bets on the dogs. It had been several hours since he spoke with the Algerian and he was due for an update. As he rose and walked outside to the nearest phone box, he tore into a fresh pack of Superkings.

The phone rang and rang. *Jesus, he always takes so long to answer.* Then the voice was there.

"It's me. What did you find out?"

"I was at the crime scene this morning. Yes, she was there at the store when your boys hit it, along with somebody else: a man. I posed as a reporter and asked to see some of the CCTV footage."

"*Uitstekend*; excellent," said the Dutchman enthusiastically. "Now remember, I just want you to tell me where she is when you find her. Don't kill her! Do you understand?"

The line went dead.

As the hitman hung up, he thought back to the images he'd seen on the CCTV footage at Dennison's. It was *that* man who bothered him the most, however. It was like he knew who he was, even though the camera offered poor visuals at best. The way he moved was just very familiar. He picked up the Rubik's Cube and had another go. *Two puzzles to solve, one in my hands and one in my head.* He was still certain that he'd find her and him.

It was ringing again—that hollow, synthetic sound. Graeme opened his eyes. He had fallen asleep on a bench close to the concourse at Victoria. He quickly glanced at his Rolex: 1:33 p.m.

"Where are you?" It was Clara.

"I'm at the concourse on Victoria."

"You need to get moving, you've got less than an hour. When you get to Notting Hill head up the stairs and out to the Gate Cinema. The door will be open and I'll meet you just inside the front entrance."

He was about to say something, but she was gone.

Placing the phone back in his coat pocket, Graeme rushed through the barrier, almost dropping his Oyster card as he hurried down the stairs to the platform. A train was just pulling in as he got there. It was fairly busy so he had to stand. Looking around him, Graeme could feel the stale underground air, peppered with different smells. He was groggy and tired. He wondered if his coat would ever dry out, and he needed a shower. All around him people just seemed to be wrapped up in their own little world, many buried in books or just simply staring at the ceiling or the floor. It was depressing; the red, blue and white of the carriage fittings doing very little to lift his mood.

At South Kensington, he managed to grab a seat. He was beginning to get nervous. What was going on? Was *this* his real life? Had he made everything up? Christ, it had seemed so real; *she* had seemed so real. It had been hard going, but he'd never felt so alive, so free and happy. And now, here he was, back to twenty-first century drudgery, broke and as far as he knew alone, apart from "Clara."

Graeme's throat was starting to get dry as the train finally rolled into Notting Hill Gate. He took the last swig from his water bottle before stepping off. Stopping on the platform for a second, he almost got mown down by passengers exiting the train who were all desperate in a rush to get seemingly nowhere.

As the mob died down, Graeme did as instructed. He headed up the stairs and out the exit of the tube station.

Walking out onto the street, he saw it. Although a listed building, the Gate Cinema seemed fairly plain on the outside. He walked through the open entrance and into the lobby, which was intimate and quaint—a throwback to a bygone era of film. There wasn't a person in sight.

Graeme waited and waited, but nobody came. He glanced at his watch. It was almost 2:35 p.m. He'd been on time. *Where the bloody hell is Clara?* he thought.

His Blackberry rang again.

"I can see you," she said. Graeme recognized Clara's distinctive, sympathetic tone. "Walk through the doors behind you and into the theater. Head to the front by the curtains."

Graeme followed her orders. Although her voice was soothing, he still felt unsettled, a little strange and somewhat frightened. His knees and hands were shaking. Nevertheless, he wanted answers. He bit his lip and walked through the door. As he did, he felt like he'd stepped back in time. The interior of the cinema was magnificent and although it was dark, he could make out the elaborate ceiling, wall decorations and velvet chairs. This wasn't a cinema; it was a proper picture house, in the old sense.

Suddenly there was light from the back of the room.

"Thank you for coming," said the smoothing, female voice. The radiance started to dim. He could see Clara's slender figure walking towards him. As she got closer, she stopped. Grabbing his hand, Graeme could feel warmth and comfort, easing his mind. Clara gazed at him with her big brown eyes and smiled.

"Graeme, *you can do this.* Her life is in your hands. You can do it. He's coming for you but you'll be ready for him."

"What do you mean? How do you know?"

"I know," she said reassuringly as she squeezed his hand.

"I don't understand." Graeme shook his head. "I came here because you asked me to and if I'm being honest Clara, I'm really starting to wonder who I actually am and what is real. Remember that dream I told you about? I've found myself in it repeatedly and the more I experience it, the more real it seems... And the more real *she* seems."

"You're not in a good place, Graeme. That's why I wanted you to come here—I had to warn you. There are things at play that you don't understand right now, but in time you will."

Graeme was trying desperately to comprehend what she meant, yet felt no closer to the truth.

Clara released her grip. "Follow me. There's something I need to give you."

Graeme wasn't sure what to think, but at the same time, felt he had nothing to lose. He followed her to the back of the theater and to the projector room.

She turned on the light and headed to the shelves on the left side. Grabbing a small box, she presented it to him.

"You need to open this," she said with her motherly tone.

He paused before releasing the metal catches. Slowly opening it, he found a key. Attached to the key was a fob with the initials ERB on it. Graeme choked.

Instinctively, he knew the significance of those letters. It had to be his partner in the "other life," Emily Braithwaite. He recalled seeing those same letters from the registration number on her Mercedes-Benz, but what was the R for? *I'm sure I'll find out soon enough. This is the only real connection to 1983.*

Clara grabbed his hand and squeezed it again. "As I told you, her life is in your hands. She needs you, Graeme."

"I don't understand. How do you know about Emily Braithwaite, my partner in my '*other life*?'"

"There's a deposit box you'll find in Paddington Station that's matched to the numbers on that key. Your answers will be waiting for you there."

Graeme was stunned. *How could Clara possibly know about Em?*

I don't like this, not one bit. Something tells me I'm not going to like what I find in that box. Perhaps it will be the final puzzle, the one thing that brings my amazing dream to an abrupt end. But then what? His mind started racing, his thoughts scattering. No matter how Graeme felt, he knew he had to get to Paddington and find out what was in that box. He took a deep breath and did his best to compose himself.

"You need to go *now*, Graeme." Clara was pushing him. "Time is not on your side." Her kind, calm aura somehow provided a feeling of comfort, even though her remarks made Graeme more unsettled than ever.

"Time isn't on my side?" What the hell does that mean? How the hell can I be living in 1983 and the twenty-first century at the same time?

He closed his eyes, trying to steady himself. When he opened them, Clara was gone.

Rushing out of the cinema, Graeme ran down the street towards Notting Hill Gate tube station.

Though Clara had said "*time wasn't on his side*," for Graeme, it felt like an age getting through the barriers and down to the eastbound platform. He waited and waited for a train to appear, rubbing his palms in anticipation. Finally, the distinctive red-fronted stock with its white and blue flanks and red doors pulled in. Graeme hopped on and took a seat by the door, hoping to make a quick exit at his stop. As the train got under way again and clattered along the line, he observed the people around him. Many were texting on their phones, while a young couple who looked like tourists from the continent were chatting away. A few others were buried in books or listening to music. The clatter from the rails and the thrum of the train's electric drive added to the feeling of routine monotony, which seemed to characterize Graeme's existence in this world—a droll reality, in which the only escape was the alternate life he'd been experiencing in "1983." *God, I hope it isn't just a dream*, he worried, as the train edged closer to his destination.

By the time he got to Paddington, it felt like hours had passed. However, glancing at his Rolex, he saw that it had only been thirty-five minutes since he'd left the cinema.

On the concourse at Paddington, he asked a young girl at the information desk about the safety deposit boxes. Presenting his key, he was led to what appeared to be a little used part of the station, adjacent to the expansive, main concourse with its distinctive, Isambard Kingdom Brunel-designed canopy and polished floors.

"It's in there," said the uniformed porter, "just make sure to check in when you've finished."

Graeme was a bag of nerves. He could feel his whole body shaking and perspiration on his forehead and down his neck as he walked into and down the narrow, faceless corridor. What on Earth would he find in that box? He kept walking, glancing at the numbered boxes on the right-side wall. Finally, he found it.

Inserting the key and opening the lock, he took a deep breath. Inside was a small, black and dented metal box that from the looks of things had been put there a long time ago.

Opening it, he almost fainted. There was a picture of him in an RAF flight suit next to a smiling young man with sandy brown hair and a darker complexion, standing next to a Harrier GR.3 in what appeared to be somewhere warm and tropical.

Graeme started to feel queasy. He also found a set of cufflinks with his initials on them, an old paper driver's license with his name and an address of 75 Stanhope Gardens, South Kensington. *My god, that's the same driving license I saw in "my flat" in "1983" just what the hell is going on?*

He discovered a letter addressed to him from a place called Tudhope Farm in Aynho, Northamptonshire. The postmark on the envelope was dated July 20, 1972. He was about to pull the letter out of the envelope when something at the bottom of the box caught his eye. Snatching it with his index finger and thumb, he pulled it out. It was a torn party invitation.

Graeme Jacob James and Emily Ruth Braithwaite formally request your company at Beaufort Hall.

The invitation was dated May 30, 1987. The back half of the invitation was missing. It was the last thing he remembered before blackness swarmed him.

Graeme felt like he was flying, arms and legs stretched out, no gravity. There were clouds and sky—they were coming in thick and fast. Then he was back there, on the farm in Aynho, learning to fix tractors and the family's cars with his father. He could see his mother's disapproval of wanting to go motor racing, his older sister telling him how dangerous it was.

He remembered his first drive in go-karts in his early teens, how he'd spun into the gravel trap during his first Formula Ford race at Mallory Park; the violent motion and ultimately, embarrassment that had resulted when he'd stalled the engine and couldn't restart it. He remembered how he desperately wanted to pursue a career in racing but that required money and there simply wasn't enough available to allow him to continue after a couple of seasons in Formula Fords.

He recalled how difficult it was to make the decision to give up his motorsport aspirations and focus on helping his parents make ends meet for a few more years.

Graeme's memory purged two recalls: he'd considered a career in the Royal Air Force once his studies were finished. He joined the local University Air Squadron at RAF Bicester in nearby Oxfordshire.

With excellent reflexes, eyesight and attitude, he'd ultimately been accepted for pilot training. He'd gone to Cranwell and became best friends with a chap named Max Willoughby. Both he and Max had shown tremendous aptitude and were selected for the Harrier training program and posted to RAF Wittering. Max had later been sent to Germany, while Graeme remained in the UK.

Having developed good skills as a rifleman and mechanic, Graeme had been chosen as part of a special squad sent to Central America to help set up a permanent British base there. Max arrived six months after Graeme, and the two of them were soon flying missions with the Harrier flight out there. During one encounter, Max's plane had suffered engine failure and he'd gone down. Graeme circled the jungle, looking for the wreckage, but no trace of Max was ever found.

Graeme had taken the loss of his friend personally; they'd been close. When it seemed accident investigators had taken an almost blasé attitude towards the case, he'd become angry.

Posted back to Wittering, he'd almost instantly been asked to go on Tactical Exercises in Norway. Fed up with the politics, and as he felt a lack of support from within the RAF, he'd resigned his commission. He took a sabbatical and spent eighteen months traveling around the Mediterranean, ending up in Cyprus.

There he met up with a couple of former RAF colleagues who were stationed on the base at Akrotiri. That's when one of life's crossroads appeared.

During a conversation one night at a local taverna in Limassol, one of his colleagues, an MP on the base, had told him that he should apply for a job at the Metropolitan Police back in the UK.

And so, a couple of months later, he did. With his marksman skills and problem-solving ability, Graeme had caught the attention of his superiors early on. He'd saved up a substantial amount of money as a single pilot, as well as fixing cars during his days off and used it to buy a flat in London.

Was this reality a dream, a premonition, or were those flashbacks of his real life? *How could I remember all that stuff if it wasn't real? And, if my life in* 1983 *IS real, then who the hell is Clara and how did she know about Em? And what the hell was that business with the box and artifacts at Paddington Station? Clues, signs, messages?* It was a lot to fathom and Graeme felt no closer to finding the truth…

Suddenly, there was a jolt.

His eyes were wide open now. "Almost there," said the ambulance technician.

How was he supposed to find them? The Algerian pondered that as he played with the Rubik's Cube. From the video footage he knew it was them who'd foiled the robbery but where to start looking? More questions that needed answers—and fast. But first he needed some food; he could feel his stomach growling. The hitman knew a little café on Fulham Palace Road, just south of the Hammersmith flyover that made good sandwiches. He grabbed the keys to the Audi, along with his Beretta and headed out the door.

CHAPTER 13

He was in the Audi, making his way towards that little café on Fulham Palace Road. It wasn't an easy spot to get to, but they were the best sandwiches he knew in London, even if that wasn't saying much. Going there was also a chance for him to reflect on making his next move. He still wondered how he'd be able to track her down; so far, he had nothing more to go on than blurry CCTV footage. No names, nor addresses.

An ambulance drove past and shot through the traffic lights close by Shepherd's Bush Green. It was almost by fate what happened next. Glancing into his rearview mirror, he saw it—a light blue Mercedes-Benz SL, sporting personalized plates, ERB 54. But it wasn't just the car. There she was, behind the wheel, he was certain. He couldn't believe his luck. He slowed down as he went around the corner, pulling to the left to let her pass. He'd follow her as far as he could, to the ends of the Earth if necessary.

Where was she going? Not that it mattered. He'd found his prize and now, he wouldn't let her out of his sight.

"What?" barked Donaldson. "When was this?"

"This morning, Guv." Tim was standing in the entrance to the super's office. Mark Hungerford sat in one of the plastic chairs facing Donaldson.

"I got a call from a Chief Inspector Wade overseeing the forensics operation at the jewelers," continued the young DC. "He said some reporter had been asking questions, had asked to see the TV footage, and then left promptly. Wade had one of his men call the *Evening Standard*, only they said the bloke in question hadn't worked for them for three years."

"Oh Christ, that's all we bloody need," said the super, scratching his crew cut. "And you said he left right after seeing the footage?"

"Yes Guv."

"Tim, I think we may have found our hit man. I want people out looking for him now. Make sure Scotland Yard is notified as soon as possible. And get his description out to as many places as you can, even the papers."

"But it's Saturday Guv, it might take a while."

"I don't care. I am not losing two of my best officers today."

"Hungerford?"

"Yes sir?" the detective replied attentively, straightening himself up in his chair.

"Grab a couple of the boys from downstairs and take one of the pool cars, will you? Start at the crime scene and see if you can trace our chap's movements. Talk to anybody outside the immediate area of Dennison's. Somebody must know where he went. I'm heading down to Charing Cross. Stay in radio contact. Tim, hand over your tasks to Wildman, you're coming with me."

Em was still behind the ambulance, about five cars back. A Scammell Routeman tipper truck in front of her made it difficult to see ahead. Seeing a gap in the traffic, she punched the throttle and zoomed past it.

As she drove, she kept thinking about James. He was on the mend and that gave Em a slight relief. Regardless, something was bugging her. *This isn't over yet, I'm sure of it. James is right, there is at least one more card to be played and he and I will likely be targeted. But where and when? Charing Cross, my flat? Good God!* Her mind started racing and that feeling of nervousness, which had plagued her the night before the robbery, started coming back again. *James, I'm counting on you.*

Had she seen him? The Mercedes had suddenly sped up. Now he was stuck behind the dirty Scammell tipper and there were just too many cars coming the other way to make a move. If he tried to overtake now, he'd draw suspicion.

He could still see her and elected to stay put. *Patience, patience,* he reminded himself as he tapped his fingers on the steering wheel and leaned his head nearly out the window, looking for that opportune moment to pass the Scammell so he could continue following his prey.

Graeme couldn't wait for his 1983 ambulance journey to end. The technician was a young lad, in his mid-twenties and cheerful. *You'd have to be to put up with this every day!* "How much further?" the inspector asked.

"About ten more minutes," came the reply as the Transit crested another bump and the interior fittings rattled.

Graeme studied his surroundings again, trying to focus on something else other than the harsh ride. The inside of the ambulance was spotless and smelled like a hospital—sanitary and official. He looked at the technician, who kept glancing out the back window and at Graeme. As the young lad beamed a genuine smile at him, Graeme tried his best to do the same, but it came out more like a grimace. This ride to Charing Cross, while well-intentioned, was punishing and the end couldn't come soon enough.

"Sierra 3, Sierra 3, come in, over."

The police radio in the gold Granada Ghia crackled as Em's distinctive voice came over the mic. "Roger, Sierra 3 responding."

"Where are you? Over," asked Donaldson.

"We're on Shepherd's Bush Road, near the Hammersmith flyover. Why?"

"I've got some further news and it's not good. Apparently somebody posing as a reporter saw you and James on the Dennison's CCTV camera earlier today. There's a good chance he might be on to you. Have you noticed anybody following you or anything suspicious?"

"Not so far, sir," Em answered.

"Alright, just stay with the ambulance and do as I instructed. I'll meet you at the hospital. I should be there in about twenty minutes."

"Roger. Sierra 3, out."

Donaldson was doing his best to get there as fast as he could, wheeling the big gold Granada in and out of traffic. In the passenger seat, Tim Charles was just about turning green.

"Do you think we'll get there in time?"

"I bloody hope so, Tim. See if you can get King on the horn. Ask him to send a couple of his SPG boys down to Charing Cross; I want some additional backup. There are multiple ways in and out of that hospital and I don't want to leave anything to chance. Em has said she hasn't noticed anything suspicious so far, but with James still wounded I'm not taking any chances. It shouldn't take them long to get there from White City."

"Right you are, Guv."

The ambulance pulled up outside the Emergency Entrance to Charing Cross Hospital. The tall, angular seventeen-story building dominated the local skyline, towering over the brown brick A&E entrance, giving the whole complex a functional, yet somehow ominous appearance.

"Right, we're here," announced the technician cheerfully.

Graeme took a deep breath and sighed. "Thank God."

Hospital staff in white coats came out and he was quickly placed on a stretcher, out of the ambulance and taken away.

As he was wheeled in, a short, bald man with a beard approached. "My name's Thompson," he said. "My team and I were instructed by DCI Donaldson to meet with you here. I understand that your partner, Detective Sergeant Braithwaite, will be here shortly, too."

Graeme nodded.

"Alright, take him to his room," Thompson instructed, "but I want you to use the service lift and be as low-key as possible. I'll see you again shortly, Inspector James." He turned and headed down the corridor.

Em, having seen the ambulance pull in, parked the Mercedes across the way. Jumping out, she ran to the main hospital entrance.

"I'm looking for Graeme James," she said, approaching a hospital porter. "He was admitted just a few moments ago."

"And you are?"

"Sergeant Emily Braithwaite, SRI," she said, displaying her badge.

"Yes, we've been expecting you," replied the porter. "Hold on one second please." As he led her to the sizeable front desk, the porter leaned forward and turned to face one of the receptionists. "Can you contact Mr. Thompson?"

"Right away."

Em sat down on one of the plastic sculpted chairs in the waiting area, breathed in and exhaled. *I'm really not relishing the thought of having to babysit James at my flat, but Donaldson* did *give me an order. I just hope we get through this and catch those bastards for good.* Picking up a dog-eared copy of *Good Housekeeping*, Em quickly started reading it, waiting for Thompson to arrive.

So that was it. She'd gone to Charing Cross Hospital, but why? It didn't really matter. He knew where she was and he could keep tabs on her.

Wheeling the Audi into the visitor's parking area, the Algerian quickly found a spot. He sat in the car for a moment, pondering what to do next. The Dutchman had said not to kill her, but to contact him once he had her in his sights. Nevertheless, he reached for the glovebox and grabbed the Beretta, just in case. He pulled out another fake ID from his assortment of similar cards before getting out of the green sedan and heading towards the main entrance to the hospital.

Graeme was being taken down multiple corridors again. How he hated hospitals, the smell, the confusion—but he knew it was all part of a plan. For now, at least, he'd go along with it.

He could feel himself getting stronger again, despite the punishing ambulance ride. Finally, after being placed in the lift and ascending a couple of floors, the staff brought him into a quieter wing and at the end of it—a fairly large recovery room with two widely spaced beds, gray walls and a nondescript suspended ceiling with uniform tiles and rectangular light fixtures.

"You must be Mr. James," said the nurse who was standing by one of the beds. She was young and attractive, probably not more than twenty-eight.

Graeme agreed.

"How do you feel?"

"Honestly? Like shit." Graeme turned and looked at her with a frank expression. "If it isn't too much to ask, I'd really like to have a wash or something."

"We'll have to wait, I'm afraid. Doctor Porritt will be in to see you shortly. It seems you're definitely on the mend but we can't do anything until we've been given the all-clear."

Graeme closed his eyes, trying to find a way to relieve his building frustration.

"You must be Sergeant Braithwaite."

She peered up from her magazine.

"My name is Thompson. Your DCS requested to meet you here."

"Ah, yes," said Em, relieved to know she was closer to getting answers regarding the whereabouts and condition of her partner. "Where's Inspector James?"

"They brought him in through the emergency entrance. If you'd like to follow me, I'll take you to him."

"How is he?" Em inquired as they walked along the corridor.

"Seems tired, a little grumpy, but doing okay. They've taken him upstairs to Ward 6. It's a quieter part of the hospital and we've got undercover police officers watching the corridor. Nobody can get in or out of the ward without us knowing about it."

"I just hope you're right," Em sighed and shook her head slightly. "The last thing we need is a shootout in a busy hospital like this."

Walking up to the entrance, the hitman smiled and handed over his badge.

"Detective Sergeant Finn, London Metropolitan Police. My colleague asked me to come here. She's blonde, early thirties."

One of the desk staff, in the midst of reading a file, looked up, just as the man flashed his convincing police ID. "Oh, you mean, Sergeant Braithwaite?"

"Yes, Sergeant Braithwaite." He nodded. "Can you tell me where to find her?"

"Ward 6, Recovery, third floor."

"Thank you." A smile curled his lips.

"Doctor, what's the synopsis? Can I take off this bloody drip yet?" Graeme was fidgeting with the IV and unable to get comfortable.

"You seem to be making an excellent recovery, Mr. James," Doctor Porritt gave him a friendly smile as he scanned Graeme's chart. "Normally I wouldn't suggest it, but I see you won't be persuaded. Let's try and see how you go. Nurse Adams will bring you some clean hospital garments and you'll be given a sponge bath. Mr. Thompson and I will be by later to check on you."

"How long do I have to stay here, Doctor?" Graeme anxiously twitched, trying to move his arms and shoulders as best he could. "I really don't like hospitals."

"We've got to keep you under observation for forty-eight hours, but you've done remarkably well, considering," Doctor Porritt explained, finishing his review of the chart. "You were very lucky. That bullet could have done a lot more damage. If you keep making progress like this, I don't see any issue in you being discharged on Monday, but we will need to keep checking on you. Sit tight." He winked at Graeme before turning around and leaving the room.

Donaldson was driving as fast as he could, belting down the A4 towards Hammersmith. As he passed Warwick Road, he failed to notice the BMW R80 police motorcycle by the curb.

"Bloody hell!" The officer, having just finished writing up the driver of a green 1978 Mini Clubman 1275GT for speeding, almost dropped his notepad as the big sedan motored past. "I'm calling this in. This is Unit 12, West Cromwell Road. I've got a speeding Ford Granada, gold in color, heading towards Hammersmith—over. Giving chase."

"What the bloody hell?" The super looked in his rearview mirror. "Tim, put the roof light on. Since we've got the cavalry in pursuit, any chance of *not* drawing attention is blown now... I simply don't have time to stop for him."

Tim did as he was told. Behind them, the motorcycle cop saw the light come on. However, he continued to follow.

The tension in his body was beginning to ease. Two nurses had managed to give Graeme a sponge bath, leaving him a little less on edge. Although still attached to the drip, he could feel his strength growing. The pain was still there but with a fresh dose of morphine, moving his left arm was becoming easier. He lay back and looked at the ceiling.

After drinking two plastic beakers of water that had been left on the stand by his bed, Graeme needed the bathroom. He hit the buzzer. Five minutes later, Nurse Adams was back, helping him sit up so he could get up and walk. He was just heading back to his bed when there was a knock at the door.

It opened, and there were Thompson and Em.

"So, here you are." Em's enthusiastic tone indicated that she was glad to see him. "How are you feeling?"

"Honestly, like arse. I'm tired, groggy, and in dire need of a proper shower. The nurses gave me a sponge bath but I'd kill for a shower. Perhaps you can join me, if you like!"

"Do grow up James. You're behaving like a teenage schoolboy and being injured is an excuse that's rapidly wearing off, at least as far as I'm concerned."

Thompson looked surprised.

"You've got a wonderful bedside manner, Sergeant," Graeme retorted. "You'd make a great doctor."

"In actuality, I probably would."

Graeme couldn't tell whether she was being sarcastic or not.

"So, what's the plan? Am I still staying here for forty-eight hours?"

"That's what your superintendent instructed," stated Thompson, "but I do get the sense you'd like to be discharged as soon as possible."

"Actually," interjected Em, "Donaldson has asked that you be discharged and taken to my flat. Quietly, of course."

"Don't tease me, Braithwaite, I'm really not in the mood."

"No, really, Donaldson thinks you'd be safer there until you can get back on your feet again. He says the location and narrow entrance mean we can have people watch who comes in and who leaves day and night."

"Right," Thompson affirmed. "I will go and try to make the necessary arrangements. If you can have your superintendent page me once he gets here, that'll be good. I'll be in A&E."

No sooner had he left the room than Em went back out into the corridor. She found one of the nurses stripping another bed in the ward.

"Hello. Sergeant Braithwaite, SRI," she said quietly in her proper Bedales English. "Can you have a Superintendent Donaldson page Mr. Thompson in A&E once he arrives?"

"Certainly, ma'am."

Em turned and headed back to Graeme's room. As she entered, she saw her partner grinning.

"And what about you, will you be watching me day and night?"

Leaning forward, Em placed her face very close to his. "We'll just have to see about that, won't we?" she whispered before drawing back.

Graeme felt the hairs on the back of his neck stand up and goosebumps on his arms, followed by a growing warm sensation within. He didn't say anything, just looked at her with a faux grin, trying to imply that her comments didn't mean anything.

"In the meantime, James, is there anything I can get you? Perhaps a cup of tea?"

"I wouldn't say no."

As she turned and headed down the corridor, Graeme felt the warmth dissipate and an uneasiness come over him. He wasn't really sure why, but he sensed as if something was about to happen—something bad. He pressed the call button for the nurse.

It took Em a little while to find some tea. The big hospital felt like a labyrinth. She stopped a young man in the corridor who was pushing a trolley full of medical supplies.

"Can you tell me the way to the cafeteria?"

"Second floor, south wing," he mumbled abruptly before hurrying on his way.

Finding the café, Em requested two cups of tea, both with milk and no sugar. She'd been quite surprised that during the first week of being paired to work with Graeme, he took his tea almost exactly the same way as she did hers.

On her way back to the ward, a man brushed past her, nearly causing one of the cups of tea to spill. She turned to give him a look and was about to say something, but instinctively changed her mind. The man turned to face her, staring blankly for a second before resuming his task. She noticed that he had sandy brown hair, piercing blue eyes, and appeared to be very fit, his outfit suggesting he might be an undercover policeman or of the government type. However, her instinct told her there was something that simply didn't seem right about him.

Em tagged down a nurse right before reaching the lift. "Sergeant Braithwaite, SRI. Can you do me a favor? Can you relay a message to reception?"

"Certainly, ma'am."

"I almost collided with a man down the corridor who seemed to be in a real hurry." She proceeded to give him a description. "...Average height, likely mid-thirties and looked very fit. He could be a policeman but there was something off about him. Can you tell reception about him, and also get them to notify Detective Chief Superintendent Donaldson as soon as he gets here?"

"Yes, ma'am, right away." The nurse started walking briskly down the corridor and towards the nearest phone.

"There, that should do it." Nurse Adams placed the water jug and two fresh beakers on the stand by Graeme's bed. "Anything else I can get you?"

"That's all for now. Thank you, Nurse," said Graeme kindly, trying to hide the fact he was becoming increasingly alert and on edge.

Nurse Adams smiled and turned to leave the room. She'd been gone a second when Em entered, carrying two cups of tea.

"I knew I could rely on you Sergeant." Graeme grinned at her as he tried to sit up.

Em was just about to place the cups down on the table by the bed when both of them thought they heard footsteps coming down the corridor. There was a scream outside and then a thud.

"Have you got your gun?" asked Graeme.

"Yes, it's in my handbag. Why?"

"Give it to me right now."

"What?"

"Just give it to me."

No sooner had he taken the gun and removed the safety switch than a bang reverberated across the room. A man walked in brandishing a 9mm Beretta and silencer.

"*Duck*!" Graeme yelled. He could see the man was trying to target Em. She dove into the bathroom. Graeme steadied the Glock in his hands as best he could and quickly fired towards the man's leg.

It was all happening in slow motion. The bullet skimmed the man's shin, causing him to lose balance.

The man tried to shoot again but his aim was off. Graeme fired another round from Em's Glock and rotated his body, sliding off the bed. He hit the floor with a thump. "*Ugh*!"

He turned his body once more, trying to catch a glimpse of the intruder from the far side of the bed and position himself to fire the Glock again. As he maneuvered to take another shot, he saw the man's oval face, his signature nose and sandy colored hair, just as the invader was attempting to steady himself again.

Graeme instantly knew who he was.

"*Max*," he breathed, the words spilling out of his mouth in shock. "*Max fucking Willoughby*!"

Graeme was overwhelmed by anger. *No fucking way! It's not possible. You fucking bastard! You were my best friend. What the bleedin' fuck!* Not thinking, he summoned every ounce of strength and tried to lunge towards his former friend, in the process pulling out the IV from his hand.

The man's eyes widened and for a moment he froze. It was a split second, but it seemed like minutes.

"Max, *you bastard*!" yelled Graeme.

The man said nothing and instead of firing another round, he turned and fled from the room, hightailing it down the corridor, past a nurse who was lying on the floor. Although limping due to his grazed shin, he was still incredibly fast.

Graeme tried to give chase but he wasn't strong enough, and his pursuit was slow and clumsy. As he managed to reach the elevators, he collided with a hospital cart, just in time to see Max staring him straight in the eye before the lift doors closed.

As soon as they did, Graeme spun around and, overcome with exhaustion and pain, collapsed in a heap on the floor.

"James!" He could hear Em calling. "*James*! Are you alright?" She was running along the corridor. As soon as she reached her partner, she slid down beside him. "You bloody idiot!" She scowled. "You could have been killed!" Despite the irate tone, there also appeared to be genuine concern in her voice. "You knew him, didn't you?"

Graeme nodded. He tried to lift himself up, but it was just too much effort on his own.

As her anger dissipated, Em softened her tone. "C'mon, let's get you back to your bed."

A group of nurses were briskly making their way from the opposite direction to help. Two stopped to assist Graeme, while a couple of others, seeing one of their colleagues lying on the floor, screamed momentarily before rushing to help.

"Are you okay sir, ma'am?" asked one of them, turning back to face the two detectives after looking further down the corridor. "We heard the commotion from way down the hall!"

"Here, let's give you a hand," said the older of the two nurses to Em. Together, they helped lift the tired copper to his feet. The other nurse had brought a wheelchair and Graeme sat in it without complaint.

As they headed to Graeme's ward, the unconscious nurse was being taken away on a wheeled hospital stretcher. Entering the room, a uniformed police officer was there, waiting.

"Did you get a good look at him?" the constable asked.

"Yes, actually I did," Graeme answered with a far-off look on his face. "It was an old friend of mine... His name is Max Willoughby, or at least it used to be. What the hell happened and just how did he get in here?" He stared piercingly, accusingly, at the uniformed copper.

"He had a badge, said he was a policeman, and that he had some information for Sergeant Braithwaite, so the lads let him through. A nurse saw him pull out his gun and screamed, so he clobbered her with it. She was knocked unconscious but it looks like she'll be okay, they've just taken her to A&E."

Heartless bastard, Graeme thought, infuriated. *That's not the Max I remember.*

"Well, that's just great," said Em angrily. "I thought your lot had this place locked down."

"We thought he was one of us," the copper replied curtly and defensively. "He seemed really genuine."

"*Shit*! Didn't you suspect anything? *Anything at all*?" She exhaled noisily. "It's the *same man* I saw earlier and asked one of the nurses to call it in! I want you to radio for more officers up here and get that man's description to as many people as you can. And," she added in a fierce, demanding tone, "make sure that we have *at least three* constables up here guarding the ward and make sure somebody meets Superintendent Donaldson as soon as he gets here. Do you understand?"

"Yes, ma'am."

"I also want your name."

"Constable, Horton, um, Paul Horton ma'am."

Clearly not used to feeling the wrath of a female detective, Horton nevertheless got on his police radio and followed her orders, heading down the corridor to find his colleagues while the two nurses helped Graeme climb back into his bed.

A few moments later, Horton returned. "We're all set, ma'am. I've got three officers just outside and the suspect's details are being sent to every department of the Met. I'll head to the lobby and wait for your superintendent."

"Good. Thank you, Constable."

One of the nurses, the older and more senior, checked Graeme's hand and the IV drip. "You were very lucky, lad."

"You're telling *me* he is," Em exclaimed. "He could have bought it back there."

The nurse gave a smile and Graeme could see that Em was doing the same. "Right, we'll let you rest now," the senior nurse remarked.

"You can stay for awhile, ma'am," said the other, slightly younger nurse, gesturing to Em. "We'll be off now, but Nurse Adams is on duty if you need anything."

Graeme lay back on the pillow, sleepy.

"James?" Em inched closer, as if she was about to say something he wouldn't forget. "Don't EVER do that to me again!"

Graeme gulped, almost in shock, before taking a deep breath. "What are you talking about?"

"You could have gotten yourself shot again, if not killed! Look," she added, speaking softly and leaning in very close to him. "I don't want to lose you, not now."

Graeme was stunned. "You really mean that?"

"Yes, I do..."

Just then, an officer popped his head through the door. "Ma'am, you're wanted downstairs."

Em drew back from Graeme. "Hold on, I won't be long." She squeezed his arm and smiled at him reassuringly as she stood up.

As Em headed out of the room, Graeme turned over and sighed. He was tired and confused. Trying to brush romantic thoughts aside was proving more and more difficult, especially in view of the increasing amount of time he was spending with this stunning woman. He shut his eyes and did his best to sleep.

The gold Granada screeched to a halt right outside the front entrance of Charing Cross Hospital, followed by the cop on the motorcycle.

The officer dismounted his bike and marched towards the big Ford on a mission. "Didn't you see me back there?" he asked, as the smartly dressed older man exited the driver's seat.

"Now's not the time, son," the super growled. "I'm Detective Chief Superintendent George Donaldson, SRI. This is official business. You give me a ticket and you'll spend the rest of your career in the typing pool. Do you understand? Now, since you're here, you might as well make yourself useful; follow me."

The officer nodded submissively.

For Max, it was a lucky escape. He had been alone in the lift and exited at the basement level.

The hitman knew they'd be crawling all over the hospital looking for him and there wasn't much time. Passing by an open storeroom, Max decided to enter and look around. He saw a janitor's coat hanging up and put it on. Grabbing a nearby mop and bucket, the former pilot turned assassin headed back into the corridor, whistling. Making his way to the service elevator, he pressed the button for the ground level. As the lift opened, he witnessed a hub of activity. There were police officers heading away from him down the corridor, along with hospital staff. Looking for a fast exit, Max breathed a sigh of relief when he saw a service entrance not far away.

Quickly and carefully, he headed towards the entrance, wheeling the mop and bucket ensemble. A police officer running down the corridor almost bumped into him. Max's heart thumped. *You stupid bastard, you should have looked away so he didn't see your face properly. What if he recognizes you? Word is probably all over the hospital now!* Max knew he could take out the copper if he had to, fast and silently. The constable quickly eyed him up, turned around and kept on going. Max opened the service entrance and stepped outside into the summer air. Taking a deep breath, he took stock.

It all made sense now: the man in the footage—it had been his old mate, Graeme James. That's why the moves on the CCTV had looked so familiar.

As for the girl, Braithwaite, she was obviously involved with him in some manner. *Lucky bastard*, he thought. *She was gorgeous.*

Max was seething. It had gone wrong. He'd contact the Dutchman and get his money, but still—he didn't like leaving loose ends. So far, he'd always been successful at every hit, but not this one. That said, he'd still figure out what to do, but he needed to get away first. Max was glad the bullet had barely missed his leg, but pulling up his left trouser, he could see the graze, which was lightly bleeding and still causing him to limp. Still looking around, the hitman was thankful that nobody seemed to be aware of him. As he made his way for the green Audi, Max hobbled along as casually as he could in order to avoid drawing any unnecessary attention.

"Nurse, can you find me some clothes?" yelled Graeme. "I've got to get out of here."

Nurse Adams entered the room. "I'm sorry, but you don't have any clean clothes. Just your suit, personal effects, keys and wallet, which were transferred from Saint Mary's."

"Great." Graeme threw up his hands in frustration. "In that case, can you ask Sergeant Braithwaite of the SRI when she gets back? She might have something for me."

"Very well."

"We got a report of shots fired," declared a young police constable, running out of the main entrance to Charing Cross and towards the Granada and police motorcycle.

"What?" the super said. "Where?"

"Third floor, recovery ward. I just came from there." Constable Horton tried catching his breath.

"Have you secured the area?"

"We have now, sir."

Donaldson gestured to the motorcycle officer. "C'mon Tim, let's go. You—stay here and coordinate backup with Constable Horton, here. I want every corridor of this hospital searched. And ask for DCI King of the SPG at Scotland Yard. Tell him Donaldson wants his boys here, NOW!"

Entering the reception area, Donaldson saw Em running towards him. "Braithwaite! Just what the hell is going on?"

"There was another attempted hit on us—myself and James."

"What? I thought we had taken the necessary precautions—that's why we transferred him here in the first place!"

"Apparently, sir, our assailant posed as a police officer. The men posted outside the ward thought he was legit. He was asking for me, said he had some questions."

"What the bloody hell?"

"That's what I thought, sir. I asked for his description to be sent to every division in the Met."

"Good, Sergeant; now, can you take me to see our Hopalong Cassidy?"

"This way, sir."

Graeme had tried to doze, but he was too restless. He lay there with his eyes open, staring at the ceiling. Just then, Nurse Adams popped her head through the door.

"You've got some visitors," she announced.

"What the bloody hell happened?" Donaldson bellowed as he entered Graeme's room, closely followed by Em and Detective Tim Charles.

"Nice to see you, too, sir," Graeme quipped sarcastically. Almost instantly, he regretted the remark. The super, with a stern look on his face, was clearly in no mood for jokes. Tim, meanwhile, tried hard not to smile.

"Somebody tried to kill us, or more specifically, me," Em reiterated. "James fired a shot but the man fled. James tried to chase after him and crashed into a medical cart near the lift. He could have bought it."

"What? Do you have a bloody death wish or something, Inspector? This isn't

Hollywood, you know. You could have been killed." The super was about to go on when Graeme stopped him in his tracks.

"I know him."

Everything in Donaldson's body froze. "You *what*?" Having collected himself, the DCS raised his eyebrows, "Tell me more."

"His real name is Max Willoughby. He's a former Harrier pilot, like me. His plane crashed in Belize almost five years ago. He was presumed dead. And, he was my best friend."

Having finally made it back to his car, Max was still trying to figure out what to do. Always priding himself on being calm and collected, the hitman was at a loss this time. Starting out as just another regular contract job, this one had now turned personal. He and James had been the best of friends.

Max opened the boot of the Audi. Inside was a small case with a tracking device that he kept exactly for situations like this. He'd plant it on her car and see where she led him. Once at the destination, it would be time to call the Dutchman and prepare for the final act.

"That's the best bloody news I've heard all day," Donaldson enthused, relaxing his shoulders. "So, what do you think happened?"

"If I know Max—certainly the *old* Max—seeing me threw him and now his plan's off-kilter. He'll try and regroup, reorganize. He knows he's been made so he'll take extra precaution to avoid being detected... But I think it also means he's more likely than ever to come for me now."

"Alright." Donaldson faced Detective Charles. "Em mentioned that she's already asked to get the word out about him, but Tim, make sure you get on the blower ASAP and tell Hungerford and his lot we've found our man. Ask them to search *all* of West London, I doubt he would have gone too far."

"Right Guv." Tim swiveled and began his way down the corridor.

"Guv," said Graeme, "I know that sounds logical, but knowing Max as I do, he's going to be a hard man to pinpoint. He's been trained in special weapons and tactics. He knows about covert operations and it's doubtful you'll ever see him again until he strikes."

"Any suggestions then, smart arse? I'm all ears." Donaldson furrowed his brow in annoyance.

"We have to lure him. I suggest we stick with the original plan and head to Sergeant Braithwaite's flat. Get SPG officers to stake out in front and back as a precaution. If he shows up there, we'll nail him. If you can set us up with a police radio at the flat, we can stay in communication should anything happen."

"What makes you so sure he'll show up?" Em analyzed.

"I know Max. There's nothing more he used to hate than unfinished business, loose ends. He'll be back, I know it. This time we need to be ready."

"I bloody hope so. Can't say I'm too thrilled about my home being blown to bits, nor having to babysit a cripple."

Graeme looked at his partner and started to shake his head.

She faked a smile.

"Alright," Donaldson interjected, "we'll get you discharged. Em, can you sort out some fresh clothes for him? We weren't able to arrange it before."

"I'll try my best sir," she said, giggling.

"Once you've been released," Donaldson continued with a sharp eye, staring at Graeme, "head back to Sergeant Braithwaite's digs and stay close to the phone, at least until the police radio is set up. We'll send a team down there to ensure it's ready for you. I want to make sure we're in touch *every hour* through this evening. Got it?"

Graeme and Em nodded.

"I'll also arrange for two SPG cars to get down there ASAP and don't try anything stupid, especially you, James—you're still not back to full strength and I don't need another dead or injured copper on my conscience, especially on a Saturday night."

CHAPTER 14

It was mid-afternoon when the British-registered DAF 2800 articulated truck rolled up by the warehouse in Zeebrugge. The driver was told to back the vehicle down the side and through the entrance. As he did, the trailer doors were opened. It seemed just like another legit load of dry produce, but amid the cans and bags, ready for loading were several small hard cases. Inside them were dismantled stolen US M16 assault rifles and a load of grenades.

They'd been smuggled off the US air base in Zaragoza, Spain and brought north through France and into Belgium via contacts in the Dutchman's former arms trafficking syndicate. Van Rooyen, at the Boss's behest, had arranged, through his contacts, to have several douaniers paid off at border crossings to ensure the "cargo" got through. It had been tricky because he was a wanted man on the continent, so it meant relying on new sources.

Be that as it may, during a weekend celebration on the base, a team disguised as US Air Force personnel and Guardia Civil had managed to get inside undetected and steal the weapons from one of the supply depots. They'd been placed in a "commandeered" US GMC M35 military truck with a bogus manifest destined for Torrejón Air Base, near Madrid. Once off the base, the load was driven to the outskirts of Zaragoza where it was switched into a civilian Pegaso 1083. Meanwhile, the GMC continued on its original route with other "cargo" to avoid raising suspicion among US Air Forces personnel in Europe.

The Pegaso, with the stolen weapons on board, was driven up to San Sebastian, where the load was switched again to a French-registered Renault TR tractor-trailer, which brought it up through France. Just outside Le Mans, another switch was made, only this time, the load was placed into two smaller Belgian-registered trucks—a Volvo F7 and MAN F8 Rigid—for delivery to the warehouse in Zeebrugge. Using locally registered trucks for the next leg of the journey would help minimize the risk of finding the weapons en route. Even though some of the customs agents were in the syndicate's pockets, Van Rooyen wasn't taking any chances. This last switch would take the load across the Channel to the prearranged delivery point just outside of London. A British trucker had been paid cash, 35,000 Belgian Francs for the "extra" cargo.

Inside the warehouse, modifications were being made to the DAF's trailer. A special hole in the floor was cut, with provisions for loading bulky items. The guns and ammo would be placed in there and sealed up. The truck was scheduled to leave the following morning, booked on a Townsend Thoresen ferry, the European Clearway, back to Blighty. Nobody would suspect a thing until it was too late.

Max saw the cavalry arrive—three liveried Rover SD1 Met patrol cars and a pair of Ford Cortinas. The officers jumped out and immediately went into the hospital. There was no sign of James or the girl, though he figured they'd try and make an exit from Charing Cross, especially now that he'd found them.

But first he needed to keep tabs. He got into the Audi, started the engine and pulled up by Em's car. Opening the boot again, he tried, with subtlety, to take out the tracking device and place it under the Mercedes, using his own car to conceal his activities. After switching it on, he drove around the car park, pulling into a space beside an old mustard-colored Morris 1100. He was sure they'd be coming out soon.

The main entrance was chaos; police officers and hospital staff were everywhere. Donaldson was on the phone behind the desk.

"Did you find anything?"

"We've started interviewing witnesses on Edgware," replied Hungerford. "One of the uniforms said he stopped him as he came to the scene of the crime. He approached him from the south side of the area."

"He must have parked up nearby. Okay, here's what I want you to do. Ask any of the shopkeepers or persons you find in the area just south of the crime scene if they saw a man, about five foot ten, sandy brown hair, blue eyes, wearing beige trousers, a white shirt and a dark blazer, getting into or out of a car between 11:00 a.m. and 12:45 p.m. today. Call me here at the hospital *immediately* if you hear anything."

"How do you know his description, Guv?" asked the DC.

"Because he was here less than twenty minutes ago and almost took out two of my officers!" Donaldson slammed down the phone. "You two," he gestured to a pair of plainclothes officers who'd just come in, "start searching this *entire* hospital from the top floor down. Report to me the minute you find anything."

"Rough day is it, sir?" a uniformed inspector approached Donaldson.

"You could say that, Brian," replied the super. "How many of your lot are here?"

"Six, with two more cars on the way. Plus, I've got some nearby foot patrols heading in, so we should have twelve to fifteen officers on the premises."

"Good, good. Now, there's a chance our man is still close, either in the building, or very nearby. I want your lot to start in the basement of the hospital and work your way up. Have a pair of them survey the car park for any suspicious activity and check all the entrances thoroughly. I really don't want this one getting away; he's extremely dangerous and probably still armed."

"Ready?" Em raised her eyebrows.

"As much as I probably can be under these circumstances," Graeme replied gruffly. He was feeling much better; perhaps the shock of seeing Max Willoughby had enabled him to take his mind off the pain in his shoulder.

With Tim on one side and his partner on the other, Graeme, dressed in some ill-fitting clothes sourced at the hospital, made his way to the lift.

On the ground floor it was bedlam. People, hospital staff and police were scurrying about along the corridors and in and out of the building. In the midst of it all, Donaldson was scratching his crew cut again. He saw his two detectives approaching and sighed.

"Guv," Graeme called anxiously, "we're ready to go. Em said I could do with some fresh clothes, though, and suggested we stop at my place first."

"Alright," Donaldson raised his voice over the increasing noise and activity, "but we'll need to give you an escort. After what just happened here, I'm not leaving anything to chance. And remember, once you're at Em's flat, stay in touch; call me as soon as you get there and follow up every hour, either via this number or my police radio and remember what I said James, don't try and play the hero."

"I'll keep an eye on him sir," confirmed Em.

The super nodded, and he was close to breaking into a smile as he did. "Right, off you go. Tim, take this walkie-talkie and join the other SPG lads on the top floor, will you?"

As they walked out the entrance and towards the car park, Graeme shook his head. "You know it's a waste of time searching the hospital, Max is long gone."

"So why didn't you tell that to Donaldson?"

"You saw the way he reacted in the ward. Besides, I'm not exactly the flavor of the week, am I? Going missing on Monday for more than forty-eight hours, showing up late to the office and then getting injured in the line of duty, plus no doubt the Southwark incident is still probably on his mind. He probably thinks I'm losing it. Maybe I am."

"It could happen to anybody." Em softened her eyes and smiled sympathetically.

"But it shouldn't happen to me. I've been trained to be the best I can be and these kinds of slip-ups are just not acceptable, not to me."

"Stop feeling sorry for yourself. I can't be doing with a partner wallowing in his own self-pity, especially now. Look, you saved my life back there, even though you almost got killed. If you're going to keep this up I might as well drive you to the Hammersmith Bridge and push you into the Thames."

He could see she was right. As they reached the Mercedes, Graeme paused for a second. He sensed somebody was watching him.

"What is it?" Em clearly noticed something had him spooked.

"Probably nothing. C'mon, let's just get to your place, shall we? I'm looking forward to being somewhere warm and comfortable."

"Don't get any ideas."

Graeme had a quick look around. He couldn't see anybody. A tall, thin plainclothes officer with a mop of dark brown hair and sporting beige jacket, white shirt and dark slacks came their way.

"Donaldson asked us to tail you back to your place," the officer turned, gesturing to another man sitting in a brown X registration Ford Cortina.

"Alright, but stay as close as you can," Graeme conceded. "I have a feeling this isn't over yet." He glanced at Em, who appeared to be a little unsettled.

"Right, Inspector James," she said authoritatively, with perhaps a twinge of sarcasm, "let's get going. Shall we?"

A few minutes later, they were on the road.

Max saw the blue Mercedes turn out of the car park and onto Fulham Palace Road, closely followed by a brown Ford Cortina with two men in it. *Looks like they've got an escort*, he thought. *No matter, I'll take them out if I have to.*

The hitman was happy his hunch had paid off. They were leaving the scene and so was he. The coppers could search every inch of that hospital, but they'd never find him. He'd seen James glance in his direction just before he and the girl had reached the Mercedes. But, sitting low-slung in the Audi, in a busy car park, Max had been tough to spot. Now they were on the move. *And with the tracking device on her car, they'll be much easier to follow.* He started the Audi and pulled out of the car park onto Fulham Palace Road, smiling to himself as he turned the corner. *You're not getting away from me this time.*

"When was this?" demanded Hungerford.

"It must have been about 12:45 p.m., I think." The shopkeeper scratched his chin.

"And you saw a man of that description getting out of a green Audi, but you don't know the registration number?"

"That's it, I remember the car; it was a light green one, literally parked outside my shop."

"Did you get a registration number?" Hungerford asked the shopkeeper again, who seemed to be a little scatty.

"No, but the last letter was an X, I think."

"Alright, thanks for your help. This we've got to call in," the detective stated eagerly, briefly clasping his hands.

One of the other lads with him, DC Thomas Bolton, smiled.

They drove in silence. Graeme was tired. The pain was still there, growing again as his mind found itself with little else to focus on. He glanced at Em. They were heading to his flat to pick up some fresh clothes and then it was on to her place at 16 Chelsea Square. He couldn't think of any place he'd rather be, but wished that circumstances were different. Their lives were still at risk and there'd be no relaxing anytime soon.

Thoughts kept racing through his mind. She was truly amazing; the most incredible woman he'd ever met. Part of him desperately wanted to be with her, entwined in the sheets, kissing every part of her body, but at the same time, he had tremendous respect for her. He'd never felt a connection to anybody like this. Injured or not, he'd do his utmost to keep her safe and alive. That's what mattered now and he'd go to the ends of the Earth to protect her. Not even his former best friend would stand in his way.

Van Rooyen was getting antsy; he'd not heard a single word from the Algerian since earlier that morning. His prized load of weapons was about to make the trip across the Channel. By Tuesday, it would be in London. If they hadn't found these bastard coppers by then, there was a good chance they could disrupt the next operation, too, and with no spoils from the Marylebone heist, things were already proving difficult.

The Boss would want answers and soon, but right now, there was nothing Van Rooyen could provide. He turned on the TV in his living room and selected channel 3, London Weekend Television. Time for a little light entertainment perhaps, not that he really enjoyed the likes of Michael Aspel or Cannon and Ball. An advert for Panama Cigars was just starting; he could think of few places he'd like to be at this moment in time than by a lagoon pool smoking one of those, perhaps with a gorgeous *meisje* or two by his side.

They'd been driving in silence for a while. "Don't know about you but I could do with some music." Switching on the SL's radio, Em tuned into BBC Radio 1, just in time to hear the beginning of Simple Minds' "Glittering Prize."

"I thought you were a jazz and classical fan." Graeme was perhaps a bit surprised at her choice of music.

"I am, but I'm also a bit of a new wave fan, as you well know."

Of course! I should have known. It all makes sense. Graeme smiled to himself. *Must be the Bedales influence,* he thought. *After all, she's more than five years "younger" than me in this world, right?*

With the music, Em, and the surroundings, he was truly reveling in the moment. *This is unbelievable, I could not have imagined it my wildest dreams and here I am! Oh how I can remember the days where songs like this and a cheap bottle of wine were about all I had to get me through in my grotty flat in Shepherd's Bush in the twenty-first century.* He turned and looked at her. She quickly glanced left and Graeme thought he saw a slight smile. *Amazing!*

They were just turning onto New King's Road. Behind them was the brown Cortina, followed by a Chrysler Alpine. Three cars back from the Alpine, behind a Renault 14, Max was in the Audi, curious to see where this next little jaunt would take them. He was still conflicted after seeing James again. It had really thrown him off balance. He could recall the times they spent together. They'd been inseparable, like close brothers. But now here he was, with a job to do, to kill the best friend he'd ever had. It wasn't going to be easy but still, he had a reputation to maintain.

The Boss was enjoying himself. A nice meal at Simpson's in the Strand, followed by a couple of Cognacs at his favorite gentleman's club and now he was at the casino, his number one mistress in tow.

It had been a disappointing week. All that preparation and the job had gone south. They needed the money. Their next job was already halfway through the planning stages and some people who'd paid coin up front to help with smuggling the weapons would be getting antsy, especially once they found out that nearly £2.5 million in jewels was now in the hands of the police. He had to find a way to get it, and to turn things around and put the odds in his favor once again.

It was all one big gamble, just like the game of baccarat he was now playing. He was already raising the stakes, his "date" swooning at the money being placed on the table. *She's incredibly shallow*, he thought. *Another worthless trophy girl, fit for a shag and not much else. Given how bad things seem to be going, I wonder if I can even be bothered to screw her tonight.*

"Pull in there," Graeme directed. Em turned right and into the Stanhope Gardens parking area, which was located behind the building and accessed by a fairly narrow alley. "Use my spot, the one on the end by the wall, next to that silver XJ-S."

"What do you need?"

Graeme paused for a second. He was tempted to say something ribald, but thought better of it. "Just a couple of pairs of trousers, underwear, socks, shirts and a jumper, that should do it." He handed her the key to his flat.

Max had managed to stay fairly close behind. He saw the blue Mercedes ahead turn left into a courtyard and then the brown Cortina pull up right in front of the entrance. *Too conspicuous, can't do it here.* He pulled over quickly and waited.

Entering Graeme's flat, Em headed for the bedroom. She found it hard not to be impressed by the place, even after all this time, and given her upbringing, she wasn't somebody who easily was. She grabbed a shirt from the big wardrobe. Heading for the dresser on the other side of the room, she found a pair of jeans and a dark blue sweater. Em smiled sweetly as she accessed the top drawer and grabbed some underwear and socks, somehow feeling comforted by the thought of gathering up his clothes. Going back into the hall, she quickly located his Reebok trainers and a blue Slazenger sports bag. *This should do*, she thought as she stuffed the belongings into the bag.

In the courtyard, it seemed like she'd been gone an eternity. From where the car was parked, Graeme couldn't see the street, nor their escort, but his gut feeling told him the chaps in the brown Cortina were there.

He saw Em come around the corner, brandishing what looked like his blue Slazenger sports bag.

"Here," she tossed him the bag as he opened the door, "put this behind the seat. Let's get a move on, James."

"Right you are, madam," replied Graeme sarcastically, a sheepish grin on his face. She just looked at him and sighed.

They were on the move again. He saw the brown Cortina back up and the Mercedes pull out on the road. *Let's see where you go now*, Max thought as he started the Audi and followed, doing his best to stay several cars behind. Even if he did lose visual sight, it didn't matter because the covert vehicle location device would still guide him to their next port of call. He glanced at the flashing receiver on the passenger seat. *You're mine now.*

Fifteen minutes later, Em steered the Mercedes right from South Parade onto the east side of Chelsea Square. Up ahead, Graeme could see a blue X registered Ford Cortina parked on the opposite side of the road. As the Mercedes drove past, Graeme caught the eyes of two men sitting in the car.

"That's got to be our boys," Graeme told Em.

Sure enough, his instincts were confirmed. The brown Cortina traveling behind them pulled up across the road from the blue one and the driver got out and walked across the road to the other car.

"Drop me off before you park, I want to have a word with them."

Em pulled up just before the courtyard entrance to the building.

"Where's my gun?" the inspector asked.

"In the boot."

"Is it locked?"

"Yes."

"Make sure you get it and bring it to your flat, won't you?"

Em didn't answer. Instead she turned to face him, tilting her head and giving a frank expression.

Graeme shrugged his shoulders, sighed briefly and got out of the Mercedes, making for the blue Cortina as she turned into the courtyard and parked.

Charing Cross Hospital was still busy with police activity as both plainclothes and uniformed officers searched every corridor looking for Graeme and Em's would-be assassin.

Chief Superintendent George Donaldson was in the main entrance, close by the reception desk, on his police radio with Detective Charles.

"Have you found anything?"

"Nothing much so far, Guv," Tim answered with a disheartened tone. "The bullet found in James' room has already been sent to ballistics. Apart from that, there appears to be no trace of our man, nor signs of an entry or exit route."

"Bastard."

"Shall we keep looking?"

The super paused. "Alright, we'll keep searching the hospital for another twenty minutes. If nothing turns up, we'll call it a day."

Donaldson sighed and briefly tilted his head back in frustration. It was obvious that the hitman had managed to evade the police. *But how? We had every exit of this building covered. Did he, in fact, escape? If that was the case, he could be anywhere. Or, maybe he was still hiding somewhere in this multi-story labyrinth?* "I'm going to find you, you bastard," the super muttered under his breath.

Just as he was being handed a cup of coffee by one of the uniformed officers, something clicked.

"My God," he said out loud. Grabbing the radio, he paged Tim.

"Yes Guv?"

"Tim, remember when we first arrived at the hospital?"

"Yes."

"Can you remember seeing a green Audi in the car park, fairly close to the front entrance?"

"Now that you've mentioned it, yes."

"That's got to be our man. Let's call this off. Get the rest of them back down here; my bet is that he's probably on the trail of James and Braithwaite again." He gestured to the uniformed inspector. "Brian, tell your lot to call it a day. Our work here is done."

"Hello, Inspector James," said the man in the driver's seat of the blue Cortina, reaching out his hand through the window. "Sergeant Tom Hogg, SPG. We've been instructed to give you this radio."

His colleague in the passenger seat got out and walked over to Graeme, handing him the device.

"Thanks, this is good," Graeme exhaled, feeling a little relieved at having the radio.

"How long have you been here?"

"About fifteen minutes."

"Anything suspicious?"

"Not that we've seen, right Tom?"

In the driver's seat, Sergeant Hogg nodded.

"Okay," continued Graeme, "but keep your eyes peeled. There's a very good chance we could be targeted tonight. If you see any cars that might be suspicious, note the registration numbers and see if and where they park. Also keep a lookout for people walking on the street. Anything—I mean, *anything*—you contact me as soon as possible. Got it?"

"Right sir. There's also a second SPG unit on its way, should be here any minute," affirmed Hogg.

"Good stuff. Can you ask them to park inside the premises so their car isn't seen?"

"Will do."

"What about us, sir?" said the moppy-haired detective from the brown Cortina. "Do you need us to stick around, at least until the second SPG squad gets here?"

"Yes, if you can stay as long as you can, that would be a big help."

Em was just walking through the front door to her flat when the phone started ringing. She headed into the living room and picked up the phone receiver from the small table next to the sofa.

"Hello?"

"Em, it's Donaldson, glad I caught you. We've got a couple of interesting updates for you. We remember seeing a green Audi at the Charing Cross Hospital car park when we first arrived, which fits the description of Max's car. There's a very good chance he might be on to you again. A shopkeeper on Edgware spotted a man that looked like him getting into such a car around lunchtime today, around the same time we heard he was asking questions at the crime scene. Ask the lads outside to keep a lookout. Remember, call within the hour. If you can't get through to me on the police radio you can reach me at this number..."

"Yes sir." Em replied wearily. "And I will make sure to stay in touch every hour."

"Good, good. And for what it's worth, Sergeant, we are going to catch the bastard this time, you mark my words."

"Thank you sir." Em let out a sigh away from the receiver and tried her best to smile. Then, she said, "We'll be in touch soon."

Hanging up, she headed into her kitchen.

Graeme was about to ring the buzzer to Em's flat when a beige Rover SD1 pulled into the complex parking area. He turned around, gesturing to the men in the car.

The one in the passenger seat got out. He had short, dark brown hair, brown eyes and a thin, oval face. "DCI King sent us. We're supposed to keep watch on you tonight."

Graeme walked towards the Rover. His strength had returned quite a bit since the incident, and he wasn't moving around with as much pain as the day before. "Are you armed?"

"We've each got a Glock in the boot," the man answered. His companion in the driver's seat got out and nodded at Graeme.

"I'd suggest getting them out right now, you're going to need them. The man who is after us is called Max Willoughby, he's an ace shooter and trained in covert operations. I would suggest you park the car facing out towards the street and stay vigilant. We don't know if he'll strike tonight, but there's a very good chance he might. Stay in touch with us on the radio, channel 7."

"Yes, sir." The man swiveled to his colleague. "C'mon Jim, let's get ready."

Em was in the kitchen as Graeme walked in.

He scanned the room, the same place where she'd tended to him two days before, after his altercation with Gerry at the garage. The breakfast bar, counters and cabinets had a real look of substance to them and that oven—it was clearly top-of-the-range by early 1980s standards. He could sense she enjoyed being in here and given the plethora of books and spices, very much liked cooking.

"I placed your Glock and your bags—the Slazenger from your place and the other from the hospital—in the living room," she mentioned, opening the door to the fridge.

"Oh, thanks."

"Fancy something to eat? I was going to whip up a quick salad and some sandwiches."

"Absolutely, I'm ravenous."

She looked at him, grimaced and then looked away.

"If you don't mind I'm just going to change out of these 'ridiculous' clothes, as you put it."

"Okay, I'm sure you know where the bathroom is."

Graeme went into the living area, grabbed his bag and his Glock and headed for the bathroom.

Once in there, he opened the Slazenger carryall from his place. In it he found a pair of jeans, his running shoes and a dark blue sweater. *Perfect. Comfortable clothing at last, and the trainers will give agility if needed.* In the bottom of the other bag from the hospital, he found his blood-soaked suit, which now reeked, and two spare, ten-round magazines for his Glock.

He looked around the bathroom. Like the rest of her flat, it was absolutely spotless, homey, and it also smelled of her—fresh, clean and comforting. He washed his face and got changed.

Walking back out into the corridor, he heard his partner calling. "Here, in the living room." She was sitting on the couch, shoes off, feet curled up and hands wrapped around a mug. "I poured one for you, it's in the kitchen."

That tracking device had worked wonders; her car had stopped in Chelsea Square, off the King's Road. As he drove towards the location, he spotted the brown Cortina and a blue one parked just across the road from it up ahead. *More fuzz,* he thought. Careful not to be spotted, Max slowed the car and gingerly turned it around. Keeping a close eye in his rearview mirror at the two Cortinas, he drove back down Manresa Road towards the King's Road and pulled up on Glebe Street, just across the way.

Taking off his jacket, he got out of the Audi and walked north, back towards the King's Road. Finding a phone box, he made the call.

"It's me," he issued into the receiver. "I've found them; 16 Chelsea Square, off the King's Road."

"*Uitstekend*," the voice replied, "I will be there shortly."

"There are police keeping the place under surveillance."

"Not a problem, we can deal with them."

"Donaldson was just on the phone," Em explained to Graeme. "He said he remembered seeing a green Audi in the hospital car park near the entrance when he and Tim were arriving this afternoon—could well be Max's car. Do you really think he'll try and attack us again tonight?"

"Honestly, I really don't know at this point. Max's preferred tactic would be to strike when we least expect it, but I don't know. I haven't seen him for five years—who knows what's happened to him since then. Did the guv say anything else?"

"That a man fitting Max's description was apparently spotted getting out of a green Audi around lunchtime today on Edgware, around the time he was posing as a reporter."

"How long ago did he call?"

"About five minutes."

"Why didn't you come outside and let me know?"

"Sorry, I got distracted for a minute."

Graeme sighed and dropped his shoulders.

"Hold on," he said. "I'll be right back."

Heading out the door, and back towards the courtyard, Graeme held up the police radio and pressed the transmit button. "Foxtrot 12, Sierra 3, over."

"Foxtrot 12 here," responded Hogg.

"Keep your eyes peeled for a green Audi, a car fitting that description is believed to be in the custody of our man."

"Roger, will do. Foxtrot 12, out."

Reaching the parking area of the complex, Graeme saw that the beige Rover had been turned around and was now pointing its nose out towards the entrance. He walked up to the driver's door. "The guy we're dealing with is highly trained. I'd suggest staying hidden as much as possible, close to the walls on each side of the entrance," the inspector guided sternly.

"Right sir."

"And stay in touch with Foxtrot 12, every fifteen minutes."

The casino was buzzing as more patrons in their black ties and evening gowns took to the tables and the bars. After a shaky start at baccarat, the Boss's luck was finally turning. He'd won the last round against his main rival, a heavyset man in his forties. The Boss liked to gamble and with his first win of the night was feeling lucky. His "date" giggled with delight as a small crowd gathered around the table. As the croupier announced the winning hand and the latest bet got ready to be paid out in the Boss's favor, a member of the casino staff approached the table who looked like he was in his early thirties, with dark, straight, slicked-back hair, olive skin and a dark suit. In fact, the man reminded the Boss of himself when he was younger.

"Sir, you have a phone call."

"At this hour?" the Boss snapped.

"Yes. Apparently it's urgent. If you'd like to follow me."

The olive-skinned man led the Boss to the far side of the casino and through a door into an office.

"Here you go, press line three. Will that be all, sir?"

The Boss nodded and the man promptly left the room.

"What is it?" he snarled roughly into the phone, annoyed at his game being interrupted.

"It's me."

"You'd better have some news for me Niels, and it had better be good news."

"Actually, I do. We've found those two coppers that made a mess of our plans yesterday. We'll be taking care of them tonight. I will contact you as soon as it is done."

"Excellent. No mistakes this time. Got it?"

"Absolutely."

As the Boss hung up the phone, a wry smile bled into his cheekbones. He headed back out to the main room and towards the baccarat table and his pretty but shallow date. *Time to make a bit more money!*

A good evening was starting to get even better.

"So, you and Max." Em frowned at Graeme slightly as he sat down on the big comfy chair, mug of tea in hand. "What was the deal?"

"We were best of friends. More like brothers, really. We almost knew how the other one thought."

"When did you first meet him?"

"At RAF Staff College, Cranwell. Why are you asking?"

"It's just you've never really told me anything about your past life before we started working together. Friends, family, girlfriends."

"Curious, are we?"

"Oh no, just wanted to see if there's anything else I should know about. I mean, the fact that you *knew* our hitman—likely the one responsible for Del's death, too—it just seems a bit, well, odd. What would you do, I mean honestly, if you saw him again?"

"Are you trying to imply something?" He was beginning to get angry.

"No, I'm *not*," Em pushed back. Graeme could sense a genuine tone in her voice.

"Look, I'll tell you something," he conceded, "and I don't say this very often. Max was a *friend*, a very good friend. We were in pilot training together and flew Harriers; it's one of the hardest jets to fly, you have to be disciplined and utterly focused to graduate training."

"I never knew that," she responded, clearly surprised. "I'd love to hear more."

Was this a seduction ploy, or was she just wanting to know more about her police partner? Graeme just didn't know for sure. He went on. "Max and I finished top of our class in pilot training," he recounted, with a hint of pride. "I could rely on him for anything, and he the same for me. His plane crashed on a training mission while we were stationed in Central America. It was because of his accident and supposed death that I left the service and joined the force—that's how and why I'm talking to you now." Then his tone changed, becoming edgier. "If you're trying to ask me what I'd do if I came face to face with him again, the honest answer is: I'd do my job."

After a moment of Em staring at him, albeit emotionally, he decided to try and put things to rest. "Please," he added, "if there is one thing I will ask of you right now it's that you don't ever question my loyalty. You know, sometimes, Braithwaite, you can really get on my nerves. Don't know about you but I could really use a sandwich." He got up and headed to the kitchen.

Em sat there for some time on the sofa, thinking about what she had just said. She'd been digging a little too deep. He had a vulnerable side, that was all too apparent right now. She got up and followed him into the kitchen.

He was turned away from her, busy cutting a sandwich.

"Graeme," she spoke softly. "Look, I'm really sorry. I didn't mean to upset you, nor to pry like that. It's just, well, I'm frightened."

He turned around with a look of surprise.

She edged closer to him. "It's as if death has been following us around all week and I feel it's going to strike again tonight and here, but I'm just not sure when."

He stared at her.

"Look," she confessed, "if I'm really being honest, I need you."

Graeme's mind started racing. *Is she trying to come on to me? If there's any time you need to keep your head, it's now.* He could see she was vulnerable, just as much as he was. The animal magnetism was almost overpowering; he could feel his body urging him to just grab her and start caressing her, but now wasn't the time. Instead, he took her in his arms and gave her a hug.

The feeling of her against him—it was special. Graeme could sense true comfort, belonging and serenity. Goosepimples reared on his arms and legs while his body tingled. Holding her seemed like an eternity, but it was barely a minute. He wanted to kiss her so badly, but his training took over and he drew back.

"You never call me Graeme," he noted.

She smiled and started laughing. "I know."

"Look, let's make sure we're prepared. I've got two spare magazine clips in my bag from the robbery yesterday. Take one. Also, since we're here, grab some steak knives, they might come in handy."

Van Rooyen was in a rush to get to his target. After yesterday's screwup, he needed a lucky break and was nervous about what would happen if this assignment didn't go according to plan. He was heading down Warwick Road in the Capri. Traffic was getting lighter. *Should be there in less than half an hour,* he calculated. In the glovebox, he had his Smith & Wesson and also a 9mm Beretta and silencer, which he'd obtained from one of his Brussels contacts. Even painted metallic gray, the Capri was fairly conspicuous even though he found himself speeding, his nerves getting to him. Turning onto Old Brompton Road, he swerved, narrowly missing a Volvo 343 coming the other way.

He saw an Austin Allegro Panda car parked on the side of the road and slowed down, trying to avoid suspicion, but it was too late. The uniformed copper in the Panda had already seen him make the corner at high speed. Getting out, he raised his hand, ordering Van Rooyen to stop.

The Dutchman pulled over, just across the road from the Allegro and lowered his window all the way.

"Do you realize how fast you were going?" asked the officer as he started walking up to the Capri. He'd barely had a chance to finish his sentence when the Dutchman fired two shots from the Beretta at the policeman's chest. As they did, the back tires of the Capri squealed as Van Rooyen gunned the throttle, causing the V-6 engine to bellow through the dual pipes as he tore down the road and into the distance.

The policeman's partner had been in a residence across the street, making inquiries when he heard the sound of gunshots and a car speeding off. As he ran out, he saw a man down with a group of people gathered round.

"Call an ambulance!" he yelled to the lady in the house he'd just come out of. "NOW!" He rushed over to the crowd. "Keep back! You! Help me get him comfortable!"

One of the women in the crowd helped the young officer hold his injured partner's head.

"Keith! Keith, can you hear me, mate?" his partner shook. "What the hell just happened?"

Keith was getting pale. "Traffic stop, shoots fire, gray Capi." Then he closed his eyes.

The officer grabbed the radio in the Allegro. "This is Lima 3-2, emergency, over. Police officer down, Old Brompton Road, Fulham, multiple gun shots. *I say again*—multiple gun shots, over."

"Roger Lima 3-2."

They were doing their best to stay prepared. "TV, or music?" Em yelled from the living room. He could see that she was trying to brighten their somewhat somber mood.

"Music," Graeme shouted in answer, thinking back to his life in the "other" world and the songs that had helped him get through. It still baffled him—the technology, the music, TV, events and people he'd never heard of—that didn't exist here. He recalled his last encounter with Clara, and wondered when he was "going back." *What had she been trying to tell me? The key, Em's initials, the locker at Paddington station and that torn invitation from "1987"? What does it all mean? This* can't *be a dream, it's just too real and I saw evidence to prove life here goes beyond the "present." But how the hell can I be living in two different time periods as the same person? Have I found a portal between the present and the past, or the ability to reach another dimension? Oh my God!* Graeme started wondering if some of those "future" events he knew about in the twenty-first century would actually come to pass. Even if they did, there was still no predicting what was going to happen where he was right now. *Keep it together man!*

He took a deep breath to try and slow his mind. As he exhaled, he reminded himself that despite the danger, he was enjoying 1983, especially being in a setting like this and with *her*. He was sure he didn't want to leave this world, nor her flat, especially once the music began.

She'd chosen Culture Club's "Time (Clock of the Heart)" 45 to put on her turntable. For Graeme, listening to the haunting, soulful melody and lyrics couldn't have been more appropriate for the here and now.

Walking into the living room, he saw she was curled on the couch again, looking into outer space.

He felt a strange sensation: comfort and edginess, both at the same time. Em's living room was warm and inviting, just like the rest of her flat. The couch and twin armchairs were big and cozy, and the decor a mix between early 1980s modern and antique. Glancing at the coffee table, TV stand and bookshelves in the corner, he could see that Em really liked quality wood. A sizable palm plant in the corner gave the room an exotic, tropical feel—paradise, perhaps? In Graeme's mind, that was exactly where he happened to be at this moment, despite the potential danger that lay ahead.

As he sat down beside her, she turned to face him as he commented, "I didn't know you had this one."

"What do you mean?"

"The single."

"Oh, that. I bought it along with a bunch of others from Our Price a few months back. Do you like it?"

"I do," he said. *In fact, I absolutely love it. And I want to hold on to this moment forever.*

Donaldson and Tim Charles were heading back to the SRI offices in the Granada when the radio burst to life.

"Sierra 1, come in."

"Hand me the mic, will you Tim?" asked Donaldson as he drove east on Cromwell Road.

"Sierra 1, over."

"Guv, you probably want to hear this," Wildman said, an anxious tone leaking from his voice. "A call just came in, apparently shots were fired and an officer was killed."

"What?!" Donaldson exclaimed as his brows raised and eyes widened. Where?

When?"

"Old Brompton Road, less than half an hour ago."

"Oh Christ, that's just down the road from here. Get some of our units on the scene and make sure an ambulance is en route—we're on our way there now."

Donaldson hit the brakes in the Granada, causing the tires to squeal and the nose to dive as weight shifted forward in the big sedan. Quickly, he spun the car around and headed south towards the scene of the crime.

CHAPTER 15

It had been a stupid move, speeding through the corner, but if the copper had identified him, he'd have been made. Van Rooyen was on the King's Road now, heading to the target. Up ahead, on the left he saw a man who appeared to be signaling to him. He pulled the Capri over and got out.

"What is it?"

"It's me."

He recognized the voice.

"Number 16 Chelsea Square is just around the corner. Manresa Road over there leads to it." Max pointed. "There's a blue Cortina parked across the road from the place with two men in it. They're watching the street, that's why I signaled to pull over. There was also a brown one with an additional two people parked right outside the entrance as well. I wasn't able to get too close otherwise they would have spotted me. I have every reason to believe they are undercover police."

Van Rooyen couldn't quite see the man's face as he talked; he was wearing a flat cap and turned away slightly while talking to him.

"Are you armed?" the Dutchman pressed.

Silence followed, but he took that as a yes.

"Then it's time to take care of some coppers."

The dead constable's name was Keith Reynolds from Cheam. He was just twenty-seven years old, with a wife and an eighteen-month-old son.

What is the world coming to? thought Donaldson, drawing on a cigarette. They'd arrived at the crime scene a few minutes before. Reynolds' body was being placed in a Bedford ambulance. His partner, PC Andy Quinlan, was sitting at the curb, leaning forward, still very much shaken at the sudden loss of his partner.

Tim Charles was taking witness statements. A crowd of people had gathered following the incident and quite a few were hysterical, making it hard for Tim to obtain any useful information. He'd gotten four accounts but so far, nothing solid had come up. It had all happened so quickly. Raising his hand, he gestured to a lady in her sixties who lived in one of the nearby flats. "Excuse me madam, did you see or hear anything?"

"I was just over there," she said pointing to the gate that led to her ground floor residence. "I was just coming out my door when I thought I heard a thud and squealing tires."

"Did you see what kind of car it was?"

"No, I didn't, but for a second I thought I saw a gray one in the distance that looked like it was going very fast."

"Guv," Tim tried to grab his boss's attention over the multiple conversations taking place. "Have you got a second?"

Donaldson turned his head. "What is it?"

"This lady says she thought she saw a gray car speeding. It could be a connection."

"Alright, but keep questioning. We need something more solid to go on."

The super walked over to Quinlan, putting his hands on his hips and stooping slightly. "So, you didn't see anything then, eh?"

"No sir." The young police constable was fidgeting, alternating between rubbing his neck and wrapping his hands together.

Looking into his eyes, Donaldson could see the uniformed copper was traumatized, a reminder of his own youth back in the Suez.

"As I said, I was in the house across the road making inquiries regarding a domestic dispute. I heard screaming and a car speeding off. I ran outside and saw a gaggle of people standing over my partner. He was lying in the road."

"You mentioned your partner said something before he died. What was it?"

"It sounded to me like 'shoots fire and gray Capi' or something, his speech was mumbled, I was trying to get him comfortable."

"You mean 'shots fired'?" asked Donaldson as he kneeled and listened intently.

"Yes sir, that's it."

"And this Capi thing, do you think he might have been trying to describe the car the suspect was driving? Say, a Ford Capri? We have a witness who says she thought she saw a gray car speeding away in the distance."

"Could be."

"Alright, thank you, Constable. I'd suggest you take a bit of time off, it's not easy seeing a colleague taken like that. If you have any issues, reach out to our department, okay?"

The super briefly placed his hand on the man's shoulder before turning around and heading back to his car.

Getting into the gold Granada, Donaldson picked up the radio and pressed the transmit button. "Control, this is Sierra 1. Over."

"Control. Go ahead."

"Wildman, I want you to relay this through all police channels. Tell them to be on the lookout for a gray Ford Capri within a twenty-five-mile radius of the crime scene. Ask everybody to keep their eyes peeled for cars being driven or parked very recently. We've got a cop killer on our hands and I want the bastard caught. Sierra 1, out."

"How's your shoulder doing?" asked Em. "You know you haven't complained much, I'm perhaps starting to worry."

"Still hurts a bit, can't really move it a great deal, but there's no point bitching about it."

"Are you always this hard on yourself?" she retorted.

"No. It's just that I'm still thinking about Max. I should know what he's planning to do, but to be honest, there's something in the back of my mind that's causing me to second guess, whether he'll come back and try and kill us and whether or not it will be tonight. I'll tell you Braithwaite, it's been a hell of a week."

"You're not kidding. At least you seem to be getting back to your old self; I was a bit worried about you back on Wednesday and Thursday, it was almost as if you were somebody else."

"What do you mean, exactly?"

"You just seemed more sensitive, perhaps more aware of what was going on around you—including me."

"You mean you don't think I'm aware of you most of the time?"

"I think you hit the nail on the head."

"Look," he raised himself off the couch. "I'm going to grab some more tea. Fancy a refill?"

She handed him her mug.

As Graeme headed out the door towards the kitchen, Em's mind was turning over. Despite the overlying tension, she was enjoying the intimate setting, the music and the atmosphere. She could see that her partner was definitely on the mend and she felt comforted—safe, perhaps—even though there was a good chance that danger—*real* danger—was still lurking in the shadows.

The moment in the kitchen when he'd held her... *That had been special*. She'd discovered that he really *did* have a sensitive side, after all—and if she was being honest, for her it had been a major turn on. Could she actually be falling for him? Things had been getting very confusing lately.

She thought back to their first day on the job, when Donaldson had introduced them. She was sitting in the super's office when he was called in.

He'd looked her up and down briefly, but hadn't even said anything until the boss introduced both of them. She'd thought it was rude; almost as if he'd had some kind of chip on his shoulder. She knew she could be haughty at times, though her work in the police force had given her a good deal of grounding. Most of the time she was well aware of how lucky she was, coming from such wealth and privilege and also that life didn't owe her anything.

But still, she was surprised that he hadn't really given her much of a second glance. She knew she had the looks. Wolf whistles, comments and dinner offers had been par for the course since joining the Met. Even during her time at St. Catherine's

College in Oxford, she'd been propositioned at least several times a week. That said, despite quite a few one-night stands and even some "experimentation," there'd only been one person who'd ever touched her heart, and that was Jonathan Llewelyn.

She had dated Llewelyn for close to three years, but somehow, she just couldn't see herself marrying him. Once she'd been accepted to join the police force, she'd broken it off for good. They'd kept in touch and were still friends, but that was it.

On the job she'd had precious time for anything else, but then she'd met Graeme. At first he'd driven her almost mad. "Ignorant" and "cavalier" were the words she'd first used to describe him but somehow she felt there was more to her partner. The Southwark incident had landed both of them in deep water and she'd been angry at him for jeopardizing both their safety and possibly their careers, especially after just a few months working together. It was as if he followed the rules, but only when they suited him and didn't really give a damn about anybody else nor the consequences of his actions.

But gradually, she'd started to warm to him. He knew how to get things done and as time passed, he seemed to develop a greater level of concern for her and those around him.

However, this past week had changed everything. She'd actually been rather fraught when he went missing and relieved when hearing he'd been found close to Leicester Square.

Em reflected. *I really felt something that day. I was really worried he could have been killed and I'm not sure it was just professional or even amicable concern. Am I crossing the line emotionally?*

She returned back to the events from Wednesday.

A couple of bobbies had radioed in that day, and she'd dispatched an ambulance to pick him up. Graeme was still unconscious when she arrived at his flat, and urged the medics to just place him on the bed. It had taken him several hours to come to, but when he did, it was as if he was suffering from amnesia.

As bizarre as his behavior had been, it seemed he'd somehow changed as a person. Now, it appeared as though he could be genuinely interested in her—his face coming close to hers at Pentonville, the flirtatious remarks over the course of the last two days, and now, the hug in the kitchen. Normally she'd have just brushed it aside, but the trouble was, she was feeling an attraction to him—one, it seemed, that was becoming harder and harder to resist.

I must have genuinely touched a nerve with this Max thing, she thought, *and I'm surprised how he reacted to it. I didn't expect him to hug me like that—in fact, I didn't even expect* myself *to react the way I did. My God, he was really turning me on. If we'd started necking right there and then, I wouldn't have minded. If he'd grabbed my breasts I wouldn't have said no. I would have probably let him have his wicked way with me. No, I can't. Stop this, Emily Ruth Braithwaite, you know better than that, he's your partner. You have a professional relationship with him, and nothing more. What the hell are you thinking?*

"Is that tea ready yet?" she called.

"Almost," came the reply from the kitchen.

Donaldson was leaning against the front wing of the Granada Ghia, drawing on another B&H. *Bollocks, our city is turning into bloody New York,* he thought. *Armed thugs running rampant.*

"Tim," he asked, walking over to the young DC, "how are those witness statements coming? Did anybody see anything at all?"

"Nothing so far, Guv; Quinlan's is the best we've got. I've still got one or two more to question; we'll see how we get on."

A small team of forensics had arrived and was now going over the Allegro Panda car and the immediate vicinity.

"Sir."

"What is it?" Donaldson spun around.

"I think you might want to take a look at this."

The super and Tim both started walking towards the Panda car.

"Looks like it could be a bullet casing from our suspect's gun," the forensics officer continued as he picked up the object with his gloved hand.

Tim looked at it closely. "What does it look like to you?" he asked the forensics expert.

"We'll have to do a proper analysis on it back at the lab, but it's a 9mm, shot from a handgun."

"Possibly a Beretta?"

"Can't tell at this point, but that's certainly possible. I'll make sure our team provides you with more details as soon as we have them."

"Guv," asked Tim earnestly, are you thinking what I'm thinking?"

"You mean that the bullet that killed the young constable earlier could be from the same gun used to mow down Em's informant at Embankment station on Wednesday night?"

"Exactly."

"Oh, Christ, that's all we need," Donaldson scoffed. "Call James and Braithwaite right now! I bet you any money our man is going to try and finish them off. You!" the super yelped to a uniformed officer. "Contact DCI King of the Special Patrol Group and have a backup squad sent to 16 Chelsea Square, NOW!"

Everyone started moving and scuffling.

"Tim, stay here and let me know of anything else that turns up," the super continued. "I'm heading down to Braithwaite's. Keep in touch on the radio."

With that, Donaldson jumped in the Granada and tore off, siren wailing, the rear tires squealing as they fought to gain traction.

The Boss had done rather well at the casino tonight. He'd won close to £30,000. Not bad for an evening's earnings at the tables.

Now he was back at the hotel. He always made sure his favorite room at the Savoy was reserved at least once a week. He was lying on the bed, smoking a cigarette while his mistress was in the bathroom. An ice bucket containing a bottle of Moët & Chandon lay on the nightstand. *It's time for a little celebration, the perfect end to a satisfying evening.*

His paramour emerged wearing a bathrobe, giving him a nervous smile. *Life is good,* he reflected. *It will be even better once those coppers are dead.*

"Now, remember, this target is mine," Van Rooyen pressed. "Don't get any ideas."

Max remained in the shadows, not wanting to show his face to the Dutchman, nor interject, even though he knew this man had little idea of just how dangerous his former friend Graeme James could be. *He'll just have to find out for himself, won't he? The big lumbering cheese head.* But then it occurred to him: the Dutchman was his client, and he'd been paid well for this job. Professionally, he'd always kept his end of the bargain and the incident with James wasn't going to change that.

"If we are going to be successful this time, we need to eliminate those staked out in front of her place," Max chimed. "There's two in that blue Cortina, two in the brown one and I feel possibly more nearby. I suggest you go on one side of the street and I the other. Walk up to the men in the cars and ask for directions. Then I will take them out. Think of it as part of the service."

The Dutchman shook his head. *I should probably take* you *out as well,* he almost said out loud. He wasn't sure how deadly the man was. So far, though, he'd eliminated his targets with ruthless precision.

Van Rooyen was nervous. He didn't trust anybody, least of all this man. At this time, however, he was proving to be a valuable ally.

The police radio crackled. "Sierra 3, Sierra 3 come in, over." It was Donaldson.

Em got off the couch and grabbed the receiver.

"Sierra 3, here."

"Em, we've had some new developments."

"What is it, sir?"

"I think you two are going to be targeted tonight and I mean soon. I've just been at a crime scene down on Old Brompton Road in Fulham; a uniformed officer was shot at close range during a traffic stop. The suspect is still at large."

"What? When?"

"Less than an hour ago. But there's more. Two bullet casings were found at the scene and it's highly possible they could be from a 9mm Beretta."

"Just like the one my informant was shot with at Embankment?"

"I'm afraid so."

Em froze, dropping the radio on the floor.

Graeme had been in the kitchen. As soon as he heard it drop, he dashed out into the landing. She was crouching over, her face in her hands. He picked up the radio with one hand, and put his other arm around his partner.

He could tell it was Donaldson on the other line.

"Guv, where are you?"

"I'm speeding down the King's Road to your place right now, I've ordered more backup, it should be on its way. Have you contacted the lads parked outside?"

"Not for the last half hour. I'll radio them right now."

"Now, James, remember what I said—*don't be a hero*. If he comes for you, do what you can to protect your partner *and try not to kill him*; I want him alive for questioning. He's now a cop killer and I want to make sure that he gets brought to justice. Understood?"

"Yes, Guv."

Em was petrified.

Graeme put the radio down and led her to the master bedroom. She wasn't saying a word. *My turn to take care of you*, he thought. His shoulder was still sore, but it was now moving more freely. He sat her down on the edge of the bed and gave her a hug. They stayed there in silence for a few minutes. The last record she'd put on had just finished and the flat was now eerily quiet. Graeme held onto his partner tightly and closed his eyes. It had come to this.

"I wonder how much longer this is going to go on for?" questioned the SPG officer in the passenger seat of the blue Cortina. "I wanted to be out on the town tonight."

"Sorry mate, probably ain't gonna happen. We've got strict orders to wait here until instructed."

"Bollocks." He heard a sound outside the car, like the tapping of feet on the pavement, edging closer. "Can you hear footsteps coming?"

"I can definitely hear something. Have you got your gun, Sam?" asked Sergeant Hogg.

The man in the passenger seat opened the glovebox and pulled it out. Glancing in the driver's door mirror, Hogg could see the shadowy silhouette of a well-built man approaching from across the road.

"Excuse me," came the voice. It was foreign, from continental Europe at least as far as Hogg could tell.

"Yes, can I help you?" replied the SPG Sergeant.

"I'm looking for Sloane Square," the silhouette replied. "I'm visiting from Holland and was asked to meet a friend. Can you tell me which way to go?"

Hogg felt uneasy. The hairs on the back his neck were standing on end and he could feel his forehead and temples moisten. The sergeant paused for just a moment. His boss, DCI King, had briefed him about a Dutchman fitting this man's description. He was reaching for the radio and about to tap the transmit button when the bullets hit him and his partner in the side of the head. Both men slumped forward almost instantly.

In Em's flat, Graeme heard the radio crackle and what he thought sounded like two shots ringing out in the background. He gently laid her down on the bed and dashed out into the corridor.

"Foxtrot 12, come in. Foxtrot 12, come in, over."

There was nothing but static.

"Fuck!" yelled Graeme. "Foxtrot 5, come in."

"Foxtrot 5 here."

Graeme steadied himself. "*Our man's here*—I repeat, *our man's here*. Make sure you stay away from the car and face the entrance with your backs to the wall on each side of the courtyard. Do it NOW! There's only one way he can get into this building. And for God's sake, make sure you're armed and ready!"

"Roger."

Graeme dashed to the kitchen, grabbed several steak knives and walked briskly to the guest bathroom. An intense, sharp focus had returned to him and his every movement. He took out the spare magazines for the Glocks. The adrenaline was pumping now. He went back to check on his partner.

The bed was empty.

"Braithwaite. *Braithwaite*, are you okay? Where the hell are you?"

"I'm all right," she uttered, quite reassuringly. "I'm just in the ensuite bathroom. Give me a second."

"*Max is here*," Graeme sputtered. His heart was racing as he tossed one of the Glock magazines on the bed. "Grab that clip I left for you. I'll wait by the bedroom door."

She did as instructed and emerged wearing jeans and a faded jumper that almost exposed her shoulders.

My God you look sexy, even in that, Graeme thought to himself. He tried not to let it distract him.

"Let's dim the lights," she suggested.

"Good plan. You head for the living room, I'll go to the kitchen. Here, take a couple of these knives with you."

They'd done as Graeme told them. One of the SPG officers from the car was crouched in the shadows with a view of the entrance. The other was on the far side.

It was almost dark now, making it difficult to see anybody coming in. Jim Garrison, radio in hand, knelt in silence, waiting for the command to strike.

"How long before your lot get to Braithwaite's?" hollered the super. He was speeding along the King's Road.

"At least another fifteen minutes," King replied.

"Well, tell them to get a bloody move on, will you? We're running out of time!"

"Roger. Will do."

Although well overdue for some rest, the super knew he couldn't relax until the killer had been brought to justice. *Killing a police officer, that was truly the lowest of the low. I'll make sure you get what you deserve you heartless bastard. And I will do whatever it takes to ensure you never again lay a finger on two of my best operatives.*

Van Rooyen was feeling increasingly uneasy. The shadowed man had taken out the two undercover police officers without breaking a sweat. He glanced up at the building across the road, trying to figure out which flat their targets were in.

"You need to view the front door," said Max. "I will watch your back. Try to stay hidden. I have a feeling more coppers are on the scene, and they will also know your face. Here, take this hat." He threw his flat cap at the Dutchman.

Van Rooyen stooped to pick it up. He tried to glance at his mysterious ally, but his face was still turned away. The tension was growing. Quickly crossing the road to the entrance, Niels held his breath as he stood against the wall.

Upstairs, Graeme decided to walk across the hall to the living room.

"What are you doing?" hissed Em. "I thought the plan was to stay put!"

"Something tells me our man is *right outside*. Since the curtains are still open I'm going to have a peek at the street."

It was almost completely dark now. Graeme crouched by the windowsill, doing his best to look below without being noticed. He saw the blue Cortina parked across the road, but everything seemed to be quiet; there was no sign of life from the car. The inspector was about to turn away when he thought he saw something not far from the car—possibly the outline of a man. He tried staring at it for a second, but wasn't sure. Graeme turned away, but the edge of his watch reflected in the moonlight.

It was just a split second, but Max had seen. It was all he needed. Swiftly, he crossed the road to the other wall of the courtyard entrance.

Van Rooyen was slowly making his way towards the front door of the building, doing his best not to be noticed, but it was too late. One of the coppers had seen him. Pressing the transmit button on his radio, the SPG officer tried to contact Graeme. "Sierra 3, this is Foxtrot 5, over."

In Em's flat, the radio crackled. "Sierra 3 this is Foxtrot 5, come in, over."

Graeme had left the radio in the hallway. He tried to get to it as fast as he could without making too much noise.

Em shook her head.

"Sierra 3 here, go ahead Foxtrot 5."

"I think your man's down here, I repeat; your man is here, in the car park."

"Has he seen you?"

"No, I don't think so," replied Garrison.

"Okay, approach him stealthily and try and grab him, try not to shoot him, Donaldson wants him alive."

"Roger. Foxtrot 5, out."

Graeme turned to face Em. "C'mon Sergeant, it looks like the SPG lads downstairs have pinpointed our man. Let's get down there, but take some of the knives with you, we might need 'em."

"I thought our boss told you not to play the hero. You're still injured, remember?" There was anger in Em's voice.

"Look, Braithwaite, *let's just go*, I don't like this any more than you do!" Graeme grabbed the radio before heading out the door.

She was right behind him.

As he headed down the stairs, Graeme pressed the transmit button on the radio. "Foxtrot 5, come in, over. What's your progress with the suspect?"

There was no answer.

He tried again. "Foxtrot 5 come in, over?"

Still, nothing.

He turned to look at his partner. She was trembling, but still trying to put on a brave face. They'd just about reached the bottom of the stairs when he was struck on the side of the head.

He was falling again, hard and fast. Then, he was awake. Graeme opened his eyes and looked around.

No, it couldn't be, it just isn't possible. Scanning his surroundings, he was horrified. He was lying on the bed in his grotty Shepherd's Bush flat. Empty beer cans were scattered on the floor. Looking down, he could see he was wearing pajama bottoms and a The Who T-shirt.

Graeme got up and went into the bathroom. Standing above the small sink, he stared into the mirror. The face looking back at him was pale and disheveled; he looked like he hadn't washed in days.

"*No, no, no*, NO!" he screamed, but nobody could hear him. Collapsing onto the floor by the sink, he started crying.

He closed his eyes tight, hoping that it would just go away. Propping himself up against the wall for what seemed like an eternity, Graeme tried to make sense of what was going on around him. *It's a dream. Just a dream*, he kept telling himself. But it wasn't any use. Whenever he opened his eyes, he was in the same spot. He scanned the unremarkable bathroom.

Now, he remembered. He'd tried to keep it as clean as possible, but there was that damp spot on the ceiling, by the shower. And the counter, which had remnants of cigarette burns from a previous tenant. Letting out an almighty scream, he raised his knees and stamped his heels into the floor, sobbing. He then began slamming his elbows hard into the wall, to the point that they started hurting.

After a while, he realized it was no use. Summoning what seemed like all the energy he had left in the world, Graeme slowly stood up. *How could it be?* Had his "life" in 1983 really been just a dream? Was this his true reality, after all? He really thought it had been real; that they *were* a team, that she cared for him, that he'd been strong, alert and despite the danger, happy.

And now, it had all come to this! He was angry and hurt, feeling cheated and defeated in equal measure. It appeared as though his mind had been playing tricks on him all along and now, here he was, firmly entrenched in "reality."

CHAPTER 16

The flat was small. The bedroom was just big enough to fit a double bed and the living area was awkwardly shaped. He just stood there and looked around, dejected. The brown pull-out sofa and the green armchair were almost threadbare on one side. He glanced towards the kitchenette, with its white cabinets, countertop and appliances.

Graeme's thoughts were racing. *Fuck! What the hell do I do? What can I do?* His hands were shaking and adrenaline was coursing through his veins. He kept darting his eyes in multiple directions. *It cannot be!!*

The anger and sadness were almost overwhelming, as was the need to drown his sorrows. *I must have some beer in the fridge,* he thought. Opening the door, he found some leftover pizza, milk, and juice. *But no sodding beer!* He looked around some more. *Ah, the wine rack.* He grabbed the last bottle of red.

In a frenzy, he searched for a corkscrew. He couldn't think of anything else but downing some wine. In his desperation, Graeme yanked open the top kitchen drawer so hard that it broke, sending cutlery scattering onto the floor.

"*Fuuuccck*!" Kneeling down, he found the corkscrew amid the scattered utensils.

He sat on the floor, opened the bottle and took a swig. It didn't taste the same as it did in a glass. *But what do I care?* It was the only thing he knew right now that could ease the pain, the frustration and the misery. Then, he thought about his arm. His left shoulder was starting to ache. The more he drank, the more he noticed the pain, along with an increasing throbbing in his head. *Just what the hell is going on?*

Graeme had downed almost two-thirds of the bottle by the time he heard the doorbell ring. He got up and stumbled towards the front of the flat.

It was still ringing. "Alright, *alright*!" he slurred. Opening the door, Graeme saw an older lady standing there, a look of disdain on her face.

"Drunk again, are we?" she said, hands on hips, her brow creased with disappointment.

It took a moment for him to figure out who she was. Then it came to him. It was that nosy Ms. Robertson from down the hall.

"What do you want?"

"These are for you," she said disapprovingly, handing Graeme a couple of Royal Mail Jiffy Bags. "They were sent to the wrong address."

Graeme took them.

"You know, it might do to say 'thank you' once in a while. I might not always be so kind."

"Thank you," said Graeme sarcastically.

"I know it's none of my business," said Ms. Robertson condescendingly, "but if I were you, I'd lay off the booze, young man." She turned and headed back to her flat, tutting under her breath, "such a waste."

Graeme went back into his unit, closing the well-worn front door. The pain in his arm was proving distracting now, further adding to the feeling of distress and despair.

He sat on the sofa, the bottle of wine in one hand and the parcels in the other. Putting the wine aside for a second, he opened the first package. In it he found a white T-shirt. On the chest it had the letters SRI and on the back, the same letters, much bigger in size, with MCMLXXXIII in simple Times New Roman font beneath them.

He wasn't sure what to make of it. *SRI? 1983. This has got to be some kind of joke.* He looked at the parcel. There was no sender's address, just a postmark: London W1. He opened the second, smaller package. Inside he found a little box. Pulling it out, he popped the lid and saw two gold keys, both embossed with "16." His eyes popped. *What the hell? That number is the same as Em's address in the other world. How can this be? Is somebody trying to tell me something?* He sat back on the couch, wondering what to make of it all. He took another swig of wine.

After a few more mouthfuls, Graeme was starting to get sleepy but the pain in his shoulder kept him from dozing off. Glancing at the cheap clock on the wall, it seemed only thirty minutes had passed. Taking another drink, he noticed a piece of folded paper on the floor. *Must have fallen out of one of the parcels.*

By now, Graeme was quite drunk and his head was starting to spin. He reached down and picked up the paper. Upon opening it, he found a typed note.

Follow these instructions.

Go to Hammersmith tube station, Piccadilly Line.

Be on the eastbound platform at 4:30 p.m. promptly on December 15.

Wait by the stairs near the concourse level for further instructions.

And bring both keys with you.

More keys, more tube trains. *What the hell does this all mean? Am I going to end up at Paddington again? And just what the hell was that T-shirt about?*

Graeme glanced at his old Rolex. It was 2:10 p.m., *December 15*. It was then that he heard a buzzing sound. It was his Blackberry. He got up and grabbed it off the small dresser by the far living room wall. It was a text message from a number he didn't recognize.

"*Did you get the packages?*" it read.

Curious to find out more, Graeme dialed the number. It rang almost endlessly, but there was no answer.

Baffled, he contemplated the next course of action. He could simply stay in the flat, but what then? Or, he could follow the instructions. Given how the booze was impacting his mental state, thoughts quickly swayed towards the latter. *Perhaps the items in the package really* do *signify something. Besides, what the hell, I don't exactly have much to lose, do I?*

His plan now set in motion, Graeme ventured into the bedroom. He found some dark blue jeans in the small, battered dresser, a jumper, underwear and socks. *Might as well try and get cleaned up.* He entered the bathroom to take a shower.

The lack of water pressure and lukewarm temperature made the shower a miserable experience, especially in winter. Washed as best as he could, he dried off and got dressed. The pain in his arm was strong enough now that getting his clothes on proved to be a bit of an ordeal. Glancing at the bottle of wine on the coffee table, he decided to finish the remnants. *Nothing to lose, have I?*

Even in a fairly drunken state, it seemed to take an eternity to walk down Shepherd's Bush Road towards Hammersmith Broadway and the aching pain only made it feel even longer. He looked at his watch. Ten minutes to go.

Graeme started to run, clenching his teeth to fight off the now considerable pangs in his shoulder and growing throb in the side of his head. The one-way system circling the Broadway development was still busy with traffic but knowing he might be late if he didn't peg it, Graeme decided to step onto the tarmac before the pedestrian sign turned green. Trying to avoid the speeding LDV delivery van, Graeme started to turn his body, but his dazed, drunken state meant he couldn't react fast enough. The van's front fender clipped him, sending Graeme flying through the air and towards the Broadway Shopping Centre entrance. Hitting the ground hard, he found himself plunged into blackness.

Graeme found himself floating, like being suspended in midair. Surrounded in total darkness, he could sense the pain in his shoulder and a strong ache from the side of his head. His face and nose were starting to feel cold and he could hear echoes—voices—followed by the sound of shuffling feet. The cool sensation was a hard stone floor.

Graeme opened his eyes. This time, he knew what was happening. Feeling down the side of his leg, he grabbed a steak knife from his pocket.

Van Rooyen had found it a piece of cake so far. The male copper had been easy. A smack to the side of the head with his Beretta and he'd tumbled to the floor—out cold. He'd grabbed Graeme's Glock, a nice weapon, but the real prize was her.

She'd resisted and stabbed him in the leg. It had hurt, but he wasn't going to let this bitch get off lightly. She was so pretty, but she needed to learn a lesson. He'd smacked her in the face and then kicked her in the knees. She was still trying to fight, but he was stronger.

"You know what I'm going to do to you?" he rasped, in his guttural tone. "I'm going to fuck you up. You cost me big yesterday and now I'm going to take it from you, I'm going to take it all."

Em tried to wrestle him, but with brute force, Van Rooyen was able to push her to the floor, causing her to hit her head on the wall as she fell.

Still putting up a fight, Em kicked and screamed. "No! No! Stop! You bastard, you'll never get away with this. Fuck you!!!"

She was strong-willed, no question, but the Dutchman wasn't going to let anything stand in his way. As she tried kicking him, Van Rooyen grasped her right leg and pinned it down. He could feel the female copper starting to weaken, no doubt a result of bashing her head against the wall. He grabbed Em's left knee and then pushed both legs apart. Reaching forward, he seized the top of her jeans and started to unfasten the buttons. He brought himself closer to her, pressing his knees on her thighs so she couldn't wriggle free.

He was in the process of unzipping his trousers when the knife struck him in the shoulder blade.

Van Rooyen, shocked at the blow, tried to turn around. *The other copper! How could that be? He was knocked out cold.* Pushing his elbows back, he managed to jab Graeme in the ribs.

Finally able to rotate his body to face the inspector, the Dutchman took a swipe at his face, causing Graeme to stagger. The copper countered, smacking Van Rooyen in the side of the nose. The Dutchman hit back, punching him in the stomach.

Graeme fell forward and to his knees.

Van Rooyen steadied himself and kicked the copper in the face, causing his nose and lips to bleed. The blow was strong enough to knock Graeme back and onto the floor.

Down and injured, Graeme heard the sound of a gun magazine clicking.

Sensing blood on his face and his teeth, he looked up. *Maybe this is it, the end.* Like a deer stunned by the headlights of an approaching car, Graeme just stared at Van Rooyen, waiting for the inevitable...

"Fucking Engels pig," the Dutchman yelled, raising Graeme's Glock and pointing it straight at him. "I'll kill you with your own gun."

Just as he was about to pull the trigger, the Dutchman stumbled and fell sideways, as if hit by a spectral fist. He tried to steady himself again, doing his best to aim at his nemesis and pull the trigger once more. Almost in synchronicity with his fingers pushing the lever back, Van Rooyen's eyes widened before glazing over, life dissipating from his body. Graeme saw blood trickle out of the villain's mouth just as the bullet shot out of the Glock.

All the inspector could do was close his eyes...

Perhaps this was it—the end of the dream. Graeme half-expected to be back in his "other" world, in the grotty flat or on the tube, but this time there was nothing; only a thud, and the weight of a heavy mass falling on him, his head being knocked backwards and then into darkness.

He could feel pain and the cold hard sensation of lying on stone. There were also sounds—echoes and sirens growing ever louder, mixed with the scent of blood and perfume. Despite being in agony and unable to move, he couldn't help but smile to himself; he'd managed to keep it together, and he wasn't going anywhere this time.

The gold Granada Ghia came tearing into Chelsea Square at breakneck speed, followed by a Ford Sierra. The screeching of tires and slamming of doors brought him back to life. Graeme opened his eyes.

She was leaning over him now. Her face was bruised and cut, but she was gazing intently at him and smiling. "We got the bastard," she said. "We got him." Her bloodied hand was stroking his face. She leaned forward, as if she was about to kiss him, when Donaldson came running up, followed by two SPG officers.

"My God!" the super exclaimed. "Just who in the hell is that?"

"Our man," replied Graeme exhaustedly as Em drew back.

"What the hell did I tell you, James? I said we wanted to take him alive for questioning. He's no fucking good to us now."

"Guv," the inspector let out a sigh. "Here me out, will you?"

"I'm all ears."

"We had no choice. He was going to kill me with my own gun. Luckily, Em stopped him and just in the nick of time, too."

Donaldson turned to address her. "Are you all right Sergeant?"

She stared at her boss blankly and didn't say a word. She turned to face Graeme again and started to smile, although as she did, they could see streams of tears streaking down her cheeks.

Just then, one of the SPG officers from the Sierra appeared. "Sir, we've got three dead and one seriously injured, an ambulance is on its way."

"You'd better order a second one, Constable, there are two more that need attention." The superintendent gestured in the direction of his protégés.

"Yes, sir." The man nodded, pressing the transmit button on his radio as he headed back towards the entrance of the courtyard.

The super walked forward and knelt, using his big burly hands to turn the lifeless body over. As he did, he saw the man's distinctive round face come into view. As he removed the flat cap, the super instantly recognized who it was.

"Van Rooyen?" yelled Donaldson, completely aghast.

"As I said," remarked Graeme, "we got our man."

"What about Max?"

"I just don't know, Guv. My instinct tells me he's long gone. There was something, a look in his eyes when he saw me. I don't think we'll be hearing from him again."

At that moment, Em started sobbing.

"What's wrong with her?" Donaldson inquired. He didn't have to wait long for an answer.

"That fucking bastard tried to rape her," Graeme blurted out.

"Graeme stopped it," Em added quickly, holding herself steady as though nothing had happened. "He stabbed him and then I shot him. Fucking bastard."

The super's eyes widened in absolute shock.

The inspector slowly stood up and limped over to his partner. "C'mon, let's get you out of here." He tried putting his arms around her but as he did, she flinched.

Graeme took a good look at her. She was still sobbing. Gently, he raised his left hand. The inspector looked at her intently for a second, before using the side of his index finger to try and wipe the tears from her right eye. She fell into him, and he just stood there, holding her tightly.

Slowly, Graeme drew back and steadied her so she was standing strong. He held onto her tightly again.

At that moment, sirens could be heard, quickly growing louder. More sirens followed. A few minutes later, an ambulance crew appeared from around the corner.

"Help this lady, will you?" asked the super.

The crew walked towards Graeme, who was still holding Em, trying to comfort her.

"We'll take it from here, sir," one of the ambulance crew nodded in respect.

Graeme carefully let the technician lead her away towards the ambulance. Em turned around to catch a glimpse of Graeme before she was whisked off.

"I'll see you around, partner."

She gazed at him, her eyes swelling with tears. Then she smiled before turning to face forward.

"Be careful with her, won't you?" Graeme asked.

"Yes sir," the lead technician acknowledged.

"By the way—where are you taking her?"

"Royal Brompton."

As they led her away, Graeme faced his boss. "Guv, I should probably go with her. I'm not one to be sentimental but right now she needs me."

The super placed his hands on his hips and shook his head. "I really wouldn't suggest it at this point. Let the hospital staff take care of her. Don't worry, we'll make sure somebody keeps an eye on Em until you're fit and able. In the meantime, you need to get yourself looked at, you're hardly in a fit state, are you?" The boss cocked his head and twitched his brow.

"You're probably right."

"You mean *always* right? C'mon, I'll give you a lift."

Epilogue

Three weeks had passed. Graeme had almost fully recovered from his gunshot wound and got his BMW back virtually good as new. Em had been kept in hospital for several days following the incident with Van Rooyen at her flat. On the third day, Graeme had gone to visit her, after being discharged from the hospital himself.

She'd been in better spirits, acting almost like the incident had never happened. *Perhaps that was her way of dealing with it?* Graeme had mused at the time. Despite some haughty remarks, the way she kept looking at him during his visit led the inspector to believe that the two of them had a special bond, cemented during some very dangerous and terrifying circumstances. After staying for a couple of hours, Graeme decided to leave—not that he wanted to, but despite enjoying being by her side, he could sense that she needed some rest.

"I've asked Donaldson to take some leave," she'd explained to him as he was about to get up and head out.

"Where will you go?"

"Back to Suffolk to be with the family, I need a break from the city."

"Will you call me before you go?"

She didn't say anything, but instead faked a smile.

That girl is taunting me again, Graeme thought. *She knows how to get inside my head.*

"Well, if you need anything, just call."

"Thank you Inspector, maybe I will."

A few days later, she'd headed up to Beaufort Hall. She'd called and left a message on Graeme's answering machine at his flat, but didn't leave a number.

If he was being honest with himself, he felt hurt that she hadn't asked him for anything just yet. But trying not to let it get the better of him, Graeme tried to busy himself as much as possible with work.

With Van Rooyen dead, the Dennison's case had been placed on the back burner. SRI officers had located the Capri and forensics had found the Dutchman's fingerprints all over it. The lockup in White City and the seized Sherpa had turned up fingerprints on Piper and Downs, while the set of keys found at the garage were found to have dabs from both Downs and Van Rooyen on them.

Some mysteries remained, however. The coroner's examination revealed that in addition to multiple stab wounds, Van Rooyen had also received a 9mm bullet to the shoulder, though no trace of the gun that fired it, nor those that had killed three of the four SPG officers at 16 Chelsea Square, had been found. The fourth officer, Jim Garrison, although suffering from leg and arm wounds, had been taken to hospital and later discharged. He'd been placed on convalescent leave until he was fit enough to work again.

Another Beretta had been found at the scene, near Van Rooyen's body. Ballistics discovered that it was the same gun used to mow down Police Constable Keith Reynolds.

Chief Superintendent George Donaldson had attended Reynolds' funeral the previous week and taken up a collection from the Met to support the young officer's widow and child. Even after all these years on the job, such acts of brutality still sickened him, especially when they took somebody who was just entering their prime of life.

Other loose ends surrounding the Dennison's case included the complete disappearance of Max Willoughby. He'd not been sighted anywhere since the altercation at Charing Cross, and there were still no solid leads on the sinister and mysterious "Boss," who was presumably, still at large.

Things had gone relatively quiet. There hadn't been any more high-profile jewelry robberies since Van Rooyen's demise and instead, SRI had been focusing its attention on a protection racket in Wandsworth and some possible connections to an arms smuggling ring.

It was Tuesday, August 9 at 9:36 a.m. As he pored over documents regarding some recently seized weapons, Donaldson took another drag of his B&H. After almost fifteen years on the police force and with the Royal Marine Commandos before that, he'd just about seen it all. As he took another puff, the super reflected. At fifty-seven years old, he knew that his habit would probably eventually get the better of him—indeed, his wife, Gladys, had been asking him to quit for years.

Yet as he saw it, a cigarette was one of few truly enjoyable pleasures he had during the long days of dealing with "bastards and bureaucracy," as he put it. A little smile glittered along his face and he sat back in the chair.

All of a sudden, there was a knock on the office door.

"What is it?" the super sighed.

It opened, and Tim Charles popped his head in. "Thought you might like to see these, Guv. We've had two more reports of local shopkeepers being severely beaten in Wandsworth. Here, take a look at this."

Tim placed the files on the desk.

"Good struth!" exclaimed Donaldson as he examined the photos. "When were these taken?"

"At the scene, yesterday Guv. Both men were taken to Westminster Hospital and they're currently under observation."

"Can we get statements from them?"

"Possibly in a couple of days, though one of them sustained quite serious injuries and is still in a coma."

"Stay on it, Tim, and in the meantime, find Braithwaite and James, will you? I want them to focus their attention on these violent bastards."

Graeme steered his white BMW onto Chelsea Square. He'd anticipated seeing his partner again and wondered how she'd be. *Did she miss me? Will we feel that same bond we did on July 16?*

As he pulled into the courtyard, he saw Em standing, waiting. She was wearing a white blouse and a black belt over dark gray trousers. She faced his car, then tilted her head and grimaced. *This is going to be interesting!* Graeme thought, but to be fair, he was almost ten minutes late picking her up.

"So, how was your trip?" he asked as she got into the BMW.

"Quite relaxing actually, nice to have a bit of tranquility, culture and no boorish policemen to deal with."

Graeme looked at her as-a-matter-of-factly. "I take it you got the call from Donaldson this morning, too."

"Do you mean the one about the protection racket?"

"That's the one. Looks like we'll be pulling surveillance duty for a while. The guv says there's a couple of restaurants in Wandsworth he wants us to keep an eye on. Here." Graeme handed Em a piece of paper with an address on it and a key. "This is where we'll be holed up for a little while. Think you can navigate there, Sergeant?"

"I can hardly read this," she snorted. "Look, just tell me the address and I'll write it down." She grabbed a pen and a small notepad from her handbag.

"It's 181 Wandsworth High Street," said Graeme a little patronizingly as he pulled out of the courtyard.

"Thank you, I've got it," she returned with equal attitude.

Maybe I deserved that, Graeme mused. He hadn't seen her for twenty days since that visit in hospital, the week following the infamous incident at Chelsea Square.

He could still remember that night, being hit over the head and Van Rooyen pointing the Glock at him. He could still hear the Dutchman's voice, feel his eyes closing and see the weight of the body falling. And then, there was the aftermath of it all—the sensation of her stroking his face, smiling at him. If Graeme was being true to himself, he'd never felt happier, nor more content than at that particular moment. He'd wanted it to last forever.

But that experience of pure joy had been laced with sadness. Em had suffered delayed trauma as the result of Van Rooyen attempting to overtake her. She'd started crying and screamed out about the attempted rape to anybody in the immediate vicinity. Graeme had decided at that moment, despite his own injuries, that the best thing he could do was comfort her, so he managed to stand up, steady himself and hold her tightly until an ambulance crew arrived to take care of her.

As Em was led away to the ambulance that day, she'd looked back at him and smiled. When she did, Graeme felt warmth within him, a real sense of happiness and belonging.

He'd tried to hold on to that feeling for as long as possible, even while Em was away at her family home. He truly sensed that they *did* have chemistry, yet the way she'd behaved this morning just indicated a reaction to dealing with a traumatic ordeal.

He felt like a child who'd just had his favorite balloon popped by that mean girl in junior school. *Maybe it was just her way of dealing with the incident at her flat, stiff upper lip and all that.*

For a while, they just drove in silence. Then, as he turned onto Chelsea Embankment, Graeme knew, deep down in his gut, that he had to say something.

"You were going to kiss me, weren't you?"

She turned his way and gave him a haughty look. "When?"

"...Just before Donaldson showed up that night at your place when Van Rooyen was killed. Why don't you just admit it?"

She paused for a moment. Graeme was sensing that he might have pushed things too far, given the attempted rape.

She stared at him intently for a few seconds, then blinked, as if whatever thought had taken hold was now gone. "Don't be ridiculous James," she snorted. "I think your mind's been playing tricks on you again."

"Formal today, aren't we?" he teased cautiously.

"At least I'm not delusional."

"What do you mean by that?"

"The fact that you think I could actually fall for somebody like you. A cavalier, brash, insensitive ego-maniac."

"That's a bit harsh, Sergeant, after all we've been through together."

In all truthfulness, that last remark was a bit cheeky, and Graeme expected a pithy comeback, but instead she softened her tone.

"Perhaps you're not altogether that bad," she commented. "I was thinking about asking for another partner the other week while I was on leave visiting my family, but I have to confess, James, you've not been as wild or unpredictable over the last little while, so I'll figure you do for now."

"*Wild*?" Graeme's head darted forward as he was surprised at her choice of words. Yet, the seed had been planted; he had to say something. "From what I hear, you're the one who has a really wild reputation, especially during your university days in Oxford."

"Who told you that?"

He turned briskly to see her staring wide eyed at him, eyebrows raised.

"A little birdie."

"Who?"

"That's all you get from me."

"Come on, who?"

"Not telling."

She sighed and looked at him.

He glanced at her for a second.

"I wasn't trying to kiss you," she declared. "I just wanted to make sure you were still breathing. I couldn't bear the thought of having a dead partner on my conscience, no matter how irritating he might be at times."

"Thanks a lot."

"Don't mention it. Now, how much longer until we get to our surveillance site?"

"About twenty-five minutes, depending on traffic."

"With you driving, so it would be about thirty-five under normal circumstances."

He was about to respond when the radio crackled into life.

"Sierra 3, come in, over." It was Donaldson.

"Roger, this is Sierra 3," Em confirmed.

"There's been an armed bank robbery in Lambeth, close to Westminster Bridge. Suspects stole some £40,000; they took off not long ago and could be heading your way, likely driving a yellow, souped-up Hillman. Where are you? Over."

"On Grosvenor Road, just past the Albert Bridge. We're on our way to that surveillance job in Wandsworth."

"Not anymore," the super relayed. "I want you to go after our robbery suspects. There's a good chance they're in your vicinity and I want them caught. Keep your eyes peeled. We've got Met patrol cars out looking and if they spot our criminals, they will give chase and vector you in. And Braithwaite, please tell that partner of yours, no stunt driving. Proceed with caution, over."

"Yes sir," said Em, wincing at Graeme.

Grinning, the inspector dropped gear, and the BMW's straight-six growled as they sped past the leafy trees on the riverside and the Georgian-era residences on the other.

"What about the surveillance job?" she wondered.

"Don't worry about that, there's already a team that's closer to our bagman's location. I'll instruct them to take the first watch. Our main priority is to get these blasted bank robbers."

"Roger, Sierra 1, over and out."

As she hung up the radio, Em leaned over to Graeme and whispered in his left ear. "Actually, I was going to."

He turned slightly. "Going to what?"

She drew back and winked at him.

Not knowing whether to laugh or cry, Graeme shook his head.

In the distance, he could see a yellow Hillman Avenger Tiger rapidly approaching from the opposite direction. Just as it passed, Graeme dropped gear and slammed on the brakes, spinning the BMW around to give chase, while Em switched on the siren.

"Here we go," he said as the 635CSi's rear tires fought for traction and the engine rumbled, thrusting the big coupe forward as Graeme stomped on the accelerator and rowed the shift lever into second and then third.

Glancing across at Em, he saw her eyes sparkle and her face break into a warm smile. The chase was on.

About Huw Evans

H uw Evans was born in Cardiff, Wales, United Kingdom. Emigrating to North America in his early twenties with not much money and a dream, he found a niche as a writer, author and editor. He developed a very unique perspective on the world while spending his formative years living in Cyprus, Gibraltar, Hong Kong, Saudi Arabia, Spain, Belgium and Greece, and different parts of the UK including Wales, Scotland, Lancashire and London. He specializes in automotive reference works, presented in a concise, informative, and easy-to-read format—one that appeals to serious enthusiasts and casual observers alike. A devoted father, entrepreneur and real estate investor, Huw currently divides time between his home in Ontario, Canada and his homeland of Wales.